WILLIAM LASHNER

is the author of the Elizabeth Webster series for young read-
ers. A former criminal prosecutor with the Department of
Justice in Washington, DC, and a graduate of the Iowa
Writers' Workshop, his novels have been published worldwide and have been nominated for two Edgar Awards, two
Shamus Awards, and selected as an Editor's Choice in the
New York Times Book Review. He also was nominated
for a Gumshoe Award in recognition of how often he steps
in gum. When he was a kid his favorite books were *The
Count of Monte Cristo* and any comic with the Batman on
the cover.

ELIZABETH WEBSTER

AND THE

PORTAL OF DOOM

BOOKS BY WILLIAM LASHNER

Elizabeth Webster and the Court of Uncommon Pleas

Elizabeth Webster and the Portal of Doom

ELIZABETH

WEBSTER
AND THE
PORTAL OF DOOM

WILLIAM LASHNER

LITTLE, BROWN AND COMPANY

New York   Boston

Little, Brown and Company

Hachette Book Group

1290 Avenue of the Americas, New York, NY 10104

Visit us at LBYR.com

First Edition: October 2020

Little, Brown and Company is a division of Hachette Book Group, Inc. The Little, Brown name and logo are trademarks of Hachette Book Group, Inc.

The publisher is not responsible for websites (or their content) that are not owned by the publisher.

Library of Congress Cataloging-in-Publication Data
Names: Lashner, William, author.
Title: Elizabeth Webster and the Portal of Doom / William Lashner.
Description: First edition. | New York ; Boston : Little, Brown and Company, 2020. | Series: Elizabeth Webster | Audience: Ages 10-14. | Summary: Elizabeth Webster and her friends return to the Court of Uncommon Pleas, this time seeking due process and freedom for Keir, a twelve-year-old boy who mysteriously does not seem to age.
Identifiers: LCCN 2020032536 | ISBN 9781368062893 (hardcover) | ISBN 9781368064965 (ebook) | ISBN 9780316592192 (ebook other)
Subjects: CYAC: Justice, Administration of—Fiction. | Lawyers—Fiction. | Vampires—Fiction. | Friendship—Fiction. | Middle schools—Fiction. | Schools—Fiction.
Classification: LCC PZ7.1.L3725 Elp 2020 | DDC [Fic] —dc23
LC record available at https://lccn.loc.gov/2020032536

ISBNs: 978-1-368-06289-3 (hardcover), 978-1-368-06496-5 (ebook)

Printed in the United States of America

LSC-C

10 9 8 7 6 5 4 3 2 1

For Nora Lee, my EW

ELIZABETH WEBSTER

WEBSTER

AND THE
PORTAL OF DOOM

A DARK AND STORMY NIGHT

When the doctor shut the latch on his black bag, a bolt of lightning split the night sky.

Am I making up the bolt of lightning? Maybe, possibly—I've been known to embellish—and this all took place a hundred years ago, so who's to say? But it really was a dark and stormy night, and a child did lie lifeless on the bed in the damp basement room, and if the lightning wasn't slashing it should have been. What happened that night happened, trust me on that if you trust me on anything, and this is how I imagine it.

The doctor mumbles something about the death certificate as he lifts the white sheet and covers the boy's lifeless face. A kneeling young mother hugs her dead child, soaking the cloth that covers him with her tears. The mother's two older sisters, the boy's aunties, bustle around the room, showing the doctor out, stopping the clock, covering the mirror.

They'd had much practice, the aunties, in the rituals of death. The influenza outbreak was sweeping through the city like a scythe. Already, three of those who lived in the servants' cottage had died and many others were deathly sick, including the boy's mother. As the aunties went about their silent work, only the moans of the mother broke the quiet.

Her parents were buried in the home country of Ireland, gone. Her husband was overseas, gone to war. Her life had become her twelve-year-old son, her darling Keir, and now he was gone with the rest. Her hands caressed the sheet that covered his face as she whispered his name into unhearing ears. Until something stopped her sobs.

The sheet that covered her son's face rose with the slightest bit of breath.

She pulled back as if from a ghost. "He's alive," she said.

"Oh, Caitlin," said one of the aunties. "I'm sorry, but the doctor said—"

"The doctor was wrong, Erin," said the mother. "My boy still breathes." She pulled the sheet from his face. "Look."

The other auntie took hold of a candle and brought the tiny flame to the boy's open mouth. They stared at the candle, the three of them, watching for the flame to twitch, but saw nothing. Nothing. And then...

"I'll run and get the doctor," said Erin.

"Not him," said the mother as she placed her hand on the boy's cold cheeks, turned blue by the sickness. "I'll not trust my boy to him again."

"Then who will you trust?"

The young mother started wrapping her boy, covering him not just with the sheet but with the thin gray blanket, too. "Can you ready the carriage, Rowan?"

The second auntie nodded. "I'll have Grady do it. He'll drive you, too, if he knows what's good for him."

"Where will he be driving you to, Caitlin?" said Erin, the oldest of the three sisters.

"Go, Rowan, run. There's not much time."

"Where are you taking him?" said Auntie Erin as Rowan rushed up the stairs.

"Where I should have taken him at the first."

"If you care for that boy's soul you won't let her near him."

"For now, sister," said the young mother, "I'll let the Lord care for his soul. I mean to care for his still-young life. Help me carry him."

"I can't. I won't. It's blasphemy."

"Then step aside." The young mother leaned over the bed, took hold of her son, and stood. She staggered under the load.

Her older sister, strong as a mule, snatched the boy from her as easily as if he'd been a loaf of bread.

The two sisters stared into each other's eyes.

"I can't have you dropping him into a puddle," said Erin, "your fever as high as it is. Now let's be going. Time's a-wasting."

The black carriage rushed forward through the rain-soaked night, rocking wildly as the horse strained under Grady's whip. The three sisters inside the carriage held tightly to the barely breathing boy. The lightning flashed. The whip cracked. The horse snorted as it galloped ever forward.

This is my favorite part of the story, the wild carriage ride through the stormy night. I like to imagine myself sitting next to Grady on the driver's bench as the carriage barrels through the corkscrew turns and past the brick church with the pointy steeple. I can feel the rain on my face, hear the thunder in my bones. I hold tight as the carriage leans wildly this way and that, almost teetering over before righting itself.

You know what they could have used in those days? Seat belts!

The reins were yanked and the horse let out a terrified neigh as it reared in front of a granite arch with a name carved into the stone: LAVEAU. Normally the gate was locked tight, but on this night its iron wings were spread wide, as if it sensed the dark desperation of their mission.

Grady pulled the horse to the left and the carriage jolted forward, diving beneath the arch and onto the gravel drive. Lanterns swinging from the roof of the carriage gouged a path through the low, overhanging branches of a grove as the horse charged on. The carriage shook so hard within the canopy of darkness it was as if it was leaving this world and entering another.

The woods ended and something wide and fearsome shone dimly on the crest of the hill, something like a great curled dragon. A slash of lightning killed the illusion—it was not a dragon at all, just a large stone house with wings stretching on either side.

At the front entrance, the two aunties jumped into the rain, carrying young Keir to the large crimson door. The mother struggled to follow. Auntie Erin held the boy as Rowan lifted the knocker and slammed it down again and again.

The young mother, bent over at the waist, whispered, "Let us in. Save my boy."

As if in response only to her plea, the door opened slowly. In the gap stood a skinny old man in black, with bony hands, long gray hair, and the blue face of a rotting corpse. Rowan gasped when she saw him and backed away from the door.

"We've come to see the Countess Laveau," said Erin.

"You are not those we were expecting," said the old man in a high-pitched warble.

"My son is fading," said the young mother. "He is on the edge of death."

The man, more bone than flesh, stared for a moment before he closed the door to them.

The wind and rain lashed their backs as they waited. There was nothing to be done but wait. And wait.

Finally the door opened again, and standing now beside the skinny blue man was a woman, tall and fierce, in a perfectly tailored man's suit with jewels at the cuffs and a red scarf at her throat. Her skin was deep brown, her cheekbones were sharp, her black hair was wound like a living thing about her face. She took the boy's rain-soaked face in her hands and raised his eyelids with her thumbs.

"Influenza?" asked the woman.

"The doctor already declared him dead," said Erin. "But still he breathes."

"How much they don't know could fill libraries," the woman said in a Caribbean accent.

"Please, Countess," said the young mother, "save my boy."

The countess looked at her as a bolt of lightning ignited the sky. In that instant the skull beneath the countess's face glowed through her flesh. "You come to me even knowing the cost?"

"He is all I have. My boy. My Keir."

"If we do save him, he can never leave this place," said the countess. "If he lives, he will be bound to me for as long as he walks this earth."

The young mother coughed and looked away. "I can't let him die."

"Do you agree to the terms?"

"Please."

Just then the eldest of the aunties, the one still holding the boy, spoke. "Surely you'll let our Caitlin see him if he lives. Surely you'll allow a mother time to visit with her only child."

The countess looked at Erin, then at Rowan, then at the mother, who was pleading with wet, red-rimmed eyes.

"Once a month, that is all," said the countess. "On this same day each month she will be allowed a visit. Do you agree?"

"Yes," said the mother. "I agree."

Without another word, the Countess Laveau seized the boy from Erin's arms, spun around, and carried him into the house. As the door slammed shut, the young mother collapsed, clutching at the ground as she cried out for her son.

The aunties were in the process of lifting their weeping sister from the wet stone when the door opened suddenly and the old man once again appeared before them. In one blue hand he held what looked like an irregular brown piece of paper, words scrawled upon it in red ink. With the other, he took from his jacket pocket a feather quill.

"Before you go, Caitlin McGoogan," he said to the young mother, "you'll need to sign."

Even in the world of the supernatural, paperwork exists. Like your middle school permanent record, it follows you through the decades of your life, past your death, and then into the long beyond, where it is up to the Court of Uncommon Pleas to decide how it rules your fate.

And that's where I come in.

Some girls play basketball. Some girls play the electric bass. Some girls dance like pogo sticks to punk rock and sleep with their headphones on. We all have our things.

My name is Elizabeth Webster and my thing is speaking for the dead.

2

TOGAS

Speaking for the dead was not my choice. I was a normal kid who only wanted what normal kids want, like a new phone, being left alone, a pool, being left alone, a butler. Was a butler too much to ask for? *Shall you have your ice cream now or after your swim, Ms. Webster?* No, a butler was not too much to ask for.

Did I have the butler? I didn't even have the pool.

Instead, about three months ago this headless ghost started calling my name in the middle of the night. It all went back to my bizarre family history, which till then I hadn't known anything about. That might seem careless of me, like I had misplaced old family stories along with my house key, but do you know who your great-great-great-granduncle was and what promises he wrestled out of the Lord Demon of the Underworld? Neither did I!

Yet somehow it all resulted in the family law firm—Webster & Spawn: Attorneys for the Damned. I'm the spawn. And because of that little detail, the dead keep asking for my help. And here's the frightening thing: if you're going to speak for the dead, you have to first speak to the dead.

I'm not complaining, mind you. There are cool things about talking to ghosts you might never imagine. For one, there is no small talk with the dead. No *How was school today, Elizabeth?* No *Are you really going to wear that outfit?* And even better, they don't have that annoying urge to tell you what your problem is.

No dead person ever said to me, like my mother, "Enough of this messing with ghosts, Elizabeth. It's time for you to choose to get serious about school."

And no dead person ever told me, like my father at the office, "Show some patience, Lizzie Face. You're always in too much of a rush."

And no dead person ever pointed out to me, like my stepfather, Stephen, at dinner, that I should stop being so moody. "Come on, Elizabeth. Turn that frown upside down." This last bit was so him it always made me want to scream. I'd try to stifle it, at least until my little brother, Peter, put his fingers in his mouth and yanked the edges of it up, turning himself into the Joker to hammer home the point. Then screaming would usually commence.

Truth is, if my parents had given me something to smile about, I would have smiled plenty. If they had given me the pool or the butler—or even better, if they had just left me alone—I would have been like JoJo the clown-faced girl.

But they gave me none of those things. All they did was tell me all the ways I wasn't making the right choices. And it's not like I didn't know they wouldn't like my outfits, or my pink hair, or the way I chewed my pencils. There was a mirror in my room, after all. They might not have forked over the butler, but they didn't stint on the mirrors.

When you think about it that way, talking to the dead was in many ways better than talking to my parents.

And then, sometimes, talking to the dead could turn into something fun. Like the February night we were all dancing in Young-Mee's basement while we waited for some Irish ghosts that were haunting her house to appear and tell us what they were complaining about.

Banshees? You bet!

I thought it would just be another chat with the dead, but it turned out to be the first step of a perilous journey that would take me from the story of that late-night carriage ride straight to the edge of the Portal of Doom. Just by the sound of it you know it's not a vacation destination. There are no character breakfasts at the Portal of Doom. And that trip, dangerous as it was, started with a toga party because, well, of course it did.

"Should Charlie turn the music down?" said Natalie Delgado, wrapped in a pretty blue sheet with red flowers because white sheets were just so ordinary. "We want to be able to hear the ghosts when they come."

"Oh, you'll hear them," said Young-Mee. "And when you do, you'll wish you didn't."

"Would you like it louder, Ms. Kwon?" said the DJ of our party, Master CF Vici, which was Charlie Frayden's DJ name. Charlie had come in a fitted plastic sheet that made him look like a pale-faced chipmunk wrapped in wax paper and bound with rubber bands. To set the mood he was playing Halloween pop songs like "Rather Be a Zombie" and "Secret Vampires."

"Any louder and it would wake the dead," said Young-Mee.

"Isn't that the point?" said Henry Harrison.

At the party there were six of us from good old Willing Middle School West, a crew sworn to secrecy about the whole I-talk-to-the-dead thing. There was Young-Mee, of course, since it was her basement and her ghosts. Then there was Natalie, my best friend since kindergarten, along with Charlie and Doug Frayden, two sixth graders who were my teammates in Debate Club. Henry Harrison, the eighth-grade swimming star and king of our middle school hallways, was also there, still recovering from being visited by his own personal ghost. And then there was me, *moi*, the teller of this tale.

"Will our ghosts want some snacks?" said Natalie.

"Snacks?" said Doug Frayden, Charlie's twin, who had become our resident ghost and ghoul expert after being given my grandfather's copy of *White's Legal Hornbook of Demons and Ghosts*.

"It could be all they want is a snack," said Natalie. "I brought some caramel popcorn."

"I don't think banshees eat popcorn," said Doug.

"Just souls," said Master CF Vici.

Young-Mee's parents, gone for the evening, had been only too happy to let their daughter host the crew for a

Shakespeare-themed educational event in their basement. That's why we were pretending to throw a Julius Caesar party taking place on the fifteenth of the month, the date that Julius was poked to death and the only night each month the ghosts appeared. The fruit punch was dark as wine, the music was punk, and a square was marked by tape in the center of the floor. Within that square we danced like a pack of Roman fools while we waited for the ghosts to come so I could ask them what they wanted.

It seemed a simple enough plan.

"Maybe they won't come at all," said Henry in the quiet between songs. "Maybe we scared them off just by being here."

"Nothing scares them off," said Young-Mee. "Not the dog, not my parents being upstairs, and certainly not the Fraydens."

"The Fraydens would scare me off if I was a ghost," said Natalie. "No offense, guys."

"None taken, Natalie," said Doug. "I think."

"But if these ghosts are Irish banshees, like Doug says," said Young-Mee, "why are they haunting us?"

"Maybe they're not haunting your family," said Natalie. "Maybe they're haunting the house. The place of some long-ago tragedy. A dead boy. A girl still in love from beyond the grave. How romantic would that be?"

"Pretty romantic, actually," said Young-Mee.

"So, what's the plan, Webster?" said Henry.

"You do have a plan, Elizabeth, don't you?" said Charlie.

"Sort of," I said, before turning to look at the corner of the room, where the seventh member of our party sat alone in one of a row of chairs. No toga there. "I'm kind of following his lead."

"Barney doesn't look very happy to be here," said Natalie.

"His name is Barnabas," I said. "And that's the way he always looks. But I'll go talk to him. I'm sure there's nothing to worry about."

I was wrong.

BARNABAS BOTHEMLY

Barnabas Bothemly sat rigidly in his chair as if he was frozen in time, which, sadly, he was.

He wore a long frock coat as black as his ruffled hair, and his long gloomy face and bony hands were so devoid of color he might have been a ghost himself. His expression could have fooled you into thinking he was terribly frightened by the impending arrival of a pack of screaming banshees, but for a very tragic reason Barnabas Bothemly, chief clerk at the firm of Webster & Spawn, was afraid of very little in this world or the next.

It's a sad story that I've told before, but the gist of it is that Barnabas's fiancée, Isabel, was tricked to the other side by the demon Redwing, and the two could only be together again when Barnabas himself died. But Barnabas, against his wishes, had been turned into an immortal by

Redwing, so the two lovers were forever yearning for each other across the boundary line of death. Talk about a tragic romance.

"It is quite a party you and your friends are tossing, Mistress Elizabeth," he said when I sat down beside him. His accent was very British.

"It's sort of cool, I admit, even with the sheets. Don't you like parties, Barnabas?"

"Oh, there were some superior parties in Sussex when I was still practicing the law."

"That must have been fun."

"The parties were not about fun, Mistress Elizabeth, they were about seeing and being seen. They were about maintaining one's position in society."

"That doesn't sound like fun at all."

"I avoided such events like the plague. I was much more content by the fire with only a book and a cup of tea to keep me company. At least until I met my Isabel. But it is good to see you and your friends enjoying yourselves before the evening takes its turn."

"Do you want to join in?"

"Certainly not. And even if I were willing to strut like a heron in a white sheet, tonight would not be the night."

"Why not tonight?"

"Because, Mistress Elizabeth, when a banshee comes, normally she comes to warn the household that one of its members is soon to journey to the other side. That means someone, possibly in this very room, is likely to die in the near future."

I turned my head and scanned my friends, who were

talking and laughing and dancing. Suddenly I felt just as sad and scared as Barnabas looked.

"Do you remember the Latin words I taught you?" said Barnabas.

"Yes, of course." I was about to repeat them when Barnabas raised a hand.

"Not now, Mistress Elizabeth. Wait until I tell you. We wouldn't want to summon the wrong spirit, now would we?"

"No, we would not," I said.

"When we hear the first mournful cries I will set this up"—he patted a long rectangle covered with black velvet by his side—"and you will recite the words I taught you and perhaps then we shall learn what these sad spirit women from the other world are trying to say."

"Will it be dangerous?"

"Not for me, I don't believe," he said without cracking a smile.

That was the thing about Barnabas, he never laughed at his own jokes, and so you never really knew if he was joking.

Just then the distant caw of a raven rose above the song Master CF Vici was playing through the speaker. The sound was so distant I wouldn't have noticed it if Young-Mee hadn't turned to us with frightened eyes.

"I believe the time has come," said Barnabas.

I stood and slashed a finger across my neck to signal Charlie to cut the music. In the sudden quiet the caw swelled, coming now from one, two, three black-winged birds, growing louder as if the ravens were swooping toward us with claws bared.

Along with the cries of the birds came the telltale breezes, swishing about us with a sulfurous stink.

"Yikes alive!" said Natalie.

"Here they come," said Young-Mee. "And they always smell like this."

"Maybe someone's making egg salad," said Henry.

"With deviled eggs," said Charlie.

The caws grew louder, harsher, turning into screeches of misery that twisted into our ears like corkscrews. The cries shot through me with such wild abandon they shook my heart, filling me not just with their bitter, painful sound but also with a sea of emotions.

It felt as if my best friend had moved away, as if my dog had just died, as if every color in the world had turned to ash.

I lost myself in the sadness and closed my eyes for just a moment to stop my tears. When I opened them again the room had changed, as if my eyes had been shut for a very long while.

THE SCRYING MIRROR

The ghosts were still screeching and the stinky drafts were still whooshing, but the room now was lit only by the tiny flames of four candles set down on each corner of the marked square and five others held by my friends, who stood against the walls. I was alone in the middle of the square, next to my backpack, with Barnabas's black-velvet-covered rectangle set on the floor in front of me.

Barnabas recited something in Latin, the official language of the dead, and the others, their faces glowing eerily in the candlelight, read from loose pages as they translated his words into English.

"*Protecti sumus*," Barnabas called out from a dark corner of the room.

"We are protected," my friends read in unison.

"*Nos autem secure*," recited Barnabas.

"We are secure."

"Spirituum quid quaeris."

"Spirits, tell us what you seek."

"Et vade in domum tuam."

"And then return to your world."

While they repeated their chants, I walked slowly up to the rectangle and lifted the black velvet from the front, letting it drop behind. Beneath the velvet was a stained and spotted mirror, what Barnabas had called a scrying mirror. Following Barnabas's instructions, I sat on the floor in front of the glass and stared at my image flickering in the candlelight. Not much to see: mussed pink hair, beady eyes, funny-looking nose, a wrinkled sheet draped over my narrow shoulders. See what I mean about mirrors?

As I continued to stare at my reflection, the screeching grew louder as the foul-smelling breezes whipped my hair and billowed my sheet. A strange fog rose to cover the edges of the room where Barnabas and my friends stood, while the square within which I sat became its own world, a landscape as gray and sad as the sound of the banshees' call.

"Now, Mistress Elizabeth," I heard Barnabas call out as if from a great distance. "Say the words I taught you."

I took a deep breath to steady my nerves and then recited a swarm of Latin. In English the words meant: "Come to me, all that are bitter in the soul."

As soon as the words left my lips, my image in the mirror faded as something seemed to dart behind the glass. The back of the mirror was still covered with black velvet, but another thing seemed to flit behind it, and another, as if the glass was now providing a window into some other world. It wasn't long before I saw them clearly: three women covered in black, swirling around each other like wisps of smoke while they sang their screeching songs.

Banshees.

Two were ancient, with spotted, wart-ridden cheeks and mouths as toothless as a baby's. But the third was young, with a lock of bright copper hair escaping from the black cloak covering her head and eyes as green as emeralds.

For a moment it was as if I could see them but they couldn't see me. Then one of the old ghosts pointed at me, and all three quieted. Barnabas and my friends were now so distant I couldn't see or hear them. All I could see was the wide gray landscape, all I could hear was the whipping of the wind.

The youngest of the women floated closer to the mirror and leaned forward to stare right at me.

"*Cé tusa?*" she said.

She reached for the mirror, as if to touch it with her forefinger, but then her arm broke through the surface. While her skin behind the mirror's glass was pale and freckled, the hand on my side of the mirror, reaching out from her drooping black sleeve, was nothing but bone.

"*Cé tusa?*" she hissed.

"Do you speak English?" I said. "Eeeng-liiish?"

Her bony finger shook at me as she said, "*Táimid ag lorg*, Elizabeth Webster."

Hearing my name in the midst of her babble felt like being shocked by a spark. Had the banshees come to warn me of my own death?

"I'm Elizabeth Webster," I said as I leaned away from her skeletal finger. I looked around for some sort of refuge, but all I saw was that gray landscape stretching out as if to the ends of the earth.

The young banshee kept pointing at me as she spoke. I didn't understand her words, but they still somehow grabbed me in the gut, filling my body with a deep sadness. And then, in the middle of it all, I thought I heard a name.

"Who?" I said.

"Keir McGoogan, *mo leanbh.*"

"Keir McGoogan?" I said. "Who is Keir McGoogan?"

When I repeated the name, her sad face cracked into tragedy. She pulled her bony hand back to her side of the mirror and hugged her chest as if she was pulling a baby close. Was Keir McGoogan her son? Was her son going to die? Was that why she had been haunting Young-Mee? Was that why she had called my name?

"You want me to save your baby?" I said. "You want me to save baby Keir?"

With tears in her eyes she nodded, as if she could understand what I was saying, though the only words that were allowed to pass her lips were ancient and strange to me. At the same time, even though she was a frightening apparition from another world, I wanted to help her. In fact, I needed to help her. That might have been my curse for being a Webster, but there it was.

"If I can help Keir," I said, "I will."

"*Seol trasna chugam é.* Keir McGoogan. *Seol mo bhuachaillín ar ais chugam.*"

"I don't understand what you're saying," I said, "but I can see in your eyes that you understand me. I will try to find your Keir and then help him however I can. You have my promise. But in order to do that, I will need two things from you."

She tilted her head, puzzled.

"First," I said, "you need to stop haunting my friend Young-Mee. If I need you, I will find a way to summon you. But this house now is off-limits to all three of you."

As the two old banshees shook their heads and cried out, the young ghost lifted her arms as if Young-Mee's house was somehow special to her. Then her hands dropped, and she nodded in agreement.

I took hold of my backpack, opened the top zipper, and pulled out a scroll of paper along with a pen. I waved the scroll in front of the mirror.

"Second," I said, "if you want me and my family's firm to help you, you need to sign a fee agreement."

As the two old banshees screamed in outrage behind her, the young ghost simply stared.

"I'll need your full name on the top and your signature at the bottom," I said over the howls of the older banshees. "As for the fee, once we save your son, either Keir can pay us in this world or we'll have someone collect our fee on the other side directly from you."

The young banshee stared for a moment longer before she, too, started to scream, a savage cry of outrage, baring her twisted teeth at me as if I was a bloodsucking demon. And, to be fair, I was a licensed barrister before the Court of Uncommon Pleas, so I could see how she could confuse me with such a thing.

As the three banshees kept up their screeching, I sat calmly and waited. My grandfather had told me it would go like this. And as my grandfather had also predicted, it wasn't long before Keir's mother quieted and her face took on a sad resignation. Once again, she reached her arm through the scrying mirror.

For a moment I thought she was reaching for my neck. But then her bony hand took hold of the pen.

As soon as the fee agreement was filled out and signed, the banshees disappeared with a final, ear-denting shriek. The breezes died, the wide gray landscape grew quiet, and my own image appeared once again in the mirror, smiling back at me even though I didn't think I was smiling.

I put my hand up to feel my mouth. No smile on my face. No hand raised in the mirror.

I waved at myself and the mirror image shook her head back at me.

I blinked twice and then everything went blank.

When I opened my eyes again my friends were huddled over me as if they were scribbling a football play with a stick and I was the dirt.

"She's awake," said Henry.

"Are you okay, Lizzie?" said Natalie.

"What just happened?" I said, sitting up and looking around. I was back in the basement and the scrying mirror was gone.

"We were hoping you knew," said Charlie Frayden, who was gripping a pitcher of water with both hands.

"Why are you holding that pitcher of water?" I said.

Charlie looked at the pitcher, then back at me. "I was thirsty?"

"You were going to dump it on me, weren't you."

"No, Elizabeth, I would never think of doing such a thing. Look," he said, and then he began to gulp from the pitcher, a wave of water rolling down his chin. "Boy, that feels good," he said before gulping some more. We couldn't stop looking as he drank and spilled, spilled and drank.

Finally I shook my head and turned to the others. "What did you guys see?"

"We were outside the box, chanting with Barney," said Natalie, "when everything grew foggy and then, bam, a second later the screeching ended and you were, like, sprawled on the floor."

"Only a second passed?" I said.

"It was quick as a snap. Then you stayed asleep for a couple of minutes."

"And Charlie got a pitcher of water," I said as I struggled to stand.

"We had to do something," said Doug.

"And that would surely have been something," I said. A wooziness swept through me, weakening my knees, before I eventually made it, with a hand on Natalie's shoulder, to my feet.

"Did you see the ghosts?" said Young-Mee. "Did you talk to them?"

"I did, actually," I said.

"What did they say? Anything about me?"

"Anything about me?" said Henry.

"Why would my ghosts talk about you?" said Young-Mee.

"I have an old friend over there," said Henry.

"No, they didn't mention you, Henry," I said. "But they agreed to stop haunting Young-Mee."

"They did? Really? Oh, Elizabeth, thank you so much," she said before giving me a hug. "You don't know how much that means to me!"

While Young-Mee continued her hugging, I looked up and saw Barnabas staring at me. He had one eyebrow raised, asking about the fee agreement.

I lifted a thumb.

WEBSTER & SPAWN

To get to the offices of Webster & Spawn from Willing Middle School West, you walk past the bus circle, keeping your head down to ignore all the kids ignoring you, and then head off to the train station, where you pick up the Willing-Pattson local to Center City Philadelphia. After arriving, you climb the station stairs, trying not to glance at the City Hall tower, where a great iron Pilgrim stares down at you with an accusing glare.

Though, to be fair, after all you and the Pilgrim have been through together, you can't say you blame him.

You walk through the City Hall courtyard, the tower looming over you all the while, and glance uneasily at the passersby—the cop twirling her billy club, the old man playing the saxophone, the guy in black with an eye patch and cane who looks like he could have come right off the tower himself—before you head for a boarded-up gray wreck of a building just north of Chestnut Street. Go around the back and slip through a gash in the chain link fence, trying not to let your coat catch on a sharp piece of wire. You'll see a knob poking out beneath the boards nailed over the rear doorway. Open the door and duck under the boards.

When the door slams shut, you need to use the flashlight on your phone as you climb the stairwell to the fourth floor, where the door is kept open just a sliver with a wedge of wood. Step through the doorway into the bright green hallway. The offices on either side are locked and the rooms are empty, but at the end of the hallway, with light leaking through its frosted-glass window, is a door.

Or, I should say, the door.

Think of a world where right side up is upside down. Think of a playground for the weird and the fabulous, where ghosts mingle with the living, where demon plots are foiled by lawyers in wigs and robes, and where long-buried judges with red-marble eyes hand out sentences like sandwiches. Think of everything you're certain about in this life and then throw it out the dusty window, because the offices of Webster & Spawn, Attorneys for the Damned, are not of this world or the next, but of someplace in between, with a single goal for the living, the dead, and the undead alike: EQUAL JUSTICE UNDER THE UNCOMMON LAW.

"There you are, dearie," said Avis to me from behind the front desk.

This was a few days after my encounter with the banshees. Avis squinted at me through narrow glasses as she used her long red nails to hunt and peck, peck and hunt on the keyboard of her old black typewriter. The typewriter was so old it didn't have a power cord. How did they even do that?

"We've been waiting for you," she said. "For you!"

"What did I do this time?" I said. Another thing about the offices of Webster & Spawn: everything I do there is wrong.

"Oh, nothing this time, dearie, though there are files to be filed and floors to be swept. But your grandfather needs to speak to you right away."

"I'll get on it."

"Right away."

"Yes, Avis. Right away."

The chairs beside Avis's desk were half filled with clients waiting to see my father or grandfather about their cases. There was a short, thin man wearing a hat and round glasses, almost like goggles, with a small animal crate resting on his lap. There was Sandy, who was often waiting in the office and had become something of a friend. She had tried to use a witch to give her blond hair a lovely sheen and was now hairy as a Sasquatch. And then—so cute—there was a little girl in a pink dress sitting alone on a chair, her shiny red shoes swinging beneath her.

Beyond them all, in his usual corner of the room, Barnabas sat on what looked almost like a lifeguard's chair, working on a document at his high desk. He raised an eyebrow, letting me know he wanted to have a word.

I smiled at Sandy as I made my way through the rows of chairs. Snuffing and whimpers came from the carrier on the lap of the man with goggle glasses.

"Puppy?" I said.

"Decidedly not," he said, as if I had just insulted him. "It's a gremlin."

"Ah," I said.

"But a friendly gremlin." A low growl came from the crate, along with a glowing red light. "Would you like to pet her, my dear?"

"I'll pass."

"She's had her shots," said the man.

"That makes one of us."

I tried to smile nicely as I moved on. When I reached the toddler, I knelt before her. "Hey, nice shoes. Is your mommy or daddy here?"

"They would be," she said with the hoarse voice of an old lady who'd smoked two packs of cigarettes every day since she was twelve, "if they hadn't been dead for twenty years. The name's Mildred. You got a match, honey? I'm dying for a cig."

I turned to look at Sandy, who shrugged. "Mildred went to the same witch," she said.

"Somebody should sue."

"Exactly!" said Sandy.

"I'm sorry, Mildred," I said, "but the sign on Avis's desk says no smoking is allowed in the office."

"Or combusting," said Sandy helpfully.

"What kind of joint is this, anyway?" said Mildred.

I couldn't help but laugh. It hadn't been long since I'd discovered my hidden history and the very peculiar office of the family firm, but somehow I was getting used to it all. Did that make me a bit peculiar, too? I was trying to figure it out when a yell came from my grandfather's office.

"Is she here yet, Avis? Has she come?"

"She's here," called back Avis. "She's come."

"Well, send her in," called back my grandfather. "What are you waiting for?"

I stood and raised a hand at Avis's exasperated expression before I headed straight over to Barnabas. "Any news on our banshee case?"

"Some," said Barnabas, "but it is quite puzzling. I had the county clerk check the records for a Keir McGoogan. One such person, a boy by that name, who resided at your friend Young-Mee's address, died in 1918 of influenza."

"The flu? Who dies of the flu?"

"Oh, it was a worldwide pandemic that year, Mistress Elizabeth, worse than what we just went through. Millions died. They called it the Spanish flu. I remember it well, another era of masks and quarantine. I volunteered my services in the wards, along with others far braver than me for obvious reasons, and I saw firsthand the toll of the sickness."

"That sounds terrible."

"It was, yes. Along with the war in Europe and the crackdown on those protesting the slaughter, it was a dark time in the city."

"But if that Keir McGoogan is our Keir McGoogan, why would his mother have turned banshee to contact me to try to save her son, who had already died?"

"It is a puzzle, as I said. But we did find one interesting tidbit that makes us—"

"Avis, you pickle-headed shrike!" shouted my grandfather

from his office. "Where is she? What have you done with her?"

"She's coming, she's coming," said Avis.

"You had better go to your grandfather, Mistress Elizabeth," said Barnabas, "before Avis flies off the handle and we're picking feathers out of the air."

THE RAINMAKER

Is that you, Elizabeth?" said my grandfather when I finally stepped into his office. "Where have you been? There is much to be done."

"I know, Grandpop," I said. "There are files to be filed and floors to be swept."

"Right you are, my dear. No use complaining, the chores always need doing. That is the first rule of the legal practice."

My grandfather's office had two desks, a fireplace, a human skull with a mop head on top, and a painting of some old dead lawyer, who happened to be a distant ancestor named Daniel Webster. The smaller of the desks, with an empty top, was mine. The larger desk, covered with towering stacks of old papers and older books, was my grandfather's. He was sitting somewhere behind the tilting piles, rummaging through his papers like a mouse.

"In my father's apprenticeship he fed the horses and mucked the stables. In your father's apprenticeship he scrubbed the front steps of this very building. We all did our chores, and they have much to teach us. How to start a job, how to finish, how to pick up horse droppings with a pitchfork. But the filing and the sweeping are not why I was so anxious to see you. What was keeping you, by the way?"

"I was in school."

"You need to get your priorities straight, girl. Will it be school or will it be the law? I know what I chose, and I never regretted it."

"You didn't go to school?"

"Oh, pish-posh, I showed my face when they needed to see it—the truant officers were rabid in those days—but I learned all I needed to learn at my father's knee. And so could you."

"Even if I wanted to skip school, my mother would never let me."

"Ah yes, the fly in our ointment." I heard a chair scrape the floor and then the tapping of a cane. "Nowadays, your mother has no tolerance for our practice of the law, but there was a time...oh, there was a time."

My grandfather appeared just then from behind the desk, short and bald, with a bent back, a round pink nose, and bushy gray eyebrows. He wore a scruffy black suit and his eyes twinkled as he looked up at me through those eyebrows. I couldn't stop myself from running over and giving him a hug.

"Careful, these bones are not what they once were. But the reason I was so anxious to see you is to offer my congratulations."

I let go and stepped back. "On what? My sweeping?"

"No, my dear, your sweeping is terrible. My congratulations come because you have made it rain."

I looked out the window. "Is it raining?"

"In a way, yes." He did a strange little jig and, with his hands in the air, said, "It's raining cases!"

My grandfather just then looked like an elf dancing at a bar mitzvah. I tried to keep myself from laughing, but I failed.

"What is so laughable?" he said as he calmed himself and patted his chest. "Business is business, always has been, always will be, and sometimes a celebration is in order. Barnabas told me about your banshee. It is one thing to see a ghost—any fool can do that—but to get the ghost's signature on a fee agreement, that takes a lawyer of the first rank."

"She wasn't happy about it."

"Of course not. Getting a fee agreement from a banshee is like getting paid by pulling gold teeth from a leprechaun, a long and bloody process. It is a wonder that Irish lawyers, in this world or the next, have any fingers at all. But you, I see, aren't missing a single digit. Well done!"

"I promised we'd help her son."

"I already put your father on it. He'll crack that nut, he always does. If he needs your help, he'll surely ask you."

"Which means he won't."

"He never liked me interfering in his cases, either. And I believe he doesn't want to burden you any further than he already has, though how the practice of law can be a burden is beyond me. The key, I suppose, is to make yourself somehow indispensable. You'll figure it out, Elizabeth, but until then I have a special treat for you. A case of your own."

"A case for me?" Did my voice squeak? Yes, I think it squeaked.

"Your reputation is rising like a rocket ship." He raised a fist into the air. "Bazoom! A new client came in just today asking specifically for you. A Mr. Topper, it is. A bit of royalty in our field. His father was the Portal Keeper many years ago, the first African-American Portal Keeper in the whole of the country, as a matter of fact. The Thurgood Marshall of Portal Keepers."

"What's a Portal Keeper?"

"There are doorways between this world and the next— portals, they are called. The superstitious call them Portals of Doom, but they are merely passageways between destinations on the ever-twisting journeys of our lives. And one of those portals happens to be quite close by. That is why we left Boston to set up our practice here in Philadelphia so many years ago. And also, the rents were low.

"Now, as I said, our new client's father was once the keeper of that portal, determining who can come and who can go. His term ended in scandal, as they usually do, but it is still quite an honor that his son has come to you for help. You might have seen him in the waiting area."

"Goggle glasses and a gremlin on his lap?"

"Precisely. And the gremlin is the root of it all."

"I didn't even know gremlins were real."

"Real as ghosts, my dear. But very rare, and ownership is tightly regulated. Now, as the son of a former Portal

Keeper, he was allowed purchase of such a creature. And that is the root of your shining new case."

"But he seems so serious. And there's so much sweeping to do. I don't think I'm ready for this—"

"Of course you are. Confidence is all. Avis!" he called out. "Avis, come quickly!"

"What is it?" she said as she hurried into the office, her head swiveling. "Where's the fire? Where?"

"No fire. Work! Do us a favor, please, and bring Mr. Topper into the office."

7

A GOAT STORY

S he is just the gentlest little thing," said Mr. Topper as the creature inside the carrier growled and scratched at the plastic floor. "She wouldn't hurt a fly. Would you want to meet her?"

"No, no," said my grandfather. "That won't be necessary."

"She can be quite affectionate." Another growl. "Are you sure?"

"Quite sure."

Mr. Topper sat on a chair in front of my grandfather's fireplace, the small pet carrier on his lap. My grandfather stood before him, leaning on his cane. I sat on the edge of my desktop, trying not to throw up.

From where I was sitting I could just catch glimpses of the thing in the carrier: a patch of green skin, a glowing red eye, a yellow horn. But it wasn't the gremlin that was clawing at my stomach. What really scared me sick was actual responsibility. And now here was this adult in serious legal trouble who for some strange reason had picked me to save him. Why would he do something as harebrained as that?

"I didn't recognize you when you first walked into the office, Ms. Webster," said Mr. Topper. "I assumed you'd be older. But I heard what you did to that nasty demon in court and I thought, who better to defend my poor Althea than you?"

Anybody else, I thought.

"Who is Althea?" said my grandfather.

Mr. Topper patted the carrier. "My sweet. I'd be so lost without her." He turned his attention to the carrier and spoke as if to a baby. "You're not a demon, are you, Althea?"

A snarl came out of the carrier, rough and high-pitched, like the quack of a deranged duck, that sounded almost like "No."

"That Moss woman who sued us, she's the demon."

Another snarl from the carrier, this time sounding like "Yes."

"Just tell us the facts, Topper," said my grandfather. "In cases like this it is only the hard facts that matter."

"The hard facts are these, Mr. Webster. About a year ago, for some unfathomable reason, Moss moved into the house right next door to me. And soon after moving in she bought a goat, an old bearded scallywag intent on clearing every piece of green in the neighborhood. There was a hedge between our properties, but the goat just chewed his way through. I was constantly asking Moss, in the most pleasant of voices, to keep that little monster on her own piece of dirt. She would use a stake and a rope and that would work for a day or two until the stake came loose or the rope was gnawed in two. Next thing you'd know, the goat was back to snacking on my rhododendron. My poor rhododendron. And they take so long to grow!"

"So what did you do?" said my grandfather.

"I did what I had to do. I got a creature of my own. I found her at a very special pet store, you know the one, Mr. Webster, in Fishtown, run by a skinwalker named Nascha."

"Oh yes, Nascha. What a delightful young lady. I met her once dressed as a groundhog."

"Why were you dressed as a groundhog?" I asked.

My grandfather looked at me like I was still wearing pajamas. "You don't know what a skinwalker is, I presume," he said. "No matter now. Go on, Topper."

"I asked Nascha for a special pet that would scare the goat away from my plants, that's all. And Nascha said she had just the thing, flown in that very week from Puerto Rico. A sweet little gremlin that goats are terrified of, for some unearthly reason. Of course I bought her, and it turned out she was the sweetest little creature. I keep her in the house mostly, she's quite the homebody. She drinks tea and watches the Shopping Channel. How adorable is that?"

"That is pretty adorable," I said.

"I named her after my mother, who was not so sweet, let me tell you. And after Althea came into my life, I'm happy to say, I had no more problems with Moss's goat. None at all."

"Until you were sued," I said.

"It is the goat's fault. It died. Goats die every day. It could have been some fast-acting goat disease. True, the beast was found in a puddle of its own blood, but what does that prove?"

"What does the complaint say?" asked my grandfather.

"Moss insists on blaming Althea. She wants me to pay for the goat and is asking for punitive damages. Punitive. That does not sound good."

"No indeed," said my grandfather. "That is compensation over and above the cost of the goat. Used to punish the offender. And what is her evidence?"

"Moss claims she saw something in the yard that night, something huge and fierce with glowing red eyes and long claws, something hairless and as big as a lion. I don't believe her, who would? But even so, it couldn't have been my Althea. She is such a sweet little girl."

The thing inside the carrier purred.

"But her eyes do glow," I said.

The purring slipped into a growl.

"They might," said Mr. Topper, "but with such an appealing color. Not really red, almost pinkish. Her eyes have a pinkish hue."

"And she does have claws, I presume," I said.

The growls turned into yaps and something slammed against the side of the carrier, making my stomach lurch.

"Little tiny things, that is all."

"Don't worry, Topper," said my grandfather. "Whatever it was that really happened, Elizabeth will the get to heart of it, I'm sure. One final question, if I may. How did the simple case of a dead goat end up in the Court of Uncommon Pleas?"

"Well, as you can imagine, the police were quite skeptical of Moss's glowing-eyed predator story," said Mr. Topper. "Who would believe such nonsense? When they came to my house asking questions, I acted just as skeptical, all the while making sure Althea was safely away in the attic. The police report attributed the death to some wild animal on the loose. After that, no responsible lawyer would take Moss's case. At least until some legal fiend showed up at her doorstep and agreed to sue me for the loss of the goat. He was the one who filed the action in the Court of Uncommon Pleas."

"Do you know the name of the lawyer?" said my grandfather.

"Yes, yes I do." From the pocket of his jacket Mr. Topper pulled out a scroll. "It says it right here on the complaint. Josiah Goodheart."

I almost fell off the desk.

You see, Josiah Goodheart was my nemesis. You would think my nemesis would be that kid in advanced math who was better at calculus than me. Or the girl at Upper Pattson Middle School who ate my lunch in our last competitive debate. But no, my nemesis was Josiah Goodheart, the barrister for the demon Abezethibou, better known in ghostly circles as Redwing. It was Redwing who had imprisoned my father in one of his dungeons on the other side. And it was Redwing who had threatened to imprison me next. I knew if I ever did land in Redwing's prison, it would be Josiah Goodheart who made it happen.

"Goodheart, you say," said my grandfather, something suddenly cold in his voice. He took hold of the scroll, untied the ribbon, and gave it a quick review.

"As soon as I was served the complaint," said Mr. Topper, "I went right to the store where I had bought Althea and showed it to Nascha. She was the one, Ms. Webster, who mentioned your victory over Mr. Goodheart in the Court of Uncommon Pleas. She suggested you might be just the barrister to win my case."

"Elizabeth will do a bang-up job, I've no doubt," said my grandfather. "I think we've heard enough. Why don't you step outside and talk to Avis. We'll need a retainer and a fee agreement."

"Of course," said Mr. Topper. "What do you think my chances are, Mr. Webster? Will I be able to keep my Althea?"

"The law, as we like to say, is the law," said my grandfather, still examining the scroll. "But Elizabeth will ensure you receive due process every step of the way."

"I will?"

"Of course you will. We are all entitled to due process, human and gremlin alike."

"Perhaps you both would be more optimistic about my case if you met her."

My grandfather's head jerked up. "That won't be necessary."

"But she really is so sweet," said Mr. Topper. "To know her is to know how impossible the claims against her are. Wouldn't you like to greet your real client? I'm sure you would."

"I'm sure we wouldn't," I said.

"Maybe some other time," said my grandfather.

"Oh, no time like the present," said Mr. Topper. "Mr. Webster, Ms. Webster, say hello to my darling Althea."

And even as my grandfather said, "Not here. Not now," in increasingly desperate tones, the goggle-glassed Mr. Topper lifted the latch on Althea's carrier and opened the door.

A GREMLIN IN THE OFFICE

The gremlin shot out of the carrier like she was being chased.

She was a little green thing, no bigger than a puppy, with glowing red eyes, sharp ears, and a line of yellow horns leading from her forehead to her poky little tail.

I lifted my legs as the gremlin dashed beneath my feet and sprinted right between my grandfather and his cane, spinning him like a top, before racing out of the office.

"Althea!" shouted Mr. Topper as he rose from his chair and lurched after her.

"Well, are you going to do something," said my grandfather, still spinning, "before I screw myself into the floor?"

I jumped off the desk and grabbed hold of him, stopping his spin. Even as the outer office filled with shouts and cries, my grandfather looked into my eyes and said, "Goodheart."

"Him again," I said. "Weird, right?"

"Something is afoot."

"You mean something other than a foot is a foot? Like a hand is a foot, or a piece of pie is a foot?"

"This is no time for joking."

"Who's joking?" I said.

"Go, go," he said, waving his hand toward the outer office. "Catch that thing before it creates a mess."

By the time I ran out the door, the outer office was in an uproar. Avis stood on top of her desk, flapping her arms, feathers and pieces of straw falling all about her. Barnabas was pressed against a far wall, his arms outstretched. Sandy stood on her chair and screamed, hairy hands over hairy eyes. And my new client, Mr. Topper, was chasing about the room with stiff legs and his arms outstretched, looking like a hyped-up zombie with goggle glasses.

Only Mildred, the young girl/old lady, was calm, sitting in her chair with her red shoes dangling, sucking on a lit cigarette. I figured the gremlin had something to do with setting it on fire.

As for Althea herself, she was nowhere to be seen, but dozens of maroon files were flying out of the file room, papers spewing everywhere. I was about to charge forward and lock her in when she darted back into the outer office and swung on the knob of a closed door, opening it just enough so she could squeeze through the crack.

The door closed behind her and suddenly Avis stopped

her flapping. Mr. Topper stopped his chasing. Barnabas's mournful face took on an expression of horror. And I understood, for Althea had entered the doorway to the temple of gloom, to the land of no smiles—the doorway to my father's office.

And then all three turned to me.

I stood there, taking in their stares, before saying, "All right. I'll get her. Geez, Louise. Does she bite?"

"Only if she's hungry," said Mr. Topper.

"That is so comforting," I muttered as I trudged to the door. I hesitated just a moment more, screwing up my courage, before gripping the knob and heading into my father's office.

We had not been getting along, my dad and I. For so many years he had been like a ghost, appearing here or there at odd moments but pretty much leaving me on my own to deal with my mother and stepfather, my brother, my life. I thought that was the worst, until he suddenly reappeared and I had to deal with him, too. Whenever he saw me in the office now, he took on a pained expression, like he was wondering how he could get me to go away.

It was enough to give a girl a complex.

Inside my father's office all was calm. It had been the firm library before my father took it over and it still had the library hush, along with walls of dark wooden shelves filled with a mishmash of old legal books. My father was working at a big desk, writing on a yellow pad. He had a wide red face and black glasses and dark hair that sort of just flopped around on his head. He glanced up when I came in, gave me one of his disappointed expressions, and then went back to his work.

"Trouble outside?" he said.

"Nothing much," I said. "A lit cigarette, a loose pet, Avis clucking about."

"The usual, then."

"You haven't, like, seen a gremlin, possibly, come into your office, have you?"

"I think I would have noticed," he said without looking up.

I spotted her right then, climbing silently up one of the bookshelves surrounding the window behind my father. She saw me looking at her and grinned.

"You would think that, wouldn't you," I said. My father was just sometimes so...

"I've been working on your banshee case," said my father as I continued to follow the gremlin's climb. "Barnabas has found a lead on Keir McGoogan. An address I'll be checking on tomorrow."

"Can I come with?"

My father looked up at me for a moment and I felt a flutter of hope, but it soon died a quick and agonizing death. You could hear the hope choke and sputter before letting out its final little cry. *I tried*, it moaned. *I really, really tried.* And then: splat!

"This case is more complicated than it appears," my father said before turning his attention back to his papers. "I think it's best if I handle it on my own. And don't you have school?"

"Like every other day, sure."

"What would your mother say?"

"Field trips can help the learning process?"

"Somehow I don't think so."

I would have been more upset at my father's dismissal of my offer to help, but I was busy watching the gremlin climb the bookshelf. When she reached the top, she leaned forward, gripping the wood with her overgrown toenails and swinging her arms.

"And I understand," my father said, still writing on his pad, "that you are getting your own case."

"Apparently."

"Something about a goat? That could be tricky." He tapped a pile of documents on his desk. "These need to be filed."

"I'll get right to it."

"And good luck finding your gremlin."

"The problem isn't so much finding her anymore."

"It's a her?"

"Her name's Althea."

"That's too bad," he said as he kept on writing. "In my experience, female gremlins are the most challenging."

Just then Althea leaped from the bookshelf to the overhead light, a round stained-glass thing hanging on a chain. Swinging back and forth, she struggled to hold on until she made another leap toward the door.

That's when I snatched her out of the air.

She turned and tumbled in my arms, hissing and scratching at my shirt, but I kept my grip until she quieted enough for me to hold her out in front of me with my hands under her arms. For all the trouble she was causing, she was pretty light.

She tilted her head to the side as if to say *Aren't I the cutest thing?*

I shook my head as if to say *Not really.*

Then she purred and licked my hand and let me hold her like a football so she couldn't do any more damage. I turned, expecting to see my father finally smiling at something I'd done in the office.

Instead he stared at me and the gremlin with disappointment creasing his eyes. "Funny," he said. "That doesn't look like a gremlin."

"Well, it's not a puppy, that's for sure."

My father stared blankly at me and then patted the documents on his desk. "Don't forget," he said.

I didn't whine, I didn't complain, I didn't yell out all the terrible things I was thinking about a father who had all but abandoned his daughter and now was treating her like a toddler. Instead I kept my mouth shut, stomped over to the desk, and, while still gripping the gremlin, grabbed the documents. I was about to storm out of the office when my father said, "Oh, one more thing."

"Something else for me to sweep?" I said.

"With the mess your little friend made, don't you have enough sweeping to do as it is?" He wasn't smiling, but he wasn't frowning, either, which was about the best I could expect from my father anymore.

He lifted a book from his desktop, something thick and old and covered in leather.

"Take this," he said.

"To Grandpop?"

"No, it's for you," he said.

I lifted the arm that held the gremlin, lifted the opposite hand, which was filled with his papers, and then shrugged. He leaned forward and stuck the old book in the gap between my jaw and my neck. Althea immediately licked the binding and let out a yummy purr, like it was the spine of a dead fish and not some old book.

"This volume belonged to your great-great-grandfather Elmer Arden Webster," said my father. "It's a book written by a man named Holmes."

"Sherlock?"

"Oliver. Give it a read. It's got stuff on contracts, fraud, and, most importantly for you, negligence."

"Really, Dad?"

"You might find it useful."

And that right there was my relationship with my father.

SOCIAL STUDIES

He's just infuriating," I said to Natalie. "The way he looks at me, like he's ashamed to be related."

"You have to cut them some slack," said Natalie. "It's a difficult time. They're getting older, their bodies are changing."

"And he's so sad when he's with me, like I've ruined his life. I just want to scream all the time."

"Their emotions are all over the place," she said. "I mean, middle age, right? You can only hope they get through it without doing too much damage."

Natalie and I were talking quietly in the back of our seventh-grade social studies class as Mr. Armbruster sat on the edge of his desk and droned on about some president named Theodore who, based on the photographs up on the screen, would run around with boxing gloves and ride horses up hills. Nice work if you can get it, but just then I wasn't so worried about Theodore and his saddle sores. I was steaming about my father. And Natalie, I must say, wasn't being so sympathetic.

"You're not being so sympathetic," I said.

"A few weeks ago you were complaining about your father never being around. And now you're complaining about him being around too much."

"That's it exactly!" I said. "And all he wants me to do is sweep and file, file and sweep. He gave me this stupid thing to look at because he says I've been negligent in my sweeping." From my pack I pulled out the old leather-bound book my father had stuck under my chin and dropped it with a thud on my desktop. "What am I supposed to do with this?"

"Read it, I suppose." Natalie took the book and weighed it in her hand. "You think it's a romance novel? I could give it to my mom. She reads a lot of romance novels."

"Are we disturbing you, Natalie?" said Mr. Armbruster from the front of the class. He was tall and his Afro was gray and he wore bow ties. Yeah, bow ties. One of those. "I wouldn't want to get in the way of your conversation with Elizabeth."

"Don't worry, Mr. Armbruster," said Natalie. "You won't."

As the class laughed, Mr. Armbruster hopped off the desk and strolled toward us. He was always so annoyingly theatrical, which sort of made his class annoyingly fun. "What's that you've got there?"

"A book?" said Natalie.

"But not your textbook. Let's see."

Mr. Armbruster lifted the book from the desk, took a look, stared at Natalie like he was staring at a fish on a bicycle, and then looked back at the book. "*The Common Law* by Oliver Wendell Holmes Junior? Why on earth are you reading this?"

"For the romance?"

"You aren't by chance doing independent research for the oral presentation that each of you will be required to give at the end of our section on the Progressive Era, are you?"

"Would that be good?" said Natalie.

"That would be thrillingly unexpected," said Mr. Armbruster. "Our Mr. Holmes here was actually appointed to the Supreme Court by President Theodore Roosevelt. Did you know that, Natalie?"

"I have the book, don't I?" she said.

"Well, that settles that. You can do your presentation on Justice Holmes and his famous book."

"An oral report on this book?"

"Just a five-minute PowerPoint. And we'll all be expecting some interesting photographs. Justice Holmes cut quite the dashing figure."

No matter how much fun it was to see Natalie squirm under Mr. Armbruster's attention, I felt right then it was my duty to step in. You know, as a friend, and as the person who actually owned the stupid book that was causing all the trouble.

"Mr. Armbruster," I said, "though I am excited to see Natalie's PowerPoint—"

"As are we all."

"I have to admit," I continued, "that the stupid Oliver-whatever book is my book, and so if anyone needs to—"

"Are you trying to steal Natalie's topic, Elizabeth?"

"No, it's just—"

"I'm very proud of her for showing such initiative. I was going to give her extra credit for bringing the book into class and discussing it with us all. And she sure could use it. But if you're trying to take that for yourself, well then—"

"That's not what I meant. I was just—"

"Maybe you should concentrate on your own work in this class. Your test on the Gilded Age was not quite so stellar. What was the line in your essay I was so taken with? Oh yes, 'Just a bunch of rich guys walking around in funny hats and getting fat at banquets.'"

"And your point is?" I said.

Mr. Armbruster was laughing with the rest of the class when there was a knock at the door and a kid came in with a note. Mr. Armbruster gave Natalie back the book and smiled at her before hurrying to the front of the room.

"Ah, this is a shame," he said after reviewing the note and sending the kid on his way. "We're going to have to finish our discussion on Elizabeth's essay at a later time. Because right now, Elizabeth, you are wanted in the office."

The classed filled with oohs and aahs and squeaks—long sad story about the squeaks.

"And take your pack with you," he added. "You might be gone for a while."

10

THE IRON GATE

When I reached the school office, I found out about the doctor's appointment that had supposedly completely slipped my mind. Silly me.

"We're sorry about this," said my father—that's right, my father—as he signed me out at the front desk. He wore a tan raincoat over his suit and didn't look at me as he spoke to Mrs. Haddad, the desk lady. "But we made the appointment with Dr. Fergenweiler months ago and it can't be changed. Elizabeth knew about it, but she left her note at home."

"Sorry about that," I said with a weak smile.

"I'll wait while you get your things from your locker," he said.

A few moments later he was walking toward his car,

parked in the bus circle, as I trudged behind in my blue coat.

"By the way," he said, "how is Dr. Fergenweiler?"

"Retired to Florida," I said. "Here's a tip, Dad. If you're going to lie to get someone out of school, it helps to know a little bit about her life."

His car was white and boring, a hybrid something, dirty on the outside with a mess of papers and cellophane wrappers across the back seat. Tragic, really. As soon as we reached it, he climbed into the driver's seat without a word and slammed the door. I stood outside, waiting. I was entitled to know a few things before I got in the car. Was he taking me to the movies? Was he taking me to a boarding school? My parents seemed to think boarding school was the answer to everything, and I was beginning to think so, too.

After a few moments he got out of the car and leaned over the roof. "Well?"

"Where are we going?"

"Just get in, Lizard Face."

What did I say? What could I say? Every time I had something I needed to say to my father, it got clogged up in my throat and the only thing that got through was a whine or a joke or, best of all, a whiny joke. But even that was now beyond me.

"Look, I don't want to do this any more than you do," he said.

"Then why are you doing it?"

"Because Barnabas told me you promised her."

"I promised who?"

"You promised the banshee that you would personally do what you could for her son."

I thought about it. "Okay, yeah," I said. "Maybe I did. So?"

"As a licensed barrister of the Court of Uncommon Pleas, you should know to be more careful with your promises. So put your huff in your pocket and get in the car."

"Put my what where?"

"Elizabeth, please," he said. "I'm trying here."

"You're not trying very hard, that's for sure."

"Get in before the woman at the front, who is right now looking out the window, starts giving us the stink-eye."

I turned around, waved at Mrs. Haddad, and then opened the car door.

It was a quiet ride. I always thought I could out-silent a rock when I put my mind to it, but I couldn't out-silent my father. Of all the things I inherited from him, that might have been the best.

As we drove out of the neighborhood and into the countryside, the road began to spiral left and right. We passed horses in sunlit pastures and a brick church with a pointy steeple. I had never before been on this route, but you had, though you might not recognize it in the bright sunlight. Imagine it on a rainy night with lightning splitting the sky and a horse-drawn carriage teetering around the corkscrew turns. Maybe the granite arch will do the trick.

Carved into the stone above us was the name LAVEAU.

"Why are we stopping here?" I said.

"Barnabas found census records that put a Keir McGoogan at this address in 1920, two years after the date of his death certificate," said my father as he looked through the windshield at the gate. "Same spelling, same birth date and birthplace, with his employment listed as 'Indentured Servant.'"

"That's peculiar."

"Not as peculiar as the owner of the property, a Marinette Laveau. She keeps appearing on the census records, the same name, but the birth date keeps changing. According to the records she's the fourth generation, but there's only ever one person by that name at this address. You know how the black widow spider kills to mate? Maybe the Laveau women kill to inherit this house."

"Must be some house. I bet there's a pool. I bet there's a butler."

"Look, I don't know what's going on, but spiders can be dangerous. Let me do all the talking. Your promise means you need to be here, but not that you have to say anything."

"Be seen but not heard. You and Mom have been telling me that since I was a baby."

"Well, maybe today for once you need to listen."

There was a thick iron gate embedded in the stone arch and beyond the gate a paved driveway that curved into a patch of overgrown woods. We couldn't see anything past all the trees, but in the sky beyond, a flock of big black birds was circling. My father opened his window, leaned out, and pressed the button on a speaker installed on a post in front of the gate.

Through the gate I could see a kid raking leaves into a messy pile. He saw us, too, but he pretended he didn't, though not very well. He was about my age, maybe younger, definitely smaller, with a red plaid jacket and a blue base-ball cap. As my father kept pressing buttons—he was good at that, my dad—I hopped out of the car and approached the gate. I stepped onto a horizontal slat at the bottom and held on to the vertical iron rods as if they were prison bars.

"Hey," I said.

"Hey yourself," the boy said without looking up from his raking. "I'm willing to bet you're lost."

"I'll take that bet," I said.

He looked up. "How much you got on you?"

"How much of what?"

"You know, fish-skins, jingle-jangle, coin."

"Just my lunch money. Four dollars."

"That's hardly worth the effort, then." The boy talked out of the side of his mouth, like he was trying to sell me a stolen ferret.

"Do you know a Mr. McGoogan?" I asked. "Keir McGoogan. Does he live here?"

"Why you looking for that old gump?"

"We just are."

He jerked a thumb to point behind him. "He should be up there, somewhere, with the rest of them."

"Up where?"

"The château, it's called. It's like a castle but creepier. I'm not sure I'd go up there if I was you."

"I don't have much choice."

"Don't say I didn't warn you."

My father was now talking to the box, but I was more interested in the boy. He had large ears and a narrow face, with two front teeth that were big and cockeyed. And he raked the leaves like he was an actor raking. A bad actor, actually, with a lock of red hair slipping from beneath his cap.

"Hey, you," I said. "Why aren't you in school?"

"Well, now, why aren't you in school?"

"My dad lied to get me out."

"Must be nice. But some of us have to work for a living."

"Is that what you're doing? I couldn't tell. I'm Elizabeth."

He stopped his raking, tilted his head, and looked right at me through the bars. "I'd have bet you'd be older."

"Then that's the second bet you would have lost," I said.

As soon as I said it the gate started shaking before swinging me away from the raking boy. As the boy waved goodbye, my father leaned over in the front seat and spoke through the open door.

"Quit playing around," he said to me, "and let's go."

There was a butler waiting for us outside the great red door of the Château Laveau.

"Welcome, Eli Webster," the butler said in a strange high-pitched voice that sounded like a penguin gargling mouthwash. "I am Egon. I'll be taking you to Miss Myerscough."

The butler was almost enough to put me off butlers completely. He was tall and skinny, with scraggly gray hairs falling from the sides of his skull. Bluish in color, he looked more like a corpse than any corpse I had seen in the movies.

As the butler spoke, I looked around. Large stone wings on either side of the main building surrounded us like a closing fist. When I glanced to my right I saw faces staring out of the dark second-floor windows before they quickly disappeared. The birds I had seen in the distance wheeled and dove above the house. They had little heads, red and featherless, and they grunted while they circled, as if they were hungry and waiting for the butler to die. Or for us.

"We came to talk to Marinette Laveau," said my father. He was still in his raincoat and held a leather briefcase, looking very official.

"The countess is not available during the day," said Egon. "But Miss Myerscough has agreed to meet with you. You should be honored. Most unexpected visitors are turned away at the gate."

He pushed open the big red door and stepped inside before facing us again. Behind him was darkness. His eyes glowed strangely. He just then seemed hungry, so hungry I wanted to give him a cupcake.

"Come, come," he said. "We mustn't keep Miss Myerscough waiting."

When we stepped inside, Egon closed the door behind us and turned the lock with a snap-click.

THE CHÂTEAU LAVEAU

We followed the butler down a checkerboard of white and black marble. The front windows were covered with heavy drapes. Beneath the staircase that rose from either side of the hallway stood a line of large rectangular boxes set upright and draped in black.

"What's inside the coffins?" I asked.

My father glared at me for speaking at all, but Egon simply said, "They're not coffins, Elizabeth Webster. They're cages for the pets."

"Puppies?" I said. "Hamsters?"

"Birds," said Egon.

"Cute."

And it did sound cute, little canaries and songbirds, until I noticed crunching sounds coming from the covered coffins,

as if beneath the coverings monstrous creatures were cracking bones in their beaks.

"Maybe not so cute," I said softly to my father.

"What did we talk about?" said my father.

"I'm just saying," I said. "Nice pictures, huh?"

High on the hallway's walls hung huge portraits of
a series of tall brown-skinned women in various outfits
changing through time. As we walked behind Egon and
the women stared out at me from their somber canvases, I
realized they were all paintings of the same woman, taken
at about the same age, with the same long black fingernails
and the same fierce and haughty expression.

And in each of these paintings, standing behind the
tall woman was another woman, pink-faced and wide-
shouldered, with a single braid of blond hair lying beside
the collar of her own ever-changing collection of dresses.
In each portrait she clasped her hands together and smiled
tightly like an impatient guidance counselor.

"This is the sitting room," said Egon as he led us into a
high-ceilinged room with a grand piano. Two chandeliers
hung from the rafters. "Would you like some tea as you
wait for Miss Myerscough?"

My father said, "No that won't be—" before I inter-
rupted him.

"Tea would be great!" I said. "I'm a bit thirsty, and I'm
sure my father is, too. Thank you, Egon."

After Egon bowed stiffly and left, my father looked at me
as if I was dressed as a teapot. "Since when do you get so
excited about tea?"

"Don't you know that detectives always ask for something to drink," I said, "so they can't be pushed out before they get all their questions answered?"

My father thought about it for a moment. "That's almost clever, Lizzie Face. Where'd you learn that? TV?"

"Natalie," I said.

Over the fireplace hung another of the series of paintings I had seen in the center hall. Here the woman in black was dressed in a modern evening gown with sequins and a scarf. *Très chic*, no? Her chin was up, her eyes peered down at me like she was peering into me. I could almost feel her digging around in there. Behind her stood the woman with the braid and the tight smile, this time in a bright print dress.

I was still staring up at the portrait when the blond woman walked into the room. She was wearing the same dress, with the same braid over the same shoulder.

"I am Miss Myerscough, and you are the Websters, I am told," said the woman in a clipped British accent. "I am sorry the countess will not be able to meet with you, but that could not be helped. I also told Egon not to bother with the tea. I don't expect you'll be staying long enough to enjoy it."

"No tea?" I said.

"No tea. Now sit."

My father tried to say, "I'm sure we can work—"

"*Sit!*" she shouted, and like two middle schoolers faced with a substitute from hell, we sat, my father and I, side by side on a couch facing the fireplace with a low table in front. Miss Myerscough sat in a chair across from us, crossed her legs, and clasped her hands together. One of her very sensible black shoes wagged with impatience.

"So," she said, "what's all this nonsense about Keir McGoogan?"

"We're looking for Mr. McGoogan," said my father, his voice calm as a nut. "He would be well over a hundred by now."

"Undoubtedly dead, then," said Miss Myerscough.

"You would think. But we have reason to believe he's still around. His mother hired our law firm to represent him."

"His mother, oh my," said Miss Myerscough. "Am I supposed to believe she's alive, too?"

"No, she's good and dead," said my father.

"So, what then? Her ghost hired you?"

"Exactly."

"How competent of the ghost. And to think we sometimes have a hard time getting a plumber. And why is she here?" Miss Myerscough said, pointing at me. "Are you babysitting or practicing law, Mr. Webster?"

"This is my daughter," said my father. "She's the one who spoke to the ghost."

She looked at me. "Come closer, dear."

I didn't move off the couch. Something about Miss Myerscough petrified me. Was it a coldness in her eyes, was it her big white teeth? My father had warned me not to speak, but he needn't have worried. Just then I'd have sooner swallowed my tongue than use it to say anything to the bizarre Miss Myerscough.

"The last record concerning Mr. McGoogan that we

could find," said my father, "had him at this address, listed as an indentured servant."

"When was that record?"

"Nineteen twenty."

"Well, if that's the best you can do, you have wasted your trip. Good day, Mr. Webster."

"If we could just have a few moments to talk with Ms. Laveau," said my father, "that might simplify—"

"Did you not understand?" said Miss Myerscough. "Should I be speaking French? *Time to go!*" She rose to her feet and smiled tightly. "Egon will show you out."

Egon now stood in the doorway, thin and hungry, with a huge black raven perched on his right arm. "This way, please."

As I rose, my father looked at Egon and his bird, then back at Miss Myerscough. I assumed it was time to go. I was hoping it was time to go. Please let's go. A shouting Miss Myerscough, a black bird, a hungry butler. I wanted to run out of there like I was running from gym class. But my father remained calmly on the couch. Following his cue, I sat back down.

"Who exactly are you?" he said.

"I am the countess's personal assistant," said Miss Myerscough.

"So you make her plane reservations," said my father, leaning back and resting his arms on the back of the couch, "and get her gowns dry-cleaned. I'm impressed." It was a show of rude arrogance that was middle-school-worthy. I was almost proud of him.

"*Egon!*" shouted the woman. As she yelled, the raven

flew off Egon's arm and flapped its wings twice, circling the room before landing on the shelf above the fireplace. The bird opened its beak and cawed.

"Ma'am?" said Egon.

"Take care of our visitors."

"Yes, ma'am," said Egon before turning around and leaving the room. What was he getting? A shotgun?

"Do you have the authority to speak for Ms. Laveau?" asked my father, still leaning back as the bird on the mantel stretched its wings.

"I assure you I have every inch of her authority."

"That's good to know." He bent over, opened his briefcase, and took out an envelope. "This is a complaint entitled *McGoogan v. Laveau*, in which we are suing your countess for the tort of false imprisonment, along with an emergency injunction, already granted by the court, that provides for the immediate release of Keir McGoogan from these premises."

Just as he lifted the envelope to hand it over, Miss Myerscough flapped her hand. The raven jumped off the mantel, flew right at us, and grabbed the envelope in its claw. It swooped up until it landed on one of the chandeliers, the envelope still it its grasp. The chandelier swung.

"Too bad," said Miss Myerscough. "You'll have to try again later."

"Not according to the uncommon law," said my father. "In the case of *Hardenhead v. Fowler*, the court held that acceptance of documents by an avian agent constitutes valid service of process. *McGoogan v. Laveau* is now alive, scheduled for the next session of the Court of Uncommon

Pleas in this district. The countess knows where to find the courtroom. When we filed this with the Prothonotorius, the clerk told us that Marinette Laveau has been sued a number of times, including for assault of a Class Three wraith, illegal concealment of a Mongolian death worm, and theft of blood."

"Theft of blood?" I said, looking at my father.

"Apparently it's a thing," said my father.

I turned and tilted my head at Miss Myerscough. "Theft of blood?"

Just then a full flock of birds flew into the sitting room, scattering everywhere, diving past our heads. One was so huge it had to stretch its wings straight backward as it whooshed sideways through the door. Its head was black, with a white ruffle about its neck, and its claws were big enough to latch on to my head. It soared around until in landed heavily on the piano. A few of the strings inside twanged. I recognized the bird from a video about the Grand Canyon they made us watch in environmental studies. A condor!

There were now so many birds in the sitting room it smelled like the bird enclosure at the zoo. They were huffing, and rustling, and dropping little gifts of white now and then. It was a good thing my father was wearing his raincoat.

"Release Mr. McGoogan into our care pending the trial," said my father, ignoring the brigade of birds, including the one that had taken a perch right behind him and, for some reason, was stepping on and off his head. "Then we'll happily leave you alone."

My father's bravery in the face of the bird swarm gave me a shot of courage. "I saw faces staring out of some windows," I said. "It was, I have to say, a little creepy. Is this some sort of prison for the damned?"

Miss Myerscough stared at me for a moment and then gave another flick of her hand. An owl swooped down and pecked at my head.

"Ouch," I said.

"Precisely," said Miss Myerscough. "Mind your own business, child."

"But Keir McGoogan is my business," I said.

"And that should worry the countess," said my father. "She might have heard of my daughter." He looked at me in a way he hadn't lately, without disappointment or worry. "Elizabeth Webster. The young barrister who stared down the demon Redwing in court and won her father's release."

Miss Myerscough startled and then looked at me more closely. "You must come again, girl, and meet the countess. You two have so much to talk about."

"We're not prepared to leave without Mr. McGoogan," said my father.

"If you insist on staying, we can make up rooms for you in the attic," said Miss Myerscough. "The chains are a bit rusty, but they should fit."

"If we have to come back—"

"You won't," she said, throwing her arms wide. And at that motion, the room exploded into a chorus of calls and flaps as the birds suddenly took flight.

Miss Myerscough lifted her left arm and the birds all flew

in that direction. She lifted her right arm and they changed course. Suddenly Miss Myerscough was moving her arms like the conductor of an orchestra, and the birds started flying in an intricate pattern around the room, swerving and diving, weaving, forming shapes, dancing to a silent symphony of insanity.

My father and I jumped to our feet and stood there in fear and fascination as the birds flew about us. We were still staring as Egon walked into the room with a silver tray covered by a large silver dome.

The birds broke from their intricate patterned flights and swerved around him.

"Tea?" I said.

"Hardly," said Egon.

He put the platter on the low table in front of us, grabbed hold of the dome, and lifted it quickly.

A pile of live mice were climbing and writhing over each other. They froze for a moment, startled by the light, and then, seeing their opportunity, made a break for it as the birds descended like a mob.

It was pure butchery. Blood and squeals. The flap of wings. Birds pushing and shoving, wrestling and clawing, fighting over their squirmy little meals. One clever mouse almost made it to the door until a raven swooped in and took it in its claws just an instant before the condor took hold of the shrieking raven.

"They get so hungry, the poor dears," said Miss Myerscough in a voice sharp enough to cut through the carnage. "Sometimes they'll go for anything not yet dead."

Through the mayhem of shrieking birds and flying

feathers, Egon grabbed a mouse for himself and bit off the head. With his hand still around the mouse's headless body and blood leaking down his chin, he looked at us calmly and said in that high strangle of a voice,

"You might want to run."

12

A STRANGE SOUND

We bolted out of the sitting room like a pair of runaway rodents.

A pack of birds gave chase down the hallway, zooming beneath the staircase and diving at our heads as we zigged and zagged across the checkerboard. Our shoes pounded the marble tiles and the birds screeched—or was that me? I think that was me.

When we reached the door I yanked at the brass doorknob. It didn't budge. I tried again, felt a wave of desperation, and then remembered the butler snap-closing the lock. While I fiddled with the bolt, my father spun around, swinging his briefcase at the birds.

Thwak!

A cloud of feathers exploded as two black birds slammed to the floor and skidded. The rest of the pack flapped away, like a parachute opening. My father swung his briefcase again as I finally turned the lock and pulled open the door.

When we were both on the outside he yanked the door closed—

"Awwwwkk!" screamed a white bird with a vicious beak, which was caught halfway out of the doorway. My father kicked the squawking bird inside and slammed the door shut.

Safe at last, we both leaned our backs against the red door. As I tried to catch my racing breath and stop myself from crying in fear, I heard my father say, "Uh-oh."

"What?" I said. He was looking up, and so did I. The birds that had been circling high over the house were now much lower, a mass of wing and beak getting closer with each turn.

"Time to go," said my father.

He dashed to the car, opened the passenger door, and dove inside. I leaped in after him, shutting the door behind me. When we were both seated, we turned to look at each other. There was a moment of calm before something thumped onto the roof of the car.

I jumped and let out an "Eeep" before instinctively putting on my seat belt.

We heard another thud. And then a bird landed heavily on the hood, one of the big black birds with little red heads. It waddled up to the windshield, looked left, looked right, and then pecked at the glass.

They all dropped on us after that, one after another, until my father's car had become a huge feathered mob. You could barely see out of any of the windows for all the flapping.

"Can we go, please?" I said loudly and not calmly. Not calmly at all.

"I was hoping to get a look inside the part of the château where you saw all those faces," said my father.

"You want to go exploring when that butler is inside chewing on a mouse and the car is being hijacked by birds?"

"Vultures," said my father calmly. "Turkey vultures, actually. I thought you loved Thanksgiving."

"Can you stop joking and just go? Please? Please?"

"Well, since you're being so polite," said my father. He pressed the start button, put the car in gear, and moved forward slowly. As the birds flew off one by one, the windshield cleared and he was able to speed up. When we reached the woods, I heard a strange sound right next to me.

I turned to look at my father. His raincoat was spotted with bird droppings, there were feathers stuck in his disheveled mop of hair, his glasses were on crooked, his cheeks were flushed, a line of blood was leaking down his temple. And he was laughing.

Laughing?

"What's so funny?" I said, suddenly angry.

He turned and tried to fight his smile. "Nothing."

"You're laughing at me."

"No, I'm not, I swear."

"Then what? You thought that was, like, fun?"

"It wasn't?" he said.

"No, it certainly was not," I said. "We were almost turned into bird feed. Bird feed! And I think one of the little devils might have pooped on my shoulder."

My father gave my coat the once-over. "No might about it."

"This was a disaster! And that Miss Myerscough—what a monster."

"She was certainly something. But you have to admit it was a little exciting."

"It was demented."

"Only in a punk rock sort of way. I thought you liked punk rock. The Misfits. The Vandals. The Dead Kennedys."

"Are they bands or clients?"

"Now who's joking?"

"I'm being serious," I said loudly, maybe too loudly. Okay, maybe I shouted it.

"Calm down, Lizzie Face. If the countess wanted to hurt us, we would have been hurt. Instead she was letting Miss Myerscough give us a friendly little warning."

"Not so friendly."

"Maybe not, but this is the business we're in. It's more than just reading old books and shouting 'Objection!' in court, though that's all fun. We also deal with the deranged and the demented and the undead. We're attorneys for the damned, and it's not all roses." He gave me a sideways glance. "Maybe instead of talking to ghosts and ducking birds, you should be out, I don't know, playing tetherball with your friends?"

"Tetherball?"

"You know, the ball on a rope attached to a pole. You knock it around and—"

"I know what tetherball is, Dad. I don't want to play

tetherball. Nobody wants to play tetherball. But if being a lawyer for the damned is so terrible, why were you laughing?"

"Well, here's the thing," said my father. "I love it. I know it's crazy, but helping dead people fills me. Do you know what that means?"

"Like eating too much coleslaw."

"Sure, with maybe a little less gas. But I also know the price I've paid. I wouldn't wish those costs on you for anything."

"Now you're sounding like Mom. She wants me to give up working at the firm and concentrate on my schoolwork, which I admit hasn't been so fantastic lately. After today I'm thinking she might be right. At least there are no vultures in middle school waiting to turn me into a meal."

"That's not how I remember it," said my father as we drove out of the woods. He tapped his fingers on the steering wheel and then said, "It's too bad we weren't able to search the château. We really need to find Mr. McGoogan before the hearing."

I thought for a moment and then said, "I think I can take care of that."

He stopped the car at the now-open gate and then looked at me. "How?"

"Pull the car ahead," I said. I waited until he was through the gate before saying, "Now stay here."

I pressed open the door, climbed out of the car, and walked back through the gate. I didn't see the boy, but I knew he'd be there, somewhere, fake-raking and waiting. When my father got out of the car to watch, I put a hand out to make sure he stayed on his side of the gate. Then I walked up to the first line of trees.

"You were right about that place being creepy," I said out loud as if to the woods themselves.

"We should have bet on that," said the boy with the narrow face and crooked front teeth, stepping out from behind a tree—the boy who was not a boy, who was instead Keir McGoogan in the flesh.

THE RAKE

I didn't realize it when I first met him. He was then just a kid who was trying to hustle me out of my lunch money. He had known I might be coming, sure, but he could have been told to look out for me by some old guy in the main house.

Except there was something about those portraits of the countess in that long center hallway. She hadn't seemed to age from one to the next. My father suspected they were each a new generation of countess, but the likenesses were too similar. I look like my mom, but I'm not a clone. I mean, have you seen my nose? I wondered if something had stopped the lady from growing old, and then I thought of the boy. Had something stopped him from aging, too? And I know you noticed he had red hair, like the banshee.

"Do you want to come with us?" I said to Keir McGoogan. "My father has a court order that says you can leave."

"What do those two ladies care about some order?" he said. "They won't ever let me go. Staying here forever and never getting old was all part of the dicker."

"Dicker?" I said.

"I thought you talked with my mam."

"I couldn't understand everything she said. She was apparently speaking something called Irish."

"Ah, that she does. But I guess she didn't read the fine print when she signed the paper."

"Paper?" My eyes widened—the legal case had just gotten more interesting. "There's a contract? Do you have a copy?"

"Fat chance of that. I've never even seen it."

He stopped, lifted his chin, cocked his head. Just then I could hear something that sounded like an agonized shriek, followed by a pack of distant yelps and then a rumble closer by. I turned to see the gates closing behind my father.

"That didn't take long," said Keir. "Time to go, Elizabeth."

"Come with us," I said quickly.

The yelps became louder, more frantic. My father grabbed hold of the iron bars of one of the closing gates and tried to stop the movement, but the iron bars pulled at him and kept pulling. His feet slid across the asphalt. He called out my name as the gates kept closing.

"Go on, Elizabeth," said Keir. "Go back to your father. And run when you do it."

I wanted to run, like he said. But something froze my

sneakers in place. This boy who was not a boy, and who was stuck here till the end of time, needed our help, my help. I couldn't run from that. And I had promised his mother.

"I won't go without you," I said.

My father called out my name as the gate kept closing, closing. He reached his arm through the gap, his fingers outstretched. I thought the closing gates would lop his whole arm off, but he pulled it back right before the iron shut with a clang.

"That's it, then," said Keir McGoogan. "I guess you'll be staying for dinner. We should bet on whether you'll be eating or eaten. Four bucks, you said?"

He laughed, maybe at something he saw on my face. My face gets all scrunchy when I'm scared, and yes, I was terrified. But there was a calm about this strange boy-man and his funny way of talking that comforted me.

"I can shake the dogs," he said. "Follow me."

Still holding the rake, he started striding toward the wall to the left. I turned to my father, gave him an *I'm okay* sign, and then ran off to catch up with Keir.

We made our way between the woods and the wall that surrounded the property until we reached a mighty tree, still leafless, that stood right next to the wall. The yelps from the dogs were getting closer and the first branches of the tree were so high it looked to be unclimbable.

"Now what?" I said.

Keir gave me a sly smile before jumping high and banging the lowest branch with the rake. Something collapsed down from the branch, unwrapping itself as it fell.

A rope ladder with wooden slats for rungs.

"Pull her up behind you when you get to the top," he said over the howls of the approaching dogs. He threw down the rake and scuttled up the ladder like a spider. As soon as he was high enough I started following, struggling my way up the swaying ropes and the tilting rungs. My feet kept slipping as I climbed, and then something grabbed hold of my sneaker and yanked.

I looked down. A dog had my foot in its slobbering jaws. The dog snarled and pulled as my other foot came loose from the ladder, leaving me dangling by my two hands.

With my free foot I kicked at the dog. He loosened his jaws just enough for me to snatch out my sneaker and start up again. Suddenly I was climbing like a pro.

When I finally caught up to Keir, he was sitting on a level platform made of wide boards nailed on top of two thick branches. Next to him was an old canvas backpack, green and stuffed full. I sat beside him and looked out over a series of rolling hills splashed with sunlight. They seemed to go on forever. The dogs howled and barked beneath us.

"Nice view," I said.

"This is the only place I feel free anymore."

"Is that why your mom hired me?"

"She said a hundred years of serving a rich lady's whims was enough. And then she met a girl on the other side who gabbed on about you."

"About me? Yikes. Who?"

"She said her name was Beatrice."

"Ah, of course. We helped Beatrice. Maybe we can help you, too. Don't you want to get out of here? See the world? Go, like, to the beach?"

"Sand, water, little metal buckets. Nothing to it." There was something just then in his voice, something sad and scared that made him suddenly seem very young.

"You've never been to the beach, have you?"

He looked at me for a moment, like I had seen through him, and then he looked down. "My mam didn't have the money to take me, and since I've been here I've never been anywhere else. What's it like?"

"Amazing," I said. "The sand is hot and strange on your bare feet. When you look out at the ocean you can see the whole curve of the world. And the waves are telling you a story that you never really understand, but you know is perfect."

"The way you talk about it, Elizabeth."

"If you leave with us, I promise to take you."

"It's a nice dream, but even with your court order thing they won't let me go. My fate is to stay right here. Forever. And maybe that's for the best."

"It's not for the best," I said. "And you can change your fate. That's what the law is all about. You can win your freedom through the law."

He lifted his face to the sky like he was looking for an answer. "I would maybe want to see that beach," he said. "All right then, we'll leave it to Fortune's call." He reached into his pocket and took out a pair of red dice, which he handed to me. "Just give them a roll. You win, I'll go with you. You lose, I get your four dollars."

"You really want my lunch money," I said before shaking the dice in my palm and spilling them onto the planks.

"The number's four," he said.

"Is that good?"

"It could be worse. Roll her again."

I did. A five and a two. "Well?"

"Isn't that a thing."

He looked at me and his crooked smile grew even more crooked. Then he grabbed the dice and stuffed them in his pocket.

"You're a lucky one, you are, Elizabeth Webster," he said. "You get to keep your lunch money for yourself."

"So I won? Just like that? What a stupid game."

"Maybe it is, but a bet's a bet." He stood up, hoisted his pack onto his shoulder, and pulled the end of a rope off a hook screwed into the trunk. "This will swing us right over the wall."

"Funny how you just happened to have a pack in the tree and a rope right there."

"One never knows when it'll be time to run. You convinced me it's finally time."

"And after we swing, then what?"

"Then we let go," he said.

14

THE LATE GREAT GENERAL TSO

When my father and I showed up at my house after our strange visit to the Château Laveau, my mother smiled tightly before reminding me in front of everyone that my grades were falling and declaring that never again was I to miss school for Websterian purposes.

"Do you understand, Elizabeth?" she said slowly, as if I was a little French girl who didn't speak English.

"I zink so," I said.

She glared at me before asking my father to join her for a little chat. He had known what was coming before we arrived, due to a series of angry text messages about my unknown appointment with some long-retired doctor. Still, he nervously adjusted his glasses before he followed her into the laundry room.

After the door slammed shut, Keir dropped his pack on

the kitchen floor and we sat in silence at the table as my mother's angry voice vibrated through the walls like, well, like the screech of a banshee.

"Your mam seems pleasant enough," said Keir.

Yes, Keir was at my house, too. Where else was my father going to take him? A few moments later my brother, Petey, wandered into the kitchen, looked around hesitantly, and sat at the table. "Are you staying for dinner?" he said to Keir.

"What are you having?" said Keir.

"Zilch. A plateful of zilch. Mom was too mad at me to cook."

"She's not mad at you," I said. "She's mad at my father and me. But what did you do this time?"

"Nothing." He looked at me with his earnest face, and then, when the face cracked, added, "Much." Peter, a second grader, was always getting in trouble. That was his superpower.

"If she didn't cook," I said, "I guess that means Chinese food."

"I never had Chinese food," said Keir. "Is it any good?"

Petey perked up. "Where have you been all your life? Chinese food is not good, it's the best. And you have to eat it with sticks. Hold on, I'll teach you." He jumped up and opened a kitchen drawer.

When my mom and dad finally came out of the laundry room with fake smiles on their faces, Keir was practicing picking up red grapes with a set of chopsticks. My mother and father stared as Keir's sticks crossed and a grape spun into the air and onto the floor.

"I guess we're having Chinese food," said my mother.

"I'm sorry I can't stay," said my father. "But Keir, you can stay. In fact, Melinda—I mean Mrs. Scali—has agreed that you can stay here until your hearing, if that's okay with you."

Keir stood up and said, "That would be a pleasure, Mrs. Scali. If I won't be a bother."

"You can stay in my room," said Petey. "I'll clear the science experiment off the spare bed. You might need a new blanket, though." He looked up at Mom. "Did you know that hydrochloric acid is, like, a thing?"

My mom narrowed her eyes at Petey for a moment before saying, "Keir can use the guest room."

Peter and I looked at each other with eyes wide. The guest room was sacred, no kids allowed. In truth, no one was allowed. Ever. We joked that my mom was saving the guest room for the Queen of England in case she ever showed up, but only if the spare bed in Peter's room was already being used. And now she was giving the guest room to Keir?

"I'll put on fresh sheets and lay out some towels for you, Keir," said my mother. "So what would you guys like to order?"

"Let's get General Tso's," said Petey.

"Who is General Tso?" said Keir.

"He was a famous general," said Petey.

"Who fought a courageous battle," I said.

"Before dying in a vat of hot oil," added Petey.

"And being buried in a sweet sauce," I said.

"Such a sad, sad story," said Petey. "Tasty but sad."

As my brother and I laughed and pounded on the table, Keir just stared at us. "I don't get it," he said.

"And you won't," said my brother through his laughter, "if you try to eat it with those sticks."

Later, during dinner, it was my stepfather, Stephen, who asked the question that would change so much.

Stephen had brought home the Chinese food—yay!—and Keir was using his fork to eat his General Tso's chicken, no knife required. There were also egg rolls, and dumplings in soup, and green beans in garlic sauce, and these little green things called bok choy. A feast! But, tragically, there was also conversation.

"Where do you go to school, Keir?" asked my stepfather.

"I don't go to school," said Keir. "The dead general is quite tasty, Mrs. Scali."

"Thank you, Keir," said my mom.

"No school?" said Stephen. My stepfather was thin and bald and spoke slowly, as if each of his words was a caramel that would stick in his teeth if he tried to finish it too quickly. But no matter how slowly the words were getting out, all this talk of school could not end well. "A boy your age has so much to learn. What do you do if you don't go to school?"

"He's homeschooled," I said, jumping in with a half-truth. I mean, Keir had certainly learned a lot at the Château Laveau, like how to avoid the dogs. "Please pass the bok choy?"

"Homeschooled," said Stephen. "That's interesting. Who homeschools you, Keir?"

"And pass the green beans, too," I said, jumping in to hijack the conversation and landing on, well, anything. "I guess I'm just on a vegetable kick. You know, Mom, we should have more vegetables. Aren't vegetables great? What's your favorite vegetable? Mine is Brussels sprouts. I just like saying it. Brussels sprouts. Let's go to the store and buy a bucket of Brussels sprouts. Yum!"

There was a moment when everybody just looked at me like a bushel of Brussels had sprouted right out of my head.

Then Keir, ignoring my really quite brilliant Brussels sprout maneuver, broke the quiet. "There are plenty of old books in the house," he said.

I gave him a stern look before adding, "And his aunt instructs him."

"My auntie?" said Keir.

"Miss Myerscough," I said. "We met her. Nice lady. She keeps pets. Birds mostly."

"She's not my auntie," said Keir. "But Miss Myerscough is very instructive."

"And very strict," I said.

"You can say that again."

"And very strict," said Petey.

My stepfather looked at me, then at Keir, and then at Peter. I thought for a moment we had sidetracked him from all this school nonsense, but no. He was a lawyer, after all—a mere patent lawyer, as my grandfather always said but a lawyer nevertheless—and it's hard to sidetrack a lawyer.

"Well," he said, "since you're staying with us for the

time being, and Miss Myerscough won't be around to guide your lessons, perhaps you could go to school here."

"I don't think that's a good idea," I said.

"It would be a shame for Keir to just waste the time," said Stephen. "And think of the friends, the classes. Lunch. They serve lunch there, don't they, Elizabeth?"

"Yes, they serve lunch."

"See," said Stephen. "Tater Tots. Who doesn't love Tater Tots? That's a vegetable, too, I believe. And you'd look out for him, right, Elizabeth? Introduce him to your pals. Show him the ropes. Gosh, I think back on my school days with such fondness."

"Mom?" I said. "Really? Can you say something, please?"

My mother would put an end to this nonsense. My stepfather looked at Keir and saw your average kid, but my mother knew better. That was why she was sticking him in the guest room. My mother understood you couldn't just dump someone like Keir McGoogan, unsuspecting and innocent, on a bunch of wild middle school delinquents who would rip him to shreds.

My mother looked at Keir for a long moment and then said, "What do you think, Keir?"

"Trust me, he won't choose to go to school," I said. "If I had the choice, do you think I'd choose school? Keir has no interest. None. And why doesn't he? Because he is sane, that is why. Tell them, Keir. Tell them how sane and normal you are."

"It might be educational, Mrs. Scali," said Keir. "I'm willing to give it a try, if you both think it best."

My mother looked at Keir and then at me and I could see

her mind working. I looked at Keir and gave him my *What are you doing?* face, but Keir just put on that tilted smile of his and shrugged.

"That's settled, then," said my stepfather. "Would you like me to call Superintendent Bartrum, Melinda? She owes me a favor after the last Board of Commissioners' meeting."

"No, dear, I'll take care of it," said my mother. "I know just whom to talk to. More beans, Peter?"

"No thank you," said Petey. "I don't want to hog the beans, since Lizzie is suddenly so hungry for vegetables. I could give you all the beans still on my plate, Lizzie, if you want, since Mom gave me so much."

"That's sweet of you," I said.

"And good news!" said Petey. "I think there are some carrots in the fridge."

Later, after things had settled down and my parents had finally gone to bed, I tiptoed to the guest room and tapped lightly on the door.

"Come in," said Keir.

He was still up, pacing around, looking at the walls, out the window. His pack was sitting on his bed, its contents spilling out. Along with some clothes there were tubes of suntan lotion. It was almost as if his mother had packed for him, his dead banshee mother.

"What got into you?" I said. Did I say it sweetly? No. Were my hands on my hips? They might have been. Did I sound like my mother? Yes, I'm sad to admit, I did. "How did you get yourself roped into going to school?"

"I don't know," he said. "My brain, it just went bonkers."

"Then tell them it was a mistake. I'll bring them in right now and you can tell them."

"Is it, really? A mistake, I mean. I don't know, Elizabeth. It might be a bit of fun."

"I'm there every day and I assure you—there's no fun. Why do you think they call it school?"

"I don't know. Why?"

"Because there's no fun!"

"I didn't last long at school my first go-round. The nuns wouldn't put up with my nonsense. Maybe I can do it right this time. You think?"

I stared at his hopeful face for a moment. "The kids are going to eat you alive."

"I'm a bit rusty in palling around, true," he said. "But if I'm to live outside the château's gates like you want me to, I'm going to have to learn to deal with people who look to be the same as me. Like I said, it might be educational."

Didn't I have enough to worry about just then? Schoolwork, and the sweeping at Webster & Spawn, and my battling parents, and the gremlin. The gremlin! Didn't I have enough on my plate without having to usher Keir McGoogan around the halls of Willing Middle School West?

Apparently not.

And the whole mess turned even messier when late that night I was woken up by something scraping and banging against my window. I tried to ignore it, but that wouldn't do. Maybe it was Natalie on the branch by my window with some secret message. Or maybe it was the squirrels, which had made a home in that tree, scrambling around like chipmunks. I grabbed the flashlight I used to read under my covers at night, slipped out of bed, and crept over to the window.

I raised the blinds and flicked on the flashlight to get a look. Then I flicked it off, lowered the blinds, jumped back in my bed, and hugged my knees to my chest.

What had I seen?

A bat is what I had seen. Except, this bat was as big as a cat. As it flapped around, it stared through the window right at me and showed me its sharp little teeth. And I began to sense what exactly we were dealing with in the strange case of Keir McGoogan.

Was I scared? Let's just say if I'd hugged my knees any tighter, they would have been behind me.

PIRANHA

There were birds in the trees outside our house the next morning, not sweet little birds twittering about love and worms, but great black birds with red heads, so heavy from the carcass bits sitting in their bellies that the branches drooped.

"Nothing to worry about," said Keir. "Just the countess's little spies."

"Not so little," I said.

The same pack was sitting in the trees outside the school when my stepdad dropped us off. They had beat us to the spot. They were clever winged things, I had to give them that.

After we climbed out of the car, Keir and I stood side by side as we faced the old stone building. He had on his red plaid jacket and his blue baseball cap, but his usual sly smile was nowhere to be seen. He stood frozen while kids streamed around us.

"Is something wrong?" I said.

"For some reason I'm feeling green around the gills," he said. "It must be the dead general I ate."

"It's not the food," I said. "You're just scared. And why wouldn't you be? This is the most terrifying building known to humankind."

"Don't be forgetting I just spent a hundred years in the queen bee's flophouse."

"This makes the Château Laveau look like a petting zoo," I said as I spread my arms wide. "Welcome to middle school."

As I led Keir McGoogan through the halls of Willing Middle School West, I tried to see the scene through his innocent eyes. Packs of wild kids shouting and jostling, pushing and shoving, calling out greetings and insults, knocking books onto the floor. Other kids staring down at their feet, wearing headphones, trying to be ignored as they headed for their lockers (my people!). Kids and more kids, a kaleidoscope of kids of all sizes and colors and cliques, with their fears and hopes, their packs and eyeglasses, their own little demons sitting on their shoulders and jabbing spears into their necks. They made the birds in the trees outside look like bath toys, the hounds look like stuffed puppies.

"It seems safe enough," said Keir.

"Not if your eyes are open," I said.

"But why is everyone squeaking? They pass us and they squeak."

"I have no idea," I lied. "Maybe their voices are changing."

"That girl there is waving at you."

"It's safer to just ignore everyone," I said. "Keep your head down and pretend you don't hear or see anything."

"Lizzie, Lizzie, over here," I heard above the shouts and laughter.

I broke my own rule, looked up, and saw Natalie standing at her locker with Henry. I put up a hand, telling them to wait, and then took hold of Keir's sleeve and guided him through the streaming crowd, like I was guiding a baby deer through a piranha-filled section of the Amazon. We made it safely to the other side, barely, and entered the school office.

"Hello, Elizabeth," said Mrs. Haddad at the front desk. "How was your doctor's appointment yesterday?"

"Eventful," I said. "This is Keir McGoogan. He's a new student? I was told he was supposed to check in at the office?"

"We've been waiting for you, Keir," said Mrs. Haddad. "Mrs. Scali told us all about you. Have a seat, and Mr. Gavigan will be with you shortly."

"Mr. Gavigan?" I said.

"Yes, of course. All new students need to be evaluated by a guidance counselor."

"Thank you, ma'am," said Keir before walking over to the row of chairs against the wall. I followed and sat down next to him.

"We have a problem," I said in a soft voice.

"What kind of problem?" said Keir.

"Mr. Gavigan. He's going to ask you all kinds of personal

questions, but he can't know anything other than that you're a twelve-year-old kid who has been homeschooled. Nothing about the countess, or your mom being a ghost, or especially about how old you really are."

"Don't worry, Elizabeth," said Keir. "I think I can handle a wee guidance counselor."

"Don't be so sure. He's going to look into your eyes and say all he wants to do is help. They're trained to do that, like seals are trained to balance basketballs on their noses. But if you let down your guard for even a moment, he'll snatch you up like a mackerel."

"Elizabeth?" said Mrs. Haddad. "Don't you need to get to homeroom?"

"I thought I'd wait with Keir," I said, "him being new and all."

"That's nice of you, dear, but I'm sure he'll be fine." She waved her fingers like she was shooing flies from her desk. "Scoot on off to class."

I gave Keir a warning look and then I scooted.

Natalie and Henry were still waiting for me when I came out of the office. Natalie was giving me one of her stern faces, the kind she gives when you snatch a French fry off her plate. Natalie's not a sharer with her food.

"I texted all night but got nothing," she said. "You ghosted me."

"What else do you expect from Webster?' said Henry.

"What was the emergency that got you out of Armbruster's class," said Natalie, "and how can I have one before I have to give my report on that stupid book of yours?"

"It was my dad," I said.

"Ah, the plot thickens," said Natalie.

"It had something to do with a case."

"Your gremlin case?" said Henry. "Natalie told me about it. Oh man, what I wouldn't give to see a gremlin. Maybe rub his head and make a wish."

"Those are genies, not gremlins," said Natalie.

"Her name's Althea," I said. "And I might need that old book back, Natalie, because I think I'm seeing her at the office this afternoon."

"Can I come, Webster?" said Henry. "Please? We're a team, right? Like when we found Beatrice's head. You, me, and Natalie, we're like the Three Musketeers."

"Now we'll be the gremlineers," said Natalie.

"Why would we be a gremlin's ears?" said Henry.

I looked at Henry, who didn't understand why Natalie was laughing at him. "I actually might need an official gremlin wrangler," I said.

Henry raised his hand. "Let me do it, Webster. Please."

"Do you have any experience with animals?"

"We had a dog," said Henry. "He died. And then we got Perky."

"Good enough. Meet me at the front door after school." I looked left, looked right, and then lowered my voice. "But that's not what yesterday was about."

"Who was that kid you took into the office?" said Natalie.

"He's what yesterday was about," I said. "Believe it or not, that was our banshee's son. That was Keir McGoogan."

"No," said Natalie.

"Yes," I said.

"That's impossible," said Henry. "He's just a kid."

"And Keir should be an old man by now," said Natalie. "He should be gray and stooped and wrinkled like a prune."

"He should, but he's not," I said.

"Yikes alive!" said Natalie. "He must have the best skin cream in the world."

But I was already getting the the idea that Keir's secret of eternal youth might be a little scarier than that.

SHINY DIMES

We were discussing the Sherman Antitrust Act in social studies—yawn—when Natalie stunned us all by actually raising her hand.

"Isn't there something about cruel and unusual punishment somewhere?" she said when called on.

"Yes, there is," said Mr. Armbruster. "In the US Constitution. Why the question, Natalie?"

"Because I think this class qualifies."

"I would expect you'd be especially interested in the Sherman Act," said Mr. Armbruster over the laughter, "since Justice Holmes, the author of your book, joined the majority in the act's most famous application, the Standard Oil case. Do you know why all our gas stations have different names?"

"The Standard Oil case?" said Natalie.

"Correct."

"Thank goodness for that," said Natalie. "Now if they could just clean the bathrooms."

That was when the door opened and Keir appeared. He looked a bit sheepish when he handed the slip to Mr. Armbruster, as if the laughter at Natalie's bad joke was aimed at him.

"So, class, we have a new student. Keir McGoogan. Take a seat anywhere, Keir."

I was sitting in my usual place, in the back row next to Natalie. I moved over a seat, leaving a gap for Keir. He walked through the desks and sat right between us.

"Where have you been?" I whispered to him.

"I was being tested," he whispered back. "I didn't do so well."

"Let me see the schedule Mr. Gavigan gave you."

He handed me the paper. Remedial math. Sixth-grade language arts. Sixth-grade earth science.

"He's making me take typing," said Keir. "What's the point of that? Will I end up working in the typing pool?"

"What does typing have to do with swimming?" I said. "You can't swim and type at the same time."

"You can almost be funny sometimes, Elizabeth."

"Who's trying to be funny?" I said. "This is going to be harder than we thought."

"So who can tell us about John D. Rockefeller?" said Mr. Armbruster to the class.

"He was, like, the richest American ever," said Juwan.

"Yes, he was," said Mr. Armbruster.

"And he built that oil company up from nothing," said Shelly.

"Yes, he did," said Mr. Armbruster. "In fact, the Standard Oil case was about breaking up the very company he built. Anything else?"

I noticed something out of the corner of my eye. Keir was raising his hand. "What are you doing?" I whispered. "Put your hand down. What did I tell you? And you don't even have the textbook—"

"Keir," said Mr. Armbruster. "It's so nice to have a new student speak up so soon. Yes, what do you know about Mr. Rockefeller?"

Keir stood and looked nervously around, like he had been caught at something, before speaking up. "He used to give dimes to the kiddies."

Mr. Armbruster's eyes widened and then he started walking toward Keir. "Yes, he did. That's an interesting little tidbit. How did you learn that?"

"I just know it," said Keir. "He would have his servants shine the dimes with spit and a rag and then he'd give a little lecture along with the dime. The papers, they lapped it up. My mam said it was so nice of him, but I figure he could have given eight bits as easy as a dime, or a plate of food if the kid was hungry, or a bed if the kid had no place to sleep. But that would have cost more than the smallest coin they had. So instead he tossed the dimes, polished with his servants' spit, and polished his own apple at the same time. The end."

When Keir sat down, Mr. Armbruster gave him a long look and then spun around to address the class. "Any comments?"

"I'd have taken the dime," said Juwan. "And maybe I'll

take Keir's dime, too, if he doesn't want it. Then I'd have two dimes."

"Enough for two whole caramels," said Natalie.

"Look, anyone wants to give me money I'll take it. Let everyone say how good he is on cable news for giving it away, who cares?"

"My dad said one of the mobsters in Philly used to give out turkeys every Thanksgiving."

"That was nice of him."

"He was a mobster!"

"But a nice mobster."

"What's eight bits, anyway?" said Natalie.

"Eight bits is a dollar," said Mr. Armbruster.

"Then I'd rather have the dollar," said Juwan.

"I'd rather have the turkey," said Natalie.

As the class laughed, I couldn't help but grow angry. I mean, here I was in the middle of a serious Keir situation, and my friend Natalie was running for class clown.

After the bell, which as far as I was concerned could not have come too soon, I pulled Keir aside in the hallway, looked this way and that, and then said in a low voice, "What was all that stuff about the dimes?"

"The teacher asked a question," said Keir.

"But why did you have to answer? Didn't I say to keep your head down and ignore everything? What about that wasn't clear? Did you hear me participate? No, you did not hear me participate."

"Don't you ever participate?"

"Only because they grade it, which is stupid. I mean, as long as I talk I get a better grade no matter what stupid things I say? How does that make sense? No, I'm not here to participate."

"Then what are you here for, Elizabeth?"

"What kind of question is that?" I stuttered around for a bit and then said, "I'm just here. I show up, I trudge from class to class, I go home. That's middle school."

"But it went over, didn't it? The dime thing. It got the class yakking."

"You're supposed to be a twelve-year-old kid. How does a twelve-year-old kid know any of what you talked about? Mr. Armbruster went to Harvard. Harvard! He's smart enough to figure out exactly who you are. You need to be more careful."

"Head down."

"That's right."

"Ignore everyone."

"See, it's not so hard. Now I probably won't see you again until school's over. Meet me outside the front door, okay, and we'll head down to my father's office."

The bell rang.

"You better get to your next class," I said. "You're already late."

I watched him saunter off, looking at his schedule and then at the numbers on the doors. Poor thing, he'd never get the hang of it.

There was a weird scene outside the building when I met up with Henry and Keir after school. Two cop cars and a blue van were parked in the bus circle and a group of adults in uniforms were standing beneath the trees where the countess's birds were still perched. Two of the adults in uniforms were carrying poles with round nets on the tops, as if they were hunting butterflies. The sign on the side of the van read ANIMAL CONTROL.

Mr. Armbruster, standing just outside the front doors, had his hands on his hips as he watched. "We're having a bird issue," he said when he saw the three of us join the group of kids already surrounding him. "A kettle of vultures."

"A kettle?" said Henry. "Are they going to boil them for soup?"

"A kettle is what you call a group of vultures, Mr. Harrison, sir," said Charlie Frayden, standing next to the teacher.

"That's correct," said Mr. Armbruster. "Like a pack of wolves and a murder of ravens."

"These vultures are actually of the genus *Cathartes* and the species *aura*," said Charlie Frayden. "Turkey vultures, to be precise."

We all turned to look at him like he was giving a speech in Latin, which he sort of was.

"Doug and I are birders," said Charlie with a shrug. "Just something to do on Sundays. This kettle has already been reported on the local bird forums. Birders are coming from all over to see it."

"I don't blame them," said Mr. Armbruster. "Magnificent creatures, actually, magnificent and disgusting at the same time. The animal control people think there must be a corpse nearby. Maybe a dead deer."

"I'm sure that's it," I said. "If they were looking for live prey, they'd probably go to one of the elementary schools. Easier pickings."

Mr. Armbruster gave me a look and then said, "A couple of the vultures attacked someone trying to visit the school. Mrs. Haddad saw it and called animal control. Now they're trying to get rid of the birds."

"Good luck on that," said Keir.

Something about that little story set me to scanning the school parking lot. That's when I spied the strange-looking man standing across the street from the school. He was dressed in black, with an eye patch and a cane, and he looked vaguely familiar. Beside him stood a large gray dog. Was this man the visitor? Who was he visiting? And why was he staring at us with his one good eye?

"The animal control people tried waving their arms, yelling out insults, hooting," said Mr. Armbruster. "Now I think they're planning to play some loud music."

"Rap?" I said.

"Ramones?" said Henry.

"Rachmaninoff," said Mr. Armbruster.

"That should do it," said Henry.

"Rakes work, too," said Keir.

"How was your first day of school, Keir?" said Mr. Armbruster.

"Instructive, sir."

"Keep up the good work."

"Thank you."

Then we were off, the three of us, heading for the train station. We hadn't gone ten feet when we heard it, a flush of sound, like the whoosh of a great gust of wind. Right then, up above us, I saw them, the kettle of vultures, rising and circling, as if they were now indeed looking for live prey and the live prey they were looking for was us.

There was a mild roar from behind us as the teachers and kids clapped and cheered at the disappearance of the birds. "Keep walking," I said, and that's what we did, but as we kept walking I looked back.

Everyone was staring up at the birds, everyone but Mr. Armbruster, who was looking straight at us. Or, more specifically, straight at Keir.

And the stranger with the eye patch? He started to follow us until one of the vultures peeled away from its kettle and flew straight at him. He lifted his arms to cover his head, turned away, and ran.

THE GIRL WITH THE WOODEN STAKE

On the train ride into the city, while Keir taught Henry one of his dice games—rolling the little red cubes on the seat between them—I finally cracked open the old book my father had given me.

It was divided into a series of lectures by this Holmes guy, some on contracts, which might come in handy on Keir's case, and some on crimes. But I was looking for something about a goat, and there was nothing in the contents about a goat. There was, however, something about cows, which was the closest I could get, so I gave it a look.

Holmes talked about a case from the 1800s called *Rylands v. Fletcher*, which told you what responsibility you had for damage done by your cow. Generally, you only had to pay up for any damage your animal caused if you didn't act like a reasonable person in taking care of your animal. That's called acting negligently.

But the *Rylands* rule said if you owned an animal that was likely to do mischief, like a cow, and then the cow escaped and chewed up someone else's lawn, then even if you acted like the most reasonable person in the world—the Queen of Reasonableness, a librarian even!—you would still have to pay. It seemed unfair, but there it was. If your pet was a dog, a cat, or a hamster? You'd be safe, because those are normal sweet little animals. A cow? You'd be in trouble. But what about a gremlin?

I had met Mr. Topper's gremlin. I had grabbed her out of the air and looked her in the eye and swept up the mess she'd made. Mischief was her middle name. As we walked through the tunnels of the underground train station next to City Hall, I was thinking that this case was going to be harder than I thought, when I looked up and spotted a girl thirty feet away running toward us through the crowd.

The girl was older than me, high school age at least, tall, with torn jeans that hung loosely, a black leather jacket, and wild hair. Was she looking right at me as she ran? Yes—or maybe she was looking just to my right, where Keir was walking along with Henry. And in her hand was a large wooden spike.

I froze as the girl in the leather jacket, still running through the scattering crowd, shouted, "This is for Travis, you undead abomination!"

She raised the stake over her head and took two more steps before she leaped.

I'd like to say I bravely stood in front of Keir McGoogan,

my client, to protect him from the deranged girl in the black leather jacket. I'd like to say I did anything other than fall into a quivering heap on the floor as the girl with her wooden stake sailed through the air with murderous intent on her face. But that would all be a lie.

All I know is when I heard another shout and then a splat, I looked up from my spot on the floor and saw the girl sprawled face-first to our side. Above her stood a man in full fighting pose.

"Begone, demon huntress," said the pale, pointy-nosed man in a black cape, with matching hat and eye patch. He waved his cane at the sprawled girl as if it was one of those thin French swords you see in old pirate movies.

The girl spun to her feet and took a graceful step forward, like a cat stalking her prey. That's when the man's dog, huge and gray, looking very wolfish with hair rising all along its spine, bared its teeth and growled.

The girl hesitated.

The dog lowered its head.

There was a moment of frozen expectation before the girl spun and sprinted away as the dog, with howls and growls, charged after her. You could chart the progress of the chase by the screams from the horrified commuters.

Still on the ground, I took a moment to check on my friends. Henry was on his feet, twisting to watch the chase, and Keir, who stood close behind him, was doing the same. I couldn't tell if Henry had bravely stood in front of Keir, or if Keir had jumped behind Henry, using the taller boy as a shield.

Still shaking, I had started struggling to my feet when a hand reached down to assist me. I looked up into the eye of the man who had saved us. I was so close I could see the scars beneath his eye patch.

"I help you up, *ja?*" he said with an accent, as if he had just come from planting tulips in Amsterdam.

"I'll be fine," I said, though I wasn't, and with my knees still shaking I grabbed his hand and let him pull me to standing.

"There, there," he said. "Calm your heart, Ms. Webster. I trust you remain unhurt."

"You know my name?" I said.

"*Ja*, of course. The famous Elizabeth Webster. Famous at least in some circles. Fortunately for you, those circles are my circles."

"Thank you for doing what you did, sir," said Henry. "I don't know what just happened, but man, that was close."

"Too close," said Keir.

"That was quite a kick you gave her," said Henry. He did a bad imitation of a karate kick. "You tumbled her right out of the air."

"It was a simple *vechtsporten* sweep," said the man. "I was afraid something like this might happen. It is why I followed you three from the school."

"Afraid what would happen?" I said.

"An unprovoked attack. Danger is all about you, Elizabeth Webster."

"About me?"

"*Ja*, who else?" said the man.

"Gulp," I said. "Who is the girl?"

"Her name is Pili. She was made crazy by grief. A sad case, a tragic case, the facts of which are better left unexplored. And I regret to say she is not the only danger for you, as long as your client is by your side. Allow me to introduce myself. I am Dr. Rudolf Van."

Dr. Van fished a card out of his vest and handed it to me.

"What kind of sawbones are you?" said Keir.

He looked at Keir closely as he answered. "I am exactly what you need, young man. I am an educator and a protector. A doctor of metaphysical science, to be precise." He smiled and then turned to me. "I would love to stay and chat—and we all have much to chat about, *ja?*—but I need to collect my pet before she gets into much trouble."

"That's some dog," said Henry.

"Her name is La Loba," said Dr. Van. "Quite cuddly, actually."

"That Pili girl, she yelled the name Travis—who is Travis?" I asked.

Dr. Van looked at me, first with amusement and then with sympathy. "He is the brother of that young girl. Was, I should say. Some tragedies provoke sadness, some provoke revenge. Goodbye, my friends, and be careful."

And just that quickly, he was gone, his cape flapping behind him as he hurried away in the same direction as the girl and the dog, which probably wasn't a dog at all.

I looked down at the card still in my hand. RUDOLF VAN, it read, DOCTOR OF THE METAPHYSICAL SCIENCES. I had never heard of such a thing. It sounded like the kind of degree you buy on the internet, like Doctor of Television Studies. But it was the next line that interested me more:

HEADMASTER OF THE SEDONA ACADEMY FOR SPECIAL CASES.

That sounded quite peculiar. I sensed just then that the Sedona Academy for Special Cases didn't specialize in teaching math.

"Let's get out of here," I said, and we did, hustling through the still-staring crowd and climbing the steps to the street.

In front of us was City Hall, and circling now in front of the cockeyed tower was the kettle of vultures, as if waiting for their turn with us.

THE STURDY BAKER

We were still talking about the attack, trying to settle our nerves, when Henry, Keir, and I showed up at the offices of Webster & Spawn. Next to the usual THANK YOU FOR NOT SMOKING OR COMBUSTING IN THE OFFICE sign was another sign with the words NO GREMLINS ALLOWED.

I wondered if Josiah Goodheart could put that sign in as evidence.

"You've come," said Avis when she saw us walking through the door. "Your grandfather has been asking for you all day." Then she squawked out, "Elizabeth has arrived!"

"Finally!" my grandfather shouted back from his office. "Have her wait!"

"He wants you to wait," said Avis.

"I guess I'll wait," I said.

"Welcome back, Henry," said Avis. "Anything we can do for you, dearie?"

"Elizabeth brought me in to help her handle the gremlin," said Henry.

"Well, somebody should," said Avis. "Did you bring a helmet?"

"Helmet?" said Henry, giving me a look. "No."

At just that moment my grandfather burst out of his office, which for him meant waddling through the doorway with his back bent, banging his cane on the floor with each shaky step, harrumphing all the while.

"Don't bother taking off your jacket, Elizabeth," he said when he saw me. "There is much to be done and we are the ones to do it. Word has come that the court is on its way to Philadelphia and the case of *Moss v. Topper* is on the docket. We must prepare. Hello, Henry, anything we can help you with today? Any more ghosts to eject?"

"He's going to handle the gremlin," said Avis. "And he didn't bring a helmet."

"A helmet would help," said my grandfather. "And steel-toed boots. Now, who is this young man?"

"Grandpop, this is Keir McGoogan. Keir, this is my grandfather, Ebenezer Webster the Third."

"Pleased to meet you, sir," said Keir.

"My son told me all about you, Mr. McGoogan, though I must admit you look spryer than I imagined. There is much work to be done on your case. We expected you here this morning."

"I had to go to school."

"School? That's peculiar for a man your age. Who had the deranged idea to send you to school?"

"My stepfather," I said.

"He's the patent lawyer, right?" said my grandfather. "I might have figured. They should have a separate bar for patent lawyers. In a dance studio! Elizabeth's father is out of the office today, Mr. McGoogan, but Barnabas will take care of you. He has many questions. Now, Elizabeth and Henry, if we are to see our gremlin we must not tarry. Walk with me, Henry, and I'll give you some gremlin pointers. First, always bring a helmet."

With those words, he hurried slowly out the door, with Henry by his side. The bangs from his cane echoed in the empty hallway.

Before following, I took a moment to look past the clients in the waiting chairs and find Barnabas at his high desk, staring straight at me. He raised an eyebrow. I tilted my head toward Keir. Barnabas nodded. I smiled. He didn't. And then, having said all I needed to say, I ran after my grandfather and Henry.

"Where are we going, Grandpop?" I said.

"To Topper's house. We have a case to build. We would do it here, but Avis has put her foot down about gremlins in the office and one doesn't ever want to get between Avis's foot and the floor."

"How are we getting there?" I said as we started down the stairs. "Taxi?"

"Nonsense. Do you know how much a taxi costs? I'm driving."

"You?"

"Of course."

"In what? A horse and carriage?"

"What makes you think that?"

"You keep talking about making the stables."

"Not making, mucking. Very different things. But I have myself a quite suitable vehicle. A Studebaker, if you must know."

"What does he bake?" I asked.

"What does who bake?"

"The Sturdy Baker."

"It's not a baker, it's a car. I've had it for years, decades in fact. Nothing is as solid as a Studebaker. Built like iron, with a horn to match. Pedestrians don't stand a chance."

The car, parked in the basement of the old gray building, was big and black, with silver lines pasted onto its sides and a front that looked like a demented smile. Best of all, there were all kinds of levers inside, including one coming right out of the floor. As my grandfather drove the car up a ramp onto the alleyway behind the building, you could have mistaken it for the Batmobile, but only if the Batman was a bald old man whose bushy eyebrows barely reached as high as the dashboard.

"Can you even see the road, Grandpop?" I said as we barged into the stream of city traffic amid a chorus of horns. I was sitting in the front seat, belted in as tightly as I could manage. Henry sat behind me.

"As much as I need to," said my grandfather.

"Wouldn't you want to buy something newer, Mr. Webster?" said Henry.

"Why? This is a Studebaker. Hardy as a weed."

"They why don't you buy a new Studebaker?"

"I would, yes indeed, but they went out of business fifty years ago. Elizabeth, I think I now know why Josiah Goodheart is involved in a simple gremlin case."

"Red light, red light," I said quickly, looking for another seat belt to put on top of the one I had already buckled.

"Oh yes, of course," said my grandfather. He slammed down both feet, the brakes squealed, the car shivered, and we stopped just short of banging into the back of a bus. "Now, where were we?"

"Josiah Goodheart?" I said.

"Oh yes. You remember I mentioned that Topper's father used to be the Portal Keeper. The old man lost the position in a scandal. It turns out our Mr. Topper wants it back."

"Is it a good job?" I said.

"One of the best," said my grandfather. "Suddenly you have many friends. And there isn't a restaurant on the other side you can't just walk into and get a table."

"Are the restaurants good on the other side?" said Henry.

"Tremendous, from what I'm told. And somehow, in the finer establishments, they are able to produce dishes from your own memories. The stew your mother made when you were a child or the fish they served at your wedding. I once had a roasted leg of lamb in Afghanistan that has haunted me ever since. That will be my first order when my time comes."

"What were you doing in Afghanistan?" I said.

"Eating lamb. Weren't you listening? Now, it turns out Topper has just recently challenged the current office holder, one Ina Brathwaite, for the Portal Keeper position before the Stygian Transit Authority. There have been grievous mistakes, he claims, and whiffs of corruption. Worst of all, he claims Portal Keeper Brathwaite is in league with Redwing."

"Why does Redwing care who the Portal Keeper is?"

"Our agents on the other side have reported the troubling rumor that Redwing is looking to expand his dominion into the world of the living."

"Yikes."

"Indeed. The demon's armies would need access to the portal, which means he would need the Portal Keeper under his one red wing. If Mr. Topper took the post from Portal Keeper Brathwaite, that would seriously upset the demon's dastardly plans."

"And so," I said, "you think Josiah Goodheart, on behalf of Redwing, brought this case to hurt Mr. Topper's chances."

"Precisely," said my grandfather. "Because the Portal Keeper often appears before the Court of Uncommon Pleas, any loss before the court could seriously damage Topper's candidacy. That is why ensuring due process for your client is so important."

"You mentioned that thing before, Grandpop. Due something. What is it?"

"Due process, my dear? Why, it is a cornerstone of the law."

"Another one?"

"There is always another one. I understand your father gave you a book by Justice Holmes. Well, Holmes himself said it best in one of his great dissents. Due process, he wrote, is at minimum a fair trial and an opportunity to be heard. That is what you must wrestle out of that moth-eaten judge when your case is called before the court."

"Do we have a strategy?" I said.

"Why are you asking me? You're the barrister in charge. I can help, yes, but the strategy must be yours. Have you come up with anything?"

"Well, I was looking at my father's book," I said. "There's this case called *Rye Bread* or something about cows wandering on other people's lawns that might be a problem."

"Oh yes, *Rylands v. Fletcher* is definitely in play. Good catch, Elizabeth. You'll just have to figure out a way around it. And be quick about it. You need to be ready when the court arrives, the case is called, and Josiah Goodheart stands before that scallywag of a judge and gives you his grin."

"I remember that grin," said Henry, "like a cat about to eat a mouse."

"And we all know who that mouse would be," said my grandfather as he stomped a pedal on the floor, pushed a lever, and roared onto the highway.

19

PUDDLE OF BLOOD

Mr. Topper lived in an old white house on a plot of land not far from where Washington crossed the Delaware to beat the British all those years ago. A win for the home team, yes!

"My father bought this property," said Mr. Topper while walking the three of us across the lawn toward his house. "He always wanted to own a part of history. Said it belonged to us as much as anyone, since our ancestors built most of it. Just imagine, the enemy was sleeping on the other side of the river while Washington's army was waiting for him right over there, in what is now the park. What a glorious moment it must have been."

"Cold," said my grandfather. "Frostbite cold, if I remember my history."

"I suppose that couldn't be helped," said Mr. Topper. "It

would have been hard to catch the Hessians napping on a bright sunny day."

"Why is that?" said my grandfather. "No better time for napping if you ask me. Where will you find me on a bright sunny day, Elizabeth?"

"Napping?" I said.

"I set up for tea in my father's study," said Mr. Topper. "Althea is looking forward to seeing you again, Miss Webster. She was quite taken with you."

"And I certainly remember her," I said. "I asked Henry to come and get to know her while we talk. Henry's good with animals and he'll take care of Althea while we're in court."

Mr. Topper looked at Henry and sniffed. "Any experience with gremlins, young man?"

"I have a cousin who my mother calls a little devil," said Henry.

"Not quite the same," said Mr. Topper. "Althea's on the porch around back playing with her dolls."

"You don't have a spare helmet, do you?" I said.

"Why, is anyone going biking?"

"I mean for Henry," I said. "When dealing with Althea."

"Oh, that won't be necessary," said Mr. Topper. "Althea is the sweetest thing." He reached into his pocket and pulled out a plastic bag filled with brown bits of something. "Just give her one of these if she starts acting up. She loves her little treats. Watch your fingers when she snatches for it. She is quite enthusiastic. But for as long as she's chewing a treat, she's gentle as a lamb."

"But not as tasty, I assume," said my grandfather, to a look of horror from Mr. Topper.

While Henry went around the house to make nice with the gremlin, my grandfather and I ended up in a library of the strange, where Mr. Topper had set out the pot and teacups.

"I hear the court is on its way back to Philadelphia," said Mr. Topper as he poured the tea.

"It should be here any day now," said my grandfather. "And to that end, Elizabeth has come with some questions."

"I have?"

"Of course you have."

"Is that one sugar or two for you, Ms. Webster?" said Mr. Topper.

"Two?" I said. Through the windows I could see Henry running crazily across the yard.

"Althea likes half a dozen cubes in her tea, the little scamp," said Mr. Topper as he handed me my teacup and a spoon.

I stirred and took a sip as I looked around at the room. On the walls were paintings of demons of all shapes and sizes, each standing beside a short, round man who looked like a pudgy Mr. Topper in a bellhop's uniform, cap included. One of the painted demons was Redwing, with his fiery horns, his burning tail, his single bloody wing. The bookshelves themselves were filled with black volumes, the word CHRONICLES printed in gold on each of the spines. And there was also a large display case with a bronze lamp, a brass helmet, a dagger made of silver, and a golden telescope all under glass.

"So, Ms. Webster," said Mr. Topper, "you had some questions?"

"One thing we have to show," I said, keeping my eye on

the window as Henry ran the other way now, holding out a treat behind him, "is that you acted like a reasonable person when taking care of your gremlin."

"Indeed," said my grandfather, nodding.

"So I was wondering how you make sure Althea doesn't leave the house at night."

"Every evening I lock the door and all the windows on the first floor," said Mr. Topper. "I also latch the door to her room on the second floor after I put her into bed. Althea of course has her own bedroom. She loves to lie under the covers and watch television late into the night."

"Is there a window in the bedroom?"

"It, too, is locked from the inside," he said. "Everything is locked, not so much to keep Althea in as to keep any intruder out. Althea isn't a danger to anyone, but one could only imagine what that devious Moss woman would do to Althea if she could."

"One can only imagine," said my grandfather. The two men were nodding together when something suddenly slammed into the window.

We all turned to look. It was Henry. The side of his face and his hands were pressed against the windowpane. He was staring at us with an expression of pure terror as he slowly slid down the glass, as if sliding straight down to his doom.

"He seems to be getting along with Althea quite nicely," said Mr. Topper.

"He is just as good with animals as you said, Elizabeth," said my grandfather. "Well done."

I shook the sight of Henry out of my head and returned

to my questioning. "Did you do all your normal closing and latching and locking on the night the goat was killed?"

"Absolutely," said Mr. Topper. "Every night. In fact, when I was woken by the commotion from Moss's property, I tried to go back to sleep but it was impossible, as you can imagine. After tossing and turning, I eventually checked on my Althea. My little lovely was in bed, snoring away, with the television on."

"What about the sheets?" I asked. "Were they dirty?"

"Althea is a very clean gremlin," said Mr. Topper.

"Has she ever attacked another animal, or a person? Has she ever needed to be pulled off some living thing?"

"Oh no, except maybe when she is showing too much affection. In case you didn't realize, this was my father's study when he was the Portal Keeper. There's so much history here, including yours, young lady."

"Mine?"

"I would think so," said my grandfather. "These volumes must be filled with the Webster name. It is often imperative that our lawyers and clients be allowed to pass through the portal."

"Oh yes, the Websters are definitely accounted for, but so is the other side of your family, Ms. Webster. Your mother has a prominent place in my father's final volume."

"My mother?"

"No need to get into that now," said my grandfather.

"How prominent?" I said.

"Oh, she was very much a part of what we Toppers call the incident. We don't like to discuss it much, but it left such a mark on our reputation."

"My mother?"

"I must ask," said my grandfather, hijacking the conversation, "is that telescope contraption in the display case what I think it is?"

"The Lens of Fate, you mean."

"Precisely. They are so rare. I've actually never seen one before. It is extraordinary that you own such a device."

"My father wrangled it in his final term," said Mr. Topper, giving me a quick glance and then turning away. "Now that it has been passed on to me, it is one of the reasons I believe I could do a better job than our current Portal Keeper. Being able to see past the border of death no matter what side you're on can be quite useful in the profession. Portal Keeper Brathwaite cares nothing about the subtleties of the job, only her regulations, and whatever bribes she has taken from one side and the next."

"You don't mean—"

"There are enough questions raised," said Mr. Topper, "to assume the answer."

As they were talking about the Portal Keeper, I looked out the window, hoping to see Henry once more, but saw nothing moving.

"I think maybe I should check on Henry," I said. "Which way is Ms. Moss's property?"

"It is the scruffy piece of land bordering us to the right if you face the river. But you should avoid that woman at all costs."

"I might have a few questions for her, too."

"Oh no, Elizabeth," said my grandfather. "Moss is being represented by a barrister of the Court of Uncommon

Pleas. That means you cannot question her except with Mr. Goodheart present. You'll have to do your questioning in court."

"You can go right out this door," said Mr. Topper. "Althea will be very excited to see you."

"That's what I'm afraid of."

I walked out of the house slowly, like I was walking into a crime scene. I remembered the way Mr. Topper had described the remains of Moss's goat, and I feared I'd find the same kind of mess now in the yard, with Henry's clothes scattered about and one of his sneakers sitting in a big puddle of blood. But there was no Henry, no gremlin, no blood, just a gentle slope down to the wide river.

"Hey, Webster," I heard from above me.

I looked up. Henry was sitting on a branch of a tree by the house. Perched beside him, as docile as a kitten, was the gremlin. Althea was chewing on something, smiling and chewing and leaning into Henry's side so sweetly it was as if she was not a gremlin at all.

"I thought you'd be in pieces by now," I said.

"Disappointed?"

"A little. I had a great speech for the funeral. What was all that running around and smashing into windows?"

"Once we figured out we'd be friends, we thought we'd put on a show."

"Ha ha," I said. "You guys are so not funny."

Henry opened the little bag, took out a treat, and held it with the tips of his fingers. Althea smoothly snatched it and popped into her mouth. "You'll never guess what this stuff is," Henry said.

"Goat jerky?"

"How did you know?"

I turned toward a thick hedge between the Topper property and the Moss property, the Mason-Dixon Line of our uncivil goat war. On the Topper side was a row of bushes with thick leaves shaped like fat fingers.

I walked up and down the property line, looking for an opening. I stopped when I found a small gap created by a mess of broken branches. I stooped down so I could peer through.

On the other side was a big oak tree, and beyond the tree I saw a woman staring in the direction of the river. She was tall and thin, with long gray hair hanging loose and a robe of some kind wrapped around her shoulders. There were stars on the robe, and planets, and swirls of space dust. I knew who it was right off. The neighbor Moss. And then she turned her head and stared straight at me, as if she knew I was there spying on her, as if she could feel my very presence.

I couldn't help but jump back from her stare like some warning message, slithery and sharp, had been sent.

Bleat.

20

MR. POPULARITY

That night after dinner, as my mother corrected papers at the kitchen table, I was tutoring Keir on how to find the area in parallelograms and trapezoids—the easiest of geometry problems, the tricycle of math!—but Keir didn't even care enough to pretend to care.

"So if you draw imaginary lines here and here," I said, "you suddenly have two right triangles and a rectangle. See?"

"Those lines aren't imaginary," said Keir. "You drew them right on the paper. How old did you say Barnabas was?"

"Older than you," I said.

Barnabas had worked with Keir on his case at the office and then, following my silent directions, had accompanied him to our house, looking out for him all the while. Barnabas stood outside the door after his mission, his hands hanging loose and his pale skin glowing, until my grandfather brought me home in the Sturdy Baker. The birds had followed them every step of the way, said Barnabas when he gave me his report, but he hadn't spied anyone or anything else following.

"No one with an eye patch and a dog?" I said.

"No, Mistress Elizabeth, and I surely would have remembered such a personage. Keir told me what happened in the train station. A very troubling development. I could wait outside through the night if you think it necessary."

"I think we'll be okay here," I said.

"Most likely yes. Your mother is a match for anyone."

"I can get Keir to school tomorrow morning, but you might want to keep an eye on him and his activities after school until the trial."

"Will do, Mistress Elizabeth," he said. "You can count on me."

A moment later Barnabas had disappeared into the night, leaving me alone with Keir and his math homework.

"Can we get back to work?" I said to Keir at the kitchen table. "Now we know how to find the area of a right triangle and a rectangle, correct?"

"Barnabas being so old," said Keir, "might explain why he's so sad."

"Barnabas is not sad, he's..."

"Sad," said Keir. "He seems stuck out of place, if you know what I mean."

"Not as out of place as you are in geometry," I replied.

Just then my brother rumbled into the kitchen and asked Keir if he wanted to play some video games up in his room.

"Video games?" said Keir. "I've heard of such things. They sound fun, but I really must do my math. How can anyone get along in this world without knowing how to draw imaginary lines? Buildings would collapse, banks would go belly-up. Unless, Elizabeth, you might..."

"Might what?" I said.

"Oh, please, Lizzie," said Petey. "I'm so bored."

"I would never ask such a thing," said Keir. "It is my homework, after all, and we all know how important homework is. But if you might just make some notes while I play with your little brother, that would be helpful when I finally roll up my sleeves and get to it."

"Yeah, I get it," I said, and I did. My mother looked up from her papers and gave me a tilted smile, as if this was just what I deserved for helping my dad bring Keir into her house. "Just go," I said. "If I spend any more time on this with you my head will implode."

"Ahh, you're a friend, you are," said Keir. "So, Petey, can you bet on these games?"

A few days later, as Natalie and I walked toward the school cafeteria, she said, "I heard you did Keir's math homework again last night."

I stopped walking. "What are you talking about?" I said as if I had no idea what she was talking about, when I really had every idea what she was talking about. Somehow my doing Keir's homework had become part of our nightly ritual.

Natalie stopped also, turned around, and leaned against a locker. "You're saying you didn't?"

"No," I said. "I did. But how did you find out?"

"Keir told me," she said as she checked her fingernails. Today they were a soft brown with darker spots, which, I had to say, were pretty sweet and something I could never pull off.

I took hold of her hand to get a better view. "New look?"

"Leopard," she said. "Do you like?"

"Rowr."

"He spilled the beans while trying to get me to do his social studies homework," she said as she took her hand back.

"But you don't even do your own social studies homework."

"I know!" she said. "That's why I told him to forget it. Besides, he wasn't even offering enough for a new pair of sneakers. I might not be diligent, but I certainly don't come cheap."

"Wait a second, what? He offered to pay you?"

"Uh, yeah. Didn't he pay you?"

"No," I said. "He certainly did not."

"Wow! Well, you can't say you don't come cheap. He paid Charlie and Doug for his science and language arts homework. Mostly with the money they owed him."

"How do they owe him money? Ice cream at lunch?"

"Not exactly. He's become quite the thing, your pal Keir. Look behind you."

Slowly I turned. There was a group moving noisily through the hallway. Henry Harrison, tall as a drum major, was seemingly leading the gang, and the two Fraydens were buzzing about, and Young-Mee was chatting and laughing with a number of other eighth-grade girls. As the roving clique moved down the hallway, kids in their path spun out of the way and jammed themselves up against lockers, like they were facing a rabid swarm of oversized bees. The whole pack seemed to be surrounding someone, someone I couldn't quite see, until Charlie Frayden skittered out of the way and there he was.

Keir McGoogan himself, long-jawed and angel-faced, with his blue cap and ears that stuck out like thumbs.

There was a sudden sourness in my mouth. Was I tasting the unwelcome tang of jealousy? Maybe. And why wouldn't I be? There was Keir, ignoring all my stern orders and finding friends in school so much more easily than I ever could. And then there was Keir giving me a sly smile and lifting a hand in a very quiet wave, like he didn't want to be rude but also didn't want to be overly connected with the likes of me. I understood—popularity is sometimes so fragile even the smallest flaw could pop it like a balloon.

"Hey, Webster," said Henry after he spun off from the group and came our way. "Natalie. What's up?"

"Keir, obviously," said Natalie.

"So, I was just wondering, Webster," said Henry, "if this gremlin-wrangling thing was a paid gig."

"I'll ask my grandfather," I said. "Why?"

"Well, you know, I could, like, use some fish-skins right about now."

"Fish-skins?" I said.

"Why don't you just do Keir's homework like everyone else?" said Natalie. "He's paying."

"I would for sure," said Henry, "but I don't have any classes with him and when I asked if I could do his math homework he said Webster had that covered."

"He said that, did he?" I said.

Henry looked at me sheepishly, and I mean that literally, like a sheep. I could have sheared him then and there. It was fortunate for his fancy high fade haircut that just then he hurried back along the corridor to join Keir's little gang.

"He's in deep to your new friend," Natalie said.

"In deep how?"

"Like the rest of them, he's been playing with Keir's dice. Something called craps."

"Is that a game, really? Who named that? And are they really betting money?"

"I suppose they'd bet lollipops, but your friend Keir doesn't want lollipops."

"I'm getting a little sick to my stomach," I said.

"Of course you are," Natalie said. "We're on the way to lunch."

A few minutes later in the cafeteria, while Natalie and I sat with our apple juices and our lunch trays, Keir and a group of kids huddled at one of the tables in the corner like they were plotting to overthrow the middle school administration.

Take the study out of study hall! Student power!

"Did you find anything on that girl who attacked us?" I asked Natalie as I watched the strange huddle.

"Nothing yet on her," said Natalie. "But I called that Academy for Special Cases in Sedona. They confirmed that

Dr. Van worked there and they offered to send me a brochure. I'm so excited. I always wanted to be a special case."

"Oh, you're special, all right," I said. Just then a groan
rose from the table. As the huddle pulled back, I could
see Keir smiling and stuffing dollar bills into a pocket. He
looked up, saw me and Natalie staring, and gave us wink.
That's right, a wink.

"Do you ever get the feeling you brought a monster into
school?" said Natalie.

"Yes," I said, still thinking of what that girl Pili had said
as she raised the stake above her head. "Yes I do." Was I
scared? I was. And angry, too.

I was trying to figure out what to do about this whole
insane thing when I saw Mr. Armbruster standing in the
doorway, hands on hips, staring with way too much interest at the huddle at Keir's table. Without another word, I
rose from my chair and headed over.

I waited by the table until Charlie Frayden lifted his head
to scan the lunchroom, saw me standing there, and ducked
back into the huddle.

"Uh-oh," I could hear him whisper.

"What is it?" whispered Doug.

"Elizabeth."

"Uh-oh," said Doug.

The whole huddle pulled back and looked at me. Keir
smiled brightly as he grabbed the dice and dropped them
into his shirt pocket. "Hello, Elizabeth," he said, his face
flushed with what I thought was excitement. "We were just
talking about—"

"All of you scram," I said. "Except for Keir."

Keir looked at me for a moment and tilted his head before saying, "Go on, now. It appears Elizabeth wants to have a chat."

It took a moment for all the dice players to sullenly grab their stuff and clear out, but eventually it was just Keir and me at the table. I sat down and clasped my hands in front of me. My mom did that whole clasped-hand thing when I crossed a line. Keir kept driving me into becoming my mother!

"Want to play?" he said with an annoying smile on his red and blotchy face. "Your math smarts should make you a pretty penny."

"I don't want any of my friends' pretty pennies," I said. "Do you even remember what I told you?"

"Keep my head down."

"Especially when Mr. Armbruster is standing in the doorway."

Keir looked around until he spied the teacher. "He's a little too curious, isn't he?"

"It's his job."

"We're just having a bit of fun is all. That's what school should be, don't you think?"

"Is it fun taking money from the other kids?"

"Yes, actually."

"And is it fun paying them to do your homework?"

"I'm only giving my pals a chance to earn back their losses. We're just playing around."

"They might be playing around, but you're not playing around, are you?"

He stared at me for a moment and then looked down at the table, as if he didn't like seeing his reflection in my eyes.

"Well, it is money, after all," he said. "When my father went away to war we were left near to starving. I guess I'm just teaching them the lessons I learned. It is a school, isn't it? Why do you care so much? You don't even like half these kids. And the things they say about you."

"What things? About my hair?"

"Why would they be talking about your hair?"

"Isn't everyone talking about my hair? It's pink!"

"Look, if it gets you so cross, I'll stop." He winked. "No more dice, I promise."

"And no more winking."

"But I give a good wink."

"Not as good as you think."

"Okay, okay. No more winking, either."

"And you'll do your own homework from here on in."

"Now you're asking too much."

I didn't say anything to that. I just gave him my angry face.

"Okay, okay, I'll do my own homework," he said finally as a drop of sweat fell from a strand of red hair sticking out from under his cap. I watched as the droplet rolled along his flushed cheek.

"Why are you sweating?"

"It's hot in here?"

"Not that hot. Are you sick? You look a little sick."

"Healthy as a horse."

"A three-legged horse, maybe, with stomach issues."

"I wouldn't want to bet on any other. Always take the long odds." He started to wink and saw my face, then stopped in the middle so that one eye stayed open and one eye closed.

Was that the end of that? Had I solved my Keir McGoogan problem? I might have thought so. Sometimes I think I'm in charge of my little world, until my little world grabs me by the ears and laughs in my face.

21

A CRAZY PACK OF SQUIRRELS

I was in my pajamas, lying in bed, reading a volume of *Vampire Knight* by flashlight—Yuki rules!—when I again heard the scraping and banging against my window. This time I rolled my eyes.

I closed the book, scooted off the bed, raised the blinds, and waved the flashlight's beam through the window without much concern. I mean, after all I had just been through was I going to be frightened again by a little bat spy fluttering around, grimacing like a fool? No, I was not, but a bat was not what I saw.

What I saw was a pack of squirrels scuttling in a frenzy to and fro across the branch by my window. As I watched, one of the critters leaped for the light as it would have leaped for a glowing acorn.

¡Splat!

It bounced back as if the window was a trampoline and landed feetfirst on the branch. Nine point eight from the Russian judge! The sound scared the rest of the squirrels and they all scampered away from the window and up the trunk, the leaper following like it'd had one too many nuts.

I leaned forward and aimed the flashlight beam back and forth through the window, trying to see what was causing all the commotion. There was nothing on the tree, nothing on the ground by the trunk, nothing in the—

Whoa.

What was that pale twisted thing in the middle of the bushes at the far end of the yard?

I aimed the flashlight beam right at it. The thing convulsed and shivered in the light before its upper half twitched toward me.

As I jumped back from the window, I dropped the flashlight and let out a yelp. Was it more like a shout? Maybe. A scream? No, not a scream, certainly not. But it might have been screamlike, and could you blame me? I wanted to dive back into bed and hide between the covers of my manga, but I didn't. Some sense of responsibility wouldn't let me. I had guessed who it might be right away, even though its face was a smear of red and it had what looked like a fake beard. The clues were in the way it stood and the way its ears stuck out.

I stepped toward the window and raised it. My flashlight was still shining on the floor, but the moon was half full and there was enough light to see the backyard. I leaned out and looked again at the bushes.

Nothing.

I looked all along the ground, the lawn, the neighbor's yard with its rusted swing set.

Nothing.

My gaze rose and my jaw dropped. Somehow Keir had twitched himself right into the tree and was now hunched on a branch, shuddering and convulsing as he peered at me from the other side of the trunk. That was when I realized his fake beard wasn't a fake beard at all, it was a dead squirrel. The squirrel's chest had been ripped apart and it was being held like a cup of fresh blood as—

Knock knock.

"Elizabeth?" The voice of my mother. "Are you awake?"

I slammed the window closed and jumped for my bed. I was under the covers when the door opened.

"Elizabeth?" my mother said.

"Mom? Mom, what?"

She switched on the light. "I thought I heard something. Did you scream?"

I sat up and rubbed my eyes like I needed to rub my eyes. "I don't think so. Maybe I was dreaming."

"About what?"

"I don't know. I was reading *Vampire Night*, so..."

"I wish you wouldn't read such books before you go to sleep. Why is that flashlight on the floor and still on?"

"I was using it to read in the dark. I must have fallen asleep in the middle of reading and dropped it."

"Elizabeth," she said, shaking her head as she walked over to the window, bent down for the flashlight, and turned it off.

When she stood up again, she looked out the window.

At first it was an idle glance, but then she looked more carefully, as if she was seeing something she didn't expect to see. Or maybe something she expected but didn't want to see. My throat tightened, and I was trying to figure out what lie to tell her, when she lowered the blinds and spun around.

"I received a text from your father," she said. "Apparently the Court of Uncommon Pleas will be in session tomorrow night. Your father said you should bring Keir." She walked over and sat on the edge of my bed. "How's Keir doing in school?"

"Fine, I guess."

"Is that the truth?"

"He's doing better than me, actually. He seems to have more friends, he gets his homework done on time."

"Which is surprising because I never see him do any."

"Why did you agree to Stephen's idiotic idea to send Keir to my school?"

"Your stepfather is quite perceptive—I mean, for a lawyer. It sounded foolish to me, too, but when Stephen proposed it Keir's face lit up. It seemed wrong to deny him the opportunity. And he'd been locked away so long I thought it might do him good. It's hard to care about other people if you don't meet them first. Is it working?"

"Well, when he talks in class, it's all about how concerned he is about everyone, especially the poor. But then, any chance he gets, he takes advantage of everyone."

"Like he gets you to do his homework for him."

"Yes, just like. Without even paying me!"

"He's still learning. I heard he wasn't so well liked in

that castle where you found him. That's why you're so good for him."

"I'm not well liked."

"Well, let's just say you're not universally despised. I'm a little worried about his safety."

"Barnabas has been looking out for him."

"Good. Barnabas is a match for anyone."

"That's funny. He said the same thing about you."

"Did he, now? How charming. Go to sleep, Elizabeth. You have a big day tomorrow. I pressed your robe. It got a little wrinkled after your last appearance, when Redwing tried to take you with him to the other side."

"Thanks for reminding me."

"I'm sure that won't happen again," she said as she stood and placed the flashlight on my night table beside my manga book. She turned the light out as she left, closing the door behind her, leaving me alone with the image of the vampire thing outside my bedroom window. What was I going to do about that?

Just then the door opened again and I saw a shadowy figure framed by the hallway light. My nerves ran around like a crazy pack of squirrels before I saw it was my mother leaning into the opening.

"Your father also mentioned something about a gremlin?" she said. "Do you have any idea what that means?"

"It's one of our cases," I said after I caught my breath. "My case, actually."

"Are you ready?"

"I sort of have a plan." I hesitated a moment and then

asked a question that had been flitting through my brain. "Mom, where did you hear about how Keir was in that castle?"

"Good luck tomorrow, dear," said my mother before closing the door behind her.

22

THE BARRISTERS' BENCH

There were seven of us snaking through the damp stone maze in the basement of Philadelphia's City Hall, eight if we count Althea, nine if we count you, following along, wondering why it took us all so long to get here.

Barnabas was leading at a brisk pace, a bundle of scrolls secured under his arm, followed by my father, in his robe and white wig, and Mr. Topper. Behind them was Henry, carrying Althea's crate, and my grandfather, who tapped his cane loudly on the stone floor. Tap tap tap. Keir and I took up the rear. I was in my black-and-purple robe, but no wig, thank you. I had enough issues with my hair without plunking an ugly white mop on top of the pink.

"Do you think the queen bee will be there?" asked Keir softly.

"If she doesn't show up, you win," I said.

"I'm not so anxious to see her again."

"Don't worry, the one place you're safe from her is in front of the judge."

"Nice fellow, is he?"

"No," I said as we hurried to keep pace.

When we reached a wooden doorway, Barnabas pulled out a long metal key with a human tooth at the end, slipped it into the lock, and spun it twice. The door creaked open, revealing a narrow circular stairway lit by flaming torches sticking out of the wall. The worn stone steps seemed to rise forever up City Hall's famous tower. Without hesitation Barnabas started up the stairs, and we all followed. Up and around and up and around.

It wasn't long before I was fighting for breath.

But Keir kept pace easily, having somehow recovered from his illness—and we both know how he had done that, don't we? Henry also had no trouble climbing, even though he was lugging Althea up the stairs—he was a swimming star, after all. What surprised me was that my grandfather banged his way up the long, twisting stairway without a rest.

"Are you okay, Grandpop?" I gasped between breaths. "This is quite a hike."

"Nonsense," said my grandfather. "I've been climbing these stairs for decades. They're more worn out than I am. There was a time I was rushing up and down this stairway four, five, six times a session. I was strong as an ox then."

"You're still pretty strong."

"But not like an ox anymore," said my grandfather. "More like an aardvark—an arthritic aardvark with an aching back. Are you ready for your case, Elizabeth?"

"I think so."

"That's the spirit. I'm sure Custer felt the same way."

"Didn't he end up losing—"

"The only way to go is boldly forward, I always say."

"But, Grandpop—"

"Ah, we've arrived."

I bent over to catch my breath on the landing at the top of the stairs as Barnabas lifted the gavel-shaped knocker on the great wooden door and slammed it once, twice, and then quickly a third time.

A moment later the plank high on the door swung open and the doorkeeper stuck his massive head through the gap. He peered down at us like a giant peering down at a flock of sheep.

"Barnabas," grunted Ivanov.

"Ivanov," replied Barnabas.

"Case?"

"Two on the docket," said Barnabas. "*McGoogan v. Laveau* and *Moss v. Topper.*"

"We've a cavalcade of Websters, I see," said Ivanov. "I suppose the judge will be in a mood today. Is that Master Harrison there?"

"Yes, sir," said Henry.

"Another ghost, young man?"

"No, sir," said Henry. "I'm just helping out with some evidence."

Ivanov sniffed the air. "What's that in the carrier? Hedgehog?"

"No, sir."

"Kinkajou?"

"Kinka what?" said Henry.

"Stop monkeying around, Ivanov," said my grandfather. "It's a gremlin."

"Oh, I hope not, Mr. Webster. The judge is not partial to gremlins, not partial at all. Last time a gremlin was in this courtroom it ended up on a spit."

"Why, that's horrible," said Mr. Topper.

"Not really, sir," said Ivanov. "With a little salt and a squeeze of lemon it was actually quite tasty. Well, it is best if you all hurry on. The court will be in session shortly."

Ivanov's huge blocky head disappeared just before his arm reached out and yanked shut the high plank. A moment later the door opened wide. Barnabas hurried through and the rest of us followed.

After Keir passed the doorway he stopped suddenly when he saw Ivanov, no taller than Keir himself, standing in his brass-buttoned uniform beside a stepladder.

"It's good to see you again, Elizabeth," said Ivanov.

"You too, Ivanov. This is our client, Keir McGoogan."

"I thought you'd be taller," said Keir.

Ivanov snorted and then said, "I thought you'd be older."

"Then we're both pleasantly surprised," said Keir.

"I have something for you, Ivanov," I said as I rummaged around in my pack. Finally I pulled out an orange knit hat with a fuzzy ball on top. "My mother made it for those cold winter sessions."

"Thank her much for me. It can get right frigid up there on the ladder." He took the hat and jammed it on his head. "How do I look?"

"Like a pumpkin," I said.

"Perfect," said Ivanov. "Go on now, both of you, before the rehanging judge makes his grand entrance."

I grabbed Keir by the sleeve of his shirt and tugged him into the courtroom. As he was yanked down the aisle, his eyes grew so wide he looked like he was walking through a fishbowl. He stared at the rows of benches filled already by the waiting crowd, at the cage hanging from the ceiling over a dark hole in the floor, at the live ram's head sticking out of the middle of the five-pointed star at the front of the room.

"Welcome to the Court of Uncommon Pleas," I said.

"What's that smell? Taffy?"

"Licorice."

"Who eats licorice? The judge?"

"The ram."

Just then a bit of glitter fell onto Keir's shoulder. He looked up at the little babies painted on the ceiling dome, who pointing at him and twittered as they flew around in their diapers.

"And who might those rascals be?" he said.

"Nobody important," I said. "They're just decorative."

My father was already at the front of the courtroom, talking to the court clerk, a tall woman with green skin and bolts in her neck. Barnabas was sitting in one of the back rows, with my grandfather, Mr. Topper, and Henry. Keir kept looking around until he froze, as if he had seen his own ghost.

"There she is," he said, "five or so rows down."

I looked over and saw the bluish back of Egon's bald head and, beside him, a woman with swirling black hair. I got the creeps just looking at them. I pushed Keir onto the bench, next to Henry and the crate, and dropped beside him.

"Mistress Elizabeth," said Barnabas, leaning over in the bench so I could see him. "You should be sitting up front."

"I thought I'd stay with Keir."

"We'll take care of Mr. McGoogan, Elizabeth, don't you worry," said my grandfather.

"Much business is conducted on the front bench," said Barnabas. "It is a place of honor. As a barrister admitted to the court, it is where you belong."

"Go on, Elizabeth," said Keir. "I'll be fine."

I gave him a false smile of confidence before rising and making my way to the front of the courtroom. I had never sat on the barristers' bench. Would the wig-headed lawyers make room for me? Would my father be proud or annoyed? Why did everything feel like the middle school cafeteria?

Whatever jitters were plaguing me turned into a swarm when Egon stepped smack in front of me, smiling his broken-toothed smile.

"We meet again, Elizabeth Webster," he said in his high-pitched voice.

Not knowing what to say, I said, "I'm still waiting for the tea."

"And we've been waiting for you. You have a great honor coming your way."

Just then the woman sitting beside Egon stood and faced me. "How nice to finally meet you, Elizabeth," said the Countess Laveau.

She was the woman in the painting, of course, in a man's pinstriped suit with a red scarf at her throat. And her hair, well, the paintings couldn't do it justice. Her hair was wild and free, swooping and winding around her face like it was alive. Its very boldness made any concerns I had about my hair seem foolish and small. Made me seem foolish and small.

"I'm not allowed to talk to you without your lawyer," I said, remembering what my grandfather had told me.

"Ah, the rules. Where would we be without the rules?" Her eyes widened. "Just imagine."

"I really have to go," I said.

"Don't let me keep you. There must be a restroom somewhere in this mausoleum."

"I didn't mean—"

"It seems everywhere I visit, all I hear is Elizabeth Webster this and Elizabeth Webster that. Now that we meet, I can only wonder why. I suppose we'll find out eventually, one way or the other. Oh dear, I didn't mean to frighten you. Does she look frightened, Egon?"

"Like a mouse in a raven's claw," said Egon.

"I must admit, I do so love seeing little eyes bounce up and down in fear. I find it as nourishing as cake. This has been delicious, hasn't it, Elizabeth? I hope we see each other again. In fact, I'll make sure we do."

And that right there was my first meeting with the Countess Laveau. So much fun!

When I reached the front of the courtroom I stared for a moment at the ram on the wall. He was chewing and staring back. He shook his big horns and let out a snort.

To the left was the barristers' bench, with its row of white wigs. Beneath each wig was a man (and they were only men), who I imagined was horrified that a mere girl was about to sit on this bench of honor.

I might have retreated from such disapproval only a few moments before, but something of the countess's electric presence had slipped into my bones and rattled them. Where Miss Myerscough was the tight-mouthed guidance counselor of my nightmares, the Countess Laveau was as wild and unconstrained as a thunderstorm. I had the peculiar thought that she was what my mother could have been had my mother made different choices, what I could be if I so chose. Maybe that's what gave me the boldness to make my way to the barristers' bench.

I could feel the disapproval as I passed one, two, three of the barristers in their haughty white wigs. Deal with it, I thought before plopping on the bench beside my father. I could hear the grumbles rise like clouds about me and I didn't care.

"I just met the countess," I said to my father.

"Interesting woman?" said my father.

"I think she's a vampire."

My father shrugged as if to say of course she was. As he was shrugging, another barrister in a white wig sat down to my right. When I turned to look at him, he gave me a brilliant smile and I slid right off the bench.

THE BANSHEE'S PLEA

Elizabeth," said my father sternly, looking at me on the courtroom floor like I was down there playing Twister. "Stop fooling around. This is a courtroom, not a playground."

"Careful there, Ms. Webster," said Josiah Goodheart, my nemesis, as he reached out a hand, took hold of mine, and helped me up. His eyes were laughing, his face was dark brown and pudgy, his smile was insanely bright. "These benches can be quite treacherous."

"Thank you, Josiah," said my father. "I don't know what came over her."

"Don't worry yourself, Eli," said Josiah Goodheart. "It is certainly no bother to give assistance to the famous Elizabeth Webster."

Before I could swallow enough air to respond, the ram

on the wall lifted his chin and bellowed before calling out in his brassy voice, "All rise."

We all rose.

I felt strange standing between my father and Josiah Goodheart, who were apparently on friendly terms—what was that about? How could two enemies be so pleasant to each other? There was still a lot of law stuff I needed to figure out.

"Oyez, oyez, oyez," called out the ram in his horselike voice. "The Court of Uncommon Pleas, sitting now in the land of Penn's Dominion, is hereby called to order."

As the ram blathered on about the court and the judge, Mr. Goodheart leaned toward me and said in his raspy voice, "I'm looking forward with keen, I say, keen interest to our little contest today."

"I'm sure you have some sneaky surprises planned," I said as a cloud of smoke burst to life behind the judge's desk.

As the smoke dissolved, Judge Jeffries appeared, coughing and hacking. He wore a red robe with a black stripe down the middle. A scraggly white wig sat atop his head. His eyes were bloodred marbles.

"Be seated," said the judge in his harsh British accent, between coughs. We all sat. "Now I warn you all, be brief in your pleadings or you'll feel my wrath. We have a long night and I hear the hounds bellowing for justice, so let us not delay."

"I expect you have your own surprises planned, Ms. Webster," whispered Josiah Goodheart as the judge kept on talking. "You might not see it, but when it comes to the legal arts, and some other things, too, I think we are birds of the same feather, if you catch my drift."

"I do not catch your drift," I said.

"No drift?"

"No drift, no feather."

"Well, time will tell," he said, maybe a little too loudly. "It always does."

The judge turned his head and aimed his red eyes at the barrister. Josiah Goodheart nodded slowly and amiably.

The judge looked down at him with exasperation and then banged his gavel. "The time has come for the law to make its mark, for good or for ill, on all of you. The clerk shall call the first case."

The tall green clerk stood and in her strangled voice shouted out, "*McGoogan v. Laveau!*"

"Eli Webster representing the plaintiffs Caitlin and Keir McGoogan in a claim of false imprisonment," said my father in a soft voice. He stood tall in his robe and wig, next to Keir, behind one of the two tables in front of the judge's bench. Standing behind the other table were the Countess Laveau, Egon, and a short, thick barrister with white wig and snuffy face.

The judge put his hands over his eyes and shook his head. "It is always an insufferable day when a Webster stands before me. Let's hope we make quick work of this. Are your clients in court today, Mr. Webster?"

"Keir McGoogan stands beside me," said my father. "He is the falsely imprisoned. His mother, Mrs. McGoogan, who initially hired our firm, is a Class Two banshee and not yet in court."

"Well, don't just stand there like a Grecian urn," barked the judge. "Time is burning while you Websters fiddle. Summon her."

My father closed his eyes and muttered to himself as his hands danced in the air. I felt it just then, the breeze slipping through the courtroom, along with the sulfurous scent of rotten eggs. The caw of a crow sounded as some dark cloud rose from the hole beneath the hanging cage and then zipped across the courtroom before settling between my father and Keir. The cloud turned ever more solid until my banshee appeared. Her face was pale, her bright red hair peeked out from her black hood, and her hands, I was glad to see, were pale and bony but not all bone.

I should have been touched at the way she leaned toward her son, kissed his forehead, and hugged him tightly, or touched by the way Keir let her do all that without pulling away, but I was too amazed by my father, standing there calmly in the courtroom, having just summoned a ghost. I didn't know he could do that.

"Welcome to my courtroom, Mrs. McGoogan," said the judge. "How long do you claim your young son has been falsely imprisoned?"

As Caitlin McGoogan began speaking, the judge cocked his head and squinted at the words. "What is that language?" he said. "Anglo-Saxon? Welsh?"

"It's Irish, Your Honor," said my father.

"Have you a translator, Webster? She won't be of much worth to you if you don't have a translator."

"I can translate," said Keir. "She says I have been imprisoned by the Countess Laveau for one hundred years, with nothing but agony and distance between a mother and her son."

"Why, that's quite a span of time," said the judge. "An unprecedented amount of time. I assume you'll be seeking extensive damages."

"We're seeking emancipation," said my father. "Freedom."

"And damages," said Keir, "if by damages you mean money."

"Generally in this court we deal with souls, young man," said the judge. "Also the occasional pound of flesh, or the surprisingly popular two pints of blood."

"Blood works," said Keir. "But we'd prefer the money."

The judge harrumphed before turning to face the barrister standing next to the countess. "Good to see you again, Mr. Locksley. Are you ready to proceed for the defendant?"

"I am ready," said the countess.

"I'll get to you soon enough, Countess. I was talking to your counsel."

"I need no one to speak for me," said the countess.

"In my courtroom you do," barked the judge. "The rules are the rules, as I have made it clear to you many times before. No one can stand before the Court of Uncommon Pleas without proper counsel."

"I am standing with proper counsel, as per your silly rules. I have hired him and paid him and instructed him to say not a word or his tongue will be my dinner. Isn't that right, Mr. Locksley?"

The snuffy-faced barrister nodded enthusiastically with his lips clasped tight.

"I will be speaking for myself in this matter," said the countess.

"Why, this is...this is...this is highly unorthodox," bellowed the judge.

"Thank you," said the countess.

The judge stared for a moment as he decided what to do about this strong woman standing before him. I couldn't help but root for her, which was weird because she was on the other side. Sometimes, I suppose, there are more than two sides.

The judge finally shook his head. "Plaintiffs claim you have imprisoned young Mr. McGoogan for over a hundred years. What is your defense?"

"The mother consented," said the countess. "She came to me on a dark and stormy night and begged me to save her son's life. She signed a contract that allowed me to keep him if I did so. His very presence here is proof that I kept my part of the bargain."

"Consent is a valid defense to false imprisonment," said the judge, nodding. "Did you sign a contract, Mrs. McGoogan?"

The banshee spoke, and when she was finished, Keir translated. "I signed, yes, to save my boy's life. I would do it again."

"And did you read the contract before you signed?"

"I was suffering from the same sickness as my boy," said

Keir, translating. "It wasn't a full day after I gave my Keir to the countess that I passed over to the other side. On the night I signed, I was too sick to read, as she very well knew."

"That brings up the issue of whether there was a true meeting of the minds here," said the judge.

"We also believe the contract is void or voidable, depending," said my father.

"Depending on what, Mr. Webster?"

"The specific language of the contract," said my father. "But the countess has not yet turned over a copy, despite our discovery demands."

"The contract was destroyed in an unfortunate fire at our estate many years ago," said the countess.

"That shouldn't matter if it was properly filed with the Portus Pactorium, as required of all supernatural contracts," said the judge. "Was that done?"

"Egon, my servant, will testify that it was," said the countess.

"I handed it to the Portal Keeper myself," said Egon in his high-pitched warble.

"We are in the process of searching the Pactorium," said my father, "but our emissaries on the other side haven't yet located the copy. Due process demands that we see the contract on which the countess bases this imprisonment."

"Due process, you say," said the judge. "Do you have a request, then, Mr. Webster?"

"In light of the crucial part the written contract plays in this case," said my father, "and our due process rights, we request a short continuance in order to find the necessary agreement."

"We don't consent to any delay," said the countess. "I will testify as to the words in the contract. Time is burning and it is dangerous to leave the young plaintiff outside my estate for too long."

"Dangerous?" said the judge.

"There are those out to do young Keir the most grievous harm," said the countess. "And the danger is not just to the plaintiff, but to all those around him, including young Elizabeth Webster."

The countess swiveled to stare at me. So did Egon, and the judge, and the ram. And so did my father. I began to shrivel under their stares, like I was a snail in salt.

"A danger to my daughter?" said my father. "What do you mean—"

The judge banged my father quiet. "Silence! So, there is a danger to a Webster. Frankly, I don't know how I'll be able to eat my steamed sponge pudding with that on my mind, but I shall try to persevere. What say you, Mr. Locksley, about the continuance? Nothing. Cat got your tongue?"

"I told you we object," said the countess.

"Yes, you did, Countess, but your counsel is silent. Normally, of course, I refuse to grant continuances, especially from a Webster. But since your counsel has not objected, and in the interest of due process, I am inclined to grant it in this case. But only until the case is called at our next session in this courtroom and not a moment more. Do you understand, Mr. Webster?"

"We do, Your Honor."

"And be aware, if no contract is found, then I expect the countess's testimony will not be healthy for your case. Mrs. McGoogan, you can return to the other side for now."

The banshee McGoogan gave her son another forehead kiss before dissolving herself back into a cloud that rose slowly into the domed ceiling. The little babies all twittered as they avoided the cloud. I thought she would keep going, right through the ceiling, but that's not what she did. Instead the cloud zipped this way and that before dropping right in front of me. A moment later the banshee was back, kneeling before me and grabbing hold of my hand with her bony fingers.

"*Seol trasna chugam é,*" she moaned. "*Seol mo bhuachaillín ar ais chugam.*"

I recognized these as the same words she had spoken to me on our first meeting. And then, after letting out a final banshee-worthy screech, she exploded into a cloud that flitted about before disappearing into the hole in the floor.

The judge gave a harrumph before he banged his gavel. "Case continued," he said.

24

THE REMEDY

The next case called in the Court of Uncommon Pleas was something involving a fight between an incubus and a librarian. As that case droned on, our team agreed to meet in the stairwell outside the courtroom to hash over what had just happened and prepare for our goat case.

As I walked out of the courtroom, I was startled to see Dr. Rudolf Van sitting in the back row. He stood and smiled as I approached. "We meet again, Ms. Webster," he said with a slight bow.

"Hopefully there will be no wooden stakes tonight," I said.

"One never knows, *ja*? That is why I am here. Better safe than sorry."

"Thank you for the other day. I was little too frazzled to tell you how grateful we all were."

"Perfectly understandable. Unfortunately, Pili got away. La Loba, my pet, was distracted by someone eating one of those cheesesteaks your city is so famous for. It was not pretty. I understand your friend, she asked for a brochure from the Sedona Academy for Special Cases."

"How do you know that?"

"The school does not send brochures to just anyone. Look it over and let the school know when you are ready to talk about Keir's future. It might be useful for Keir to have options no matter how the case turns out." Then he put a finger to his lips. "Shhhhh. Court is still in session."

When I finally made it to the stairwell, Barnabas was discussing Keir's case with Keir, my father, and my grandfather. "The judge has made it clear," Barnabas said, "that without the contract, Master Keir's case is doomed."

"I'm going to have to go to the other side myself and look for it in the Pactorium," said my father, "as long as Portal Keeper Brathwaite allows me to pass."

"If Topper were in the post, he would let you pass," said my grandfather. "His father was very kind to the Websters."

"Was there really a fire that destroyed the countess's copy of the contract?" I asked Keir.

"There was a fire, at least," said Keir. "Right after I showed up at the estate. But in the years that followed, the countess blamed much on it. She has a shifty way with the truth, she does."

"So a copy could still be in the château," said my grandfather.

"I might have an idea where if we want to look for it," said Keir.

"Go back into that creepy bird house?" I said. "No thank you."

Just then the courtroom door swung open and out came Egon, his bones jangling. The Countess Laveau was still in the courtroom, her face turned to where Dr. Van was sitting. She bared her teeth and hissed so loudly it was like a pack of snakes had gotten loose.

"We could settle this dispute right now," said the countess to my father after she stepped into the stairwell, "if you'd be willing to talk reasonably."

"Freedom isn't reasonable," said my father calmly.

"The idealism of fools," said the countess.

"Of Americans," said my father.

"Have it your way," she said. "Keir, darling, when you've gotten into enough trouble and you come to your senses, just tell one of the birds. I'll send Egon to pick you up in the car."

"I'll bring along a snack, Keir McGoogan," said Egon.

"Don't hold your breath," said Keir.

"What's holding his breath going to do to Egon?" said the countess. "Kill him?"

They chuckled, the two of them, as they started down the stairs.

"Oh, Countess," said my father, "one more thing."

The countess stopped, turned around, and looked up. She didn't like my father, you could tell by the expression on her face, but by the expressions on her face you got the sense she didn't like anyone.

"If anything happens to my daughter," said my father, "I'll hold you responsible."

"Of course you will," said the countess almost cheerfully. "A child's death, an earthquake, a plague—because I am different I am always to blame. The fire that burned the contract you so badly need? It was in the time of the same sickness that killed Keir's mother. Despite how many I saved, Keir included, the mob decided I was responsible for the influenza, so they came with their torches. They would have burned me alive if they could have found me, and they would have laughed at my screams. Why would I expect anything better from you?"

We stayed silent, all of us, as the countess turned and continued down the steps. Egon followed. We could hear his bones bumping each other in the quiet.

"We should return to the courtroom," said Barnabas. "They're liable to call Mistress Elizabeth's case any moment now."

"Yes indeed," said my grandfather. "Back to the courtroom."

I waited out in the hallway as my grandfather and father accompanied Barnabas back through the great wooden door. As Keir started to follow, I grabbed him by his collar and yanked him back.

"Is the countess right?" I said as I stared into his green eyes. "Am I in danger?"

"Not from me, Elizabeth. You're a friend."

I stared at him a little longer; then for some reason I had to turn away. "Like the friendly little squirrels?" I said. "And what about our friendly schoolmates? What about Petey?"

"Ah, Petey's a good kid."

"That's not what I asked."

"Look at me, Elizabeth," Keir said, and when I didn't, he said it again. "Look at me."

I turned, and the Keir McGoogan I saw just then was different from the boy who had been standing in front of me a moment before. There was no sly smile, there was no hint of deceit in his emerald-green eyes.

"I swear I'd sooner stay locked up in the countess's prison for all eternity than have anything happen to you or them because of me. I'd sooner die."

I stared at him a moment longer and then I nodded. Did I believe him? Yes, actually, I did. Was I a fool? Probably. I mean, we all know Keir had lied to me before—all it took was a quick search on the game of craps to learn that. But he always hesitated, like he felt a shot of guilt before he delivered the lie. This time, there was no hesitation, no false sincerity or barely contained smile. Maybe I'm the worst kind of sucker, but there it was. I believed him.

"That guy from the train station, that Dr. Van, was in the courtroom," I said.

"I saw him," said Keir. "I don't like the way he looks at me. He gives me the creeps."

"He saved you once already," I said. "Maybe he's not so bad to have around. And that school of his might be something to look at."

"I'm happy enough at Willing Middle School West," said Keir.

"Really? Happy? In middle school?"

"It beats the flophouse."

"Maybe," I said. "Barely. So tell me this. When your

mother grabbed my hand and said something in Irish, what did she say?"

Keir hesitated just long enough for me to notice before he said, "She thanked you for helping her. She thanked you for helping her little boy."

"It's not over yet."

"It will be when we get that contract," said Keir.

"And then what?"

"Like your father said. Freedom. Whatever that means. Chocolates on the beach, I suppose. And I hear amusement parks are fun."

"Only if you like puking your guts out from rides that spin you upside down."

"Excuse me, Elizabeth." I looked up and saw Ivanov standing in the doorway, with his navy-blue uniform and orange pumpkin cap. "The case of the delinquent incubus is almost concluded. You don't want to keep the judge waiting when your case is called."

I followed Keir back into the courtroom and slid onto the bench where Henry sat with the animal carrier by his side.

"How's Althea doing?" I said.

"She's a bit antsy," said Henry. "I'm keeping her fed."

"Good. Stuff her like a piñata. Don't come up when the case is called. Wait until I ask for you."

"Got it," he said before taking a dried brown morsel out of his shirt pocket and holding it before the opening in front of the crate. A small green hand with three claws emerged from between the bars and snatched at the snack.

The gremlin let out a sweet little "Oooh."

Just then the judge banged his gavel, found for the librarian, and ordered the clerk to call the next case.

In the front of the courtroom the green clerk stood up and called out in her garbled voice, "*Moss v. Topper.*"

A moment later I was standing nervously next to Mr. Topper at one of the front tables.

At the other table, Josiah Goodheart stood next to the tall and thin Ms. Moss, now in a long-sleeved black dress with a striped hat that rose to two sharp points, like the horns of a zebra if zebras had horns. She wore small rectangular sunglasses and her long gray hair streamed down loose and magnificent. You couldn't say she hadn't dressed for the occasion.

"Josiah Goodheart at your service, Your Honor. I'll be representing Ms. Moss in her action against Mr. Topper and his gremlin."

"And you, Webster, announce yourself for the record."

"I'm Elizabeth?" I said. "Elizabeth Webster of the firm Webster and Spawn?"

"Is that a question or a statement?"

"A statement?" I said.

"Then say it like you mean it," said the judge.

"Elizabeth Webster of the firm of Webster and Spawn, Your Honor. I am here to defend Mr. Topper and his gremlin."

"Better. Much better. Now pray tell, Mr. Goodheart, what do you claim the gremlin did?"

"What it did, Your Honor, is so brutal, so horrible, so lacking in the simplest level of mercy that I am hard-pressed to—"

"Spare me the theatrics, Goodheart. State your claim in simple legal terms."

"The gremlin trespassed upon Ms. Moss's property and killed her goat."

The ram let out a gasp as the judge shook his head and said, "A goat, you say. And what remedy are you seeking?"

"What the law not only allows," said Josiah Goodheart, "but compels. We are demanding, I say, demanding monetary and punitive damages."

"The monetary damages I understand," said the judge. "A good goat is worth its weight in goat meat. But what kind of punitive damages are you seeking?"

"As my dear departed mother used to say," said Goodheart, "what is good for the goat is good for the gremlin. To pay for its crime, the remedy we demand is simply this: that Topper's gremlin be destroyed forthwith."

"Forthwith?" said the judge over Mr. Topper's gasp.

"Indeed," said Josiah Goodheart.

"Not my sweet little pet," said Mr. Topper. "You couldn't."

"Quiet in the court," ordered the judge after a bang of his gavel. "I assure you, Mr. Topper, that I could, and I probably will. Well, let's get to it, Mr. Goodheart. Call your first witness."

THE DEVOURING

State your name for the record," said Josiah Goodheart.

"Cassandra Moss," said the witness in a soft, breathy voice.

"And what do you do, Ms. Moss?"

"What do I do?" I had to lean forward to hear her. "I summon the sun in the morning and the stars at night, Mr. Goodheart. I reach my hand into the earth and touch the souls of all those who walk on its surface or swim in its seas. In short, I dance beneath the light of the cosmos and the universe dances with me."

"I meant as your profession," said Josiah Goodheart.

"Oh, I misunderstood," she said. "I am a dental hygienist."

"Quite a useful occupation," commented the judge before sucking on one of his undead molars.

"And how long have you been living next to the defendant, Topper?" said Barrister Goodheart.

"About a year," she said in her whispery voice.

Just then the front of the judge's great desk swung open with a bang.

Filling the space within the desk was a creature I had never seen before, huge and gray, with the face of a potato. His back was pressed against the desktop, and his legs were curled tightly beneath him. Before him was a little desk of his own with a lantern and an open ledger. In the thing's thick-fingered hand was a feather quill.

"The witness needs to speak up," said Potato Man in a gravelly voice rich with annoyance. "I can't hear a word. How can I keep a record if I can't hear a word?"

The judge turned to the witness. "You'll need to raise your voice, Ms. Moss, so Bittman can hear what you say."

"I'll try."

"You'll do more than try," said the potato-faced Bittman, "or there won't be a record. And without a record, where would we be?"

"Indeed," said the judge.

Bittman gave us all a glare from his potato eyes before slamming closed the front of the judge's desk.

"So now, Ms. Moss," said Josiah Goodheart, "tell us all, in a voice as loud as possible for the troll's sake, the sad and terrifying story of your goat."

And so she did.

Every year, halfway between the winter solstice and the spring equinox, Cassandra Moss celebrated the coming of spring with a bonfire and feast with friends and family. For last year's celebration, in her new house, it was suggested she roast a goat for the holiday table, so she purchased a live goat to fatten for the feast. For a while she kept the goat in a makeshift pen outside the shed where he slept, but soon she let him run free, as free as the wind, the way goats were meant to run on this good earth. She fed him table scraps and rubbed his beard and in exchange the goat kept her yard neatly trimmed.

She grew to admire and then love the goat. It was an old soul, she believed. She called him Magwitch. As the feast approached, when she was faced with the prospect of killing and eating Magwitch, she began having second thoughts, no matter how delicious roasted goat could be— especially when marinated in yogurt and orange juice and then spiced with coriander and cumin before the roasting. She ended up buying a lamb carcass at a warehouse store and roasting that instead, letting Magwitch chew on the scraps. Magwitch's joyful bleats from outside had the effect of sanctifying the joyous festival meal.

It wasn't long before Magwitch became Ms. Moss's closest companion. They sat out together in the sun, both she and the goat wearing sunglasses. She asked him questions and he answered with his right hoof, one tap for yes and two taps for no. Ms. Moss had been married for a decade once and she could attest that this was the better relationship.

Occasionally Magwitch broke through the hedges of the yard and ended up on one or the other of her neighbors' properties. The neighbor on the right simply placed a call and she went over to fetch Magwitch and bring him back. But when Magwitch wandered onto Mr. Topper's property it was never so simple. The goat was seized, the police were called, insults were thrown about.

She tried tying the goat to a post in the yard, but Magwitch was a wily little creature and had a developed a taste for rhododendron. Occasionally he would escape to snack in Mr. Topper's yard. Ms. Moss offered to buy more plants for Topper, but all he did was call the police and complain about how long it took for rhododendron plants to grow.

One day Mr. Topper came to Ms. Moss's house and banged on her front door. He told her he had bought a beast of his own and that she should now take all precautions to keep her goat away from his yard. "Consider yourself forewarned," he said ominously.

After that visit, she could hear Topper's creature growling from the other side of the hedge. Ms. Moss never really got a good view of the animal, just heard the sound of it and glimpsed the glowing light of its eyes, but the change in Magwitch was immediate. He bleated in fear and hovered by the house. He shook whenever the beast was loose in Topper's yard.

Then came the night of the devouring.

"Tell us what happened that terrible, terrible evening, Ms. Moss," said Josiah Goodheart.

Cassandra Moss put a hand on her throat as if she was swallowing a sharp bone.

"I know it's hard, Ms. Moss," said the judge. "But do try."

"It was a lovely summer night," she said, "and so I left Magwitch outside his shed to enjoy the night air. To avoid any problem with Mr. Topper, I kept Magwitch on the rope.

I remember looking out, and my sweet was lying down, his head high, looking around nervously. I went up the stairs to take a bath. I lit the scented candles, turned on the music. When I came back down, forty or so minutes later, and looked out the kitchen window, all I could do was scream."

"What had you seen, Ms. Moss?" said Barrister Goodheart. "Spare us no detail of the horror you witnessed."

"Magwitch was gone, just gone. There was a great puddle of blood, there were bones, there was a head, yes, with eyes wide and the darling little beard, but it was no longer attached to anything. It was just lying there on the ground, staring at me. And feasting on the grisly mass of bone and blood was the beast."

"What beast?"

She pointed her finger straight at Mr. Topper. "His beast," she said. "It was Topper's gremlin, I tell you."

I stood up and said meekly, "Objection?"

"What's that, girl?" said the judge.

"I think I'm kind of objecting?"

"Then you need to do a better job than that. If you have something to say, say it like you mean it."

"Objection!" I shouted.

"Better," said the judge. "Much better." And then he shouted back, "Overruled!" His voice calming again, he said gently to the witness, "Go on, Ms. Moss."

"But, Your Honor," I said, "don't you want to hear why I objected?"

"Not really, no."

"But, sir..."

"Oh, go ahead and make your piddling little argument."

"It just doesn't seem right," I said. "Ms. Moss said she had never seen Mr. Topper's gremlin, but then she is very quick to say that the thing she saw snacking on her goat was the very gremlin she never saw."

The judge stared at me with his bloodred eyes as if I had just said the stupidest thing ever uttered in his courtroom. I could see his face redden, and I was already flinching when he turned his head to stare at Mr. Goodheart. "Well, Counsel? What say ye to that? Seems pretty reasonable to me."

"We'll withdraw the statement," said Mr. Goodheart.

The judge banged his knuckles on the desktop. The door of the desk opened and Bittman stuck his potato head out. "Be a good troll and cross out the statement about it being Topper's gremlin," said the judge. "It's off the record."

Bittman scratched at the book with his feather pen. "Done."

"Splendid," said the judge as the desk door slammed shut. "Go on, Ms. Moss, and just describe for us the beast you saw."

"It was horrible," said Moss. "It was huge, at least six feet tall and hunched, its body a sickly brown and completely furless. Its hands were huge gnarled claws, its feet were even larger, and all along its back were razor-sharp spikes. When it heard me scream, it turned its horrible blood-smeared face toward me, a face as hairless as a skull, with long twisted teeth and yellow gums. And then there were the eyes, Mr. Goodheart, glowing red eyes that burned with hatred."

"You are sure of what you saw?" said Josiah Goodheart.

"I will never forget it. The vision of that beast haunts my days and darkens my dreams. It was death itself that crawled into my yard and took my Magwitch. Death itself, I say, and it belonged to Topper."

26

My Roll of the Dice

When it was my turn to ask questions of the whispery Cassandra Moss, I stood unsteadily at the table.

It wasn't just the witness's story I was up against, there were also the pictures that Goodheart had put into evidence, horrible photographs of the blood and bones of poor dead Magwitch. And along with those pictures was a photograph of the hole in the hedge, through which, Josiah Goodheart had proclaimed in his most theatrical voice, the evil gremlin had journeyed from Topper's property to seize the goat.

And what did I have in defense? Not much, really, except maybe one little trick up my sleeve. But I hadn't just been sweeping and filing in my time at Webster & Spawn, I had also been learning what my grandfather called the lawyerly arts, which always sounded to me like a bunch of lawyers trying to finger-paint. And one of those lawyerly arts was the art of cross-examination, for which there were all kinds of rules. Don't blather on too long. Ask short questions that get you yes-or-no answers. Don't ever ask a question you don't know the answer to. I was lectured about all that by my two fathers, my grandfather, and Barnabas. At night, as I was falling asleep, I made up cross-examination questions for the ghosts in my dreams.

But I was told by all my teachers that the Number One Rule of Cross-Examination—Number One!—was to never, ever ask the one question too many. I honestly had no idea what that rule meant, but I was about to find out.

"You never really got a good look at Mr. Topper's gremlin, did you, Ms. Moss?" I said.

"Not until it ate my goat," she said.

"Something ate your goat, that's for sure," I said. "But you couldn't have given a description of Mr. Topper's gremlin before the night of the attack because you had never gotten a good look at it, isn't that right?"

"I said its eyes glowed and it growled."

"Could you describe its color or its size?"

"No," said Cassandra Moss. "Not its color or size."

"Are you aware, Ms. Moss, of the many precautions Mr. Topper took to keep his gremlin on his side of the property?"

"As far as I know he took none."

"As far as you know? So you couldn't testify as to what he did or didn't do?"

"That's correct."

"The way he locked his gremlin in the house each night. The way he checked on her constantly."

"Objection," said Josiah Goodheart. "Is the defense counsel testifying now? Are we going to let her reach a verdict, too?"

"Is that allowed?" I said. "Because I'd be willing."

"Objection sustained," said the judge. "You're assuming facts not in evidence, Ms. Webster. Don't."

"And I fail to see the relevance in this entire line of questioning," said Goodheart. "What is the point here, Judge?"

"Ms. Webster?" said Judge Jeffries.

"It's about that case, you know, the one about the cows."

"Cows?"

"That *Rylands v. Fletcher* case thing?" I said uncertainly, wincing.

"*Rylands v. Fletcher*?" said the judge sharply. He thought on it a bit and repeated the name to himself, "*Rylands v. Fletcher*," before he turned to Josiah Goodheart. "*Rylands v. Fletcher*," he said. "Overruled. Very good. We are talking about a gremlin here and not a cow, but continue."

"So, Ms. Moss," I said, "your testimony is that Mr. Topper could have done everything a reasonable person would have done—that's the standard, right, Judge?"

"Indeed," said the judge.

"He could have done all that, and you wouldn't know, isn't that correct?"

"Whatever he did, it wasn't enough. His gremlin killed my goat."

"Your Honor?" I said.

The judge nodded and knocked his desktop with his knuckles. The front swung open and Bittman said, "What's that?"

"Strike that last line, Bittman," said the judge.

"Will do, Judge," said the troll before slamming the front closed again.

"And the witness will only testify as to what she saw," said the judge. "Go on, Ms. Webster."

"Why did you move next to Mr. Topper?"

"A friend suggested the house for sale might be perfect for me."

"Was that the same friend who suggested you buy a goat?"

"Possibly."

"And who was that friend, Ms. Moss?"

"Objection," called out Josiah Goodheart. "Relevance."

"Is this relevant to the case at hand, Ms. Webster?"

"Well, don't you want to know?" I said. "Doesn't it all seem curious?"

"Mere curiosity is hardly the standard for relevance," said the judge. "Objection sustained."

"But, Judge—"

"Move on."

"Fine," I said with a pout. "Then let's talk about your goat's last night, Ms. Moss, shall we? You testified Magwitch was nervous but alive before you took your bath."

"That's right."

"Then you went upstairs and got undressed, right?"

"It was a bath."

"And took off your glasses."

"Of course."

"And with the candles lit and the water warm, you leaned back and relaxed."

"Yes."

"Maybe even fell asleep."

"I don't think so."

"But maybe? Possibly?"

"It has been known to happen."

"And sometime after that, you climbed out of the bath, wrapped yourself in a robe, wandered down the stairs, and looked out the window to see a creature like something out of a nightmare?"

Was the last word a bit much? Maybe it was a bit much, because Ms. Moss gave me a look like I was a piece of lint. "I was not asleep, I was wearing my glasses, and I saw what I saw," she said, just as defiant and angry as I'd hoped she would be.

"And the creature was six feet tall or so," I said.

"At least."

"With spikes on its back and a wide chest."

"Yes, yes."

"And this huge beast was strong enough to break through a hedge, and hungry enough to devour a whole goat, and hateful enough to stare at you with the eyes of death."

"That is what I said."

I gave her a little smile. This was the do-or-die moment of the trial. Everything had been leading up to this. Yes, Mr. Topper would testify next, but that wouldn't matter much if this worked, and it wouldn't matter at all if it blew up in my face. I was rolling the dice—I guess a little bit of Keir had rubbed off on me after all.

I turned around and looked at Henry and said in a

voice loud with false confidence, "Mr. Harrison, could you come up to the front of the court and bring the crate with you?"

The ram on the wall sniffed the air as Henry came closer. When Henry finally stood beside me, with the crate lying on the table, the ram stared with a fearful curiosity as he chewed and chewed, a black twist of licorice leaking from his mouth.

"This is highly irregular," said Josiah Goodheart. "Highly irregular."

"As will I be if this goes on any longer," said the judge. "What are you doing here, Mr. Harrison? Another ghost?"

"He is our gremlin wrangler," I said.

"I hope you brought a helmet, young man," said the judge. "I am not an admirer of gremlins, you know, but I'll let you go on, Ms. Webster, just so we can finish up and be done with it."

"Thank you, Judge," I said. "Now, Ms. Moss, I'd like you to look at this crate sitting on the table in front of me. Could the thing you claimed to see that terrible night, the big-skulled, broad-chested, six-foot-or-more spiked-backed beast that supposedly ate your goat, could that thing fit into this tiny little crate?"

"Don't be ridiculous," she said. "Of course not."

"And if I told you that Mr. Topper's gremlin was small and cute and adorable and inside this crate, would you believe that?"

"No. Never."

"Well, maybe, Ms. Moss, it is time for you to actually

meet Mr. Topper's gremlin," and before Cassandra Moss could react or Josiah Goodheart could object, I reached for the latch of the crate.

The ram's head on the wall bellowed in fear as I swung open the door.

THE ONE QUESTION TOO MANY

Althea didn't bolt right through the opening like she had in my grandfather's office. Instead she cautiously stuck out her head and looked around. At that very same moment the ram's head reared up—as far up as it could rear, stuck as it was on the wall—and it bellowed so loudly that the licorice stick fell out of its mouth.

Althea stepped slowly out of the crate, hunched as if afraid of the ram, before Henry gently lifted her into his arms. She looked up at Henry with her big glowing eyes and she cooed.

That's right, she cooed. Was Henry Harrison the greatest gremlin wrangler of all time or what?

"Is this your gremlin, Mr. Topper?" asked the judge.

Mr. Topper stood. "Yes, it is, Judge. My very sweet little Althea."

"Althea?" said the judge. "I once knew an Althea. She was the mistress of an estate in Lancashire." His bloodred eyes grew distant. "She was quite a spirited woman."

"It was my mother's name, Your Honor," said Mr. Topper.

"You don't say," said the judge. "How extraordinary."

"Ms. Moss," I said. "Have you ever before seen the gremlin that is cooing now at Henry?"

Cassandra Moss stuttered a bit and then said, "I don't know."

"Would you like a better look? Henry, please bring Althea closer to the witness."

"That won't be necessary," said the suddenly nervous witness. "Not necessary at all."

"Maybe we all need a closer look," said the judge. "Come forward, Mr. Harrison, and bring Althea with you."

Henry carried the gremlin around the table and toward the witness. Althea hung on to Henry's neck and muttered as if she was terrified of what Ms. Moss would do to her. The ram's head on the wall was making such a commotion that the judge turned around and pointed his gavel at it.

"Bailiff," said the judge. "Control thyself."

"Y-y-yes, sir," neighed out the ram.

"Look closely at Althea, Ms. Moss," I said. "How tall would you say she is?"

"I don't know," said the witness.

"She's surely not six or so feet tall, is she?"

"I'd say not," said the judge.

"And what is its color?"

"Something green?" said the witness.

"Not gray. And though its eyes glow, as you said before, you wouldn't say they burn with hatred, would you?"

Just then Althea tickled Henry's chin and giggled her gremlin giggle.

"In fact," I said, "while Althea matches the glimpses you got of her while she was on Mr. Topper's property, she is nothing like the beast you claimed devoured your goat."

"It doesn't make any—"

"Maybe, getting out of the bath without your glasses and then looking out the window, you were confused by what you saw."

"I suppose that—"

"And yet you are seeking to destroy this sweet little animal, isn't that right?"

"Objection, Your Honor," said Josiah Goodheart. "This is simply too much to bear. Ms. Webster is parading this beast around the court as if it's a baby in a beauty pageant."

"*Rylands v. Fletcher*, Mr. Goodheart," said the judge. "There is a question as to whether this innocent little creature was the one that indeed attacked the goat in question. But beyond that, without any showing of negligence—and Ms. Webster has ably established that the plaintiff has no knowledge of the care defendant took or didn't take in protecting the neighborhood from his gremlin—the question becomes whether this gremlin is the kind of animal likely to do mischief. For that we need to judge the creature on a case-by-case basis. Let me get a closer look. Lift her up to me, Mr. Harrison," he said, tapping the top of his desk. "Put her right here next to me."

Henry looked at me and I nodded. He took a snack out

of his pocket and gave it to Althea. As she was chewing, he lifted her onto the desktop next to the judge. Henry looked again at me and I gestured to him to step back, leaving the judge and Althea alone at the judge's bench.

I couldn't help but flinch when the judge reached his pale, wrinkled finger toward the gremlin. Would the gremlin bite it off? Would she set it on fire with her eyes or use it as a step to climb onto his head before leaping up to the chandeliers hanging from the ornate ceiling? I had gambled the entire case on the behavior of a gremlin. What kind of idiot would do such a thing?

Exactly!

But Althea didn't snap off the judge's finger with her teeth. Instead she wrapped her little hand around it and started laughing. The judge ruffled the tuft of hair beneath the gremlin's ear, and the gremlin snickered. The judge wagged his gavel back and forth, and the gremlin's little head wagged back and forth with the hammer, forth and back. It was more than cute.

"Why, this is a delightful creature," said the judge. "She is such a sweet, peaceful thing, with a lovely name. And you seek to destroy her, Mr. Goodheart?"

"The law is the law, Your Honor."

"The law may be the law, but it contains an element of mercy in all its provisions," said the judge. "Do you have any other witnesses, Mr. Goodheart?"

"No, Your Honor."

"And you, Ms. Webster, will you be foolish enough to call a witness of your own?"

I looked at my father sitting on the barristers' bench. He

shook his head slightly, just enough for me to see. "No, Your Honor," I said.

"Very wise. I believe I'm ready to rule. In the matter of—"

There was a banging from the back of the courtroom. The judge stopped speaking and peered up the aisle to the courtroom door. We all turned and looked as the door slowly opened.

Then it appeared, through the now-open door, ambling in without an ounce of concern for where it might be or what it might be disturbing, looking left, looking right, searching for a tuft of grass as it moseyed ever forward toward the judge.

A goat.

That's right, a goat. I looked at the goat and then turned to look up at Althea, who was staring at the goat with eyes glowing ever redder.

I swiveled my gaze back to the goat, then back to the gremlin. The judge was also twisting his head back and forth, facing first the goat, then Mr. Topper's gremlin. He pulled away from the gremlin as Althea let out a little exclamation that sounded like,

"Uh-oh."

Uh-oh was right. *Uh-oh* had never been righter. *Uh-oh* was my new life motto. Sew it onto my flag, write it into the chorus of my personal anthem. *Uh-oh, daddy-o, a goat has come to court.*

As I turned back to see what the goat was up to, my gaze snagged on the face of Josiah Goodheart. His eyes were smiling, his lips were smiling, the teeth peeking through his smile were smiling. When he saw me looking, he gave the tiniest shrug, which told me just how bad this *uh-oh* was going to be.

That was when Althea started to change. Her body swelled, as if she was a balloon being blown up. Her arms grew longer, her nails turned into claws, her teeth lengthened into twisting spears. The cute little horns running down her back sharpened into vicious spikes as her green skin turned gray.

The ram within the five-pointed star on the wall above the judge's desk began to screech. His rounded horns banged into the wall behind him, cracking the plaster. And then the ram let out a call that shook the courtroom so much that the chandeliers swayed and the flying babies held on to the painted dome for dear life. And this is what the ram called out in all his terror:

"*Chupacabra!*"

The goat stopped, looked up.

He didn't know it, the poor little goat, but he himself was the one question too many. And the answer, trust me when I tell you, wasn't pretty.

28

HAMLET'S GHOST

Chupacabra?" said Doug Frayden, leafing through my grandfather's copy of White's Legal Hornbook of Demons and Ghosts. When he found the right page he tapped a finger on one of the entries. "Uh-oh," he said. "Not good, Elizabeth. Not good at all."

"Tell me about it," I said.

We were sitting on the floor in Young-Mee's basement, all the kids from the original Julius Caesar banshee experience—like a ride at Disney World!—along with Keir, the banshee's son. We had asked Barnabas, still guarding Keir, to join us inside, but he said he was more comfortable keeping an eye on the perimeter of the house. Good old Barnabas.

"According to the hornbook," said Doug, "we're talking

about a vampire for goats." He glanced uneasily at Keir before continuing. "From the Spanish words *chupar*—"

"Which means 'to suck,'" said Natalie.

"And *cabra*," said Doug.

"Which means 'goat,'" said Natalie.

"Hence, chupacabra," said Doug.

"Goat sucker," said Natalie.

"Sounds like a milk shake," said Charlie Frayden. "I'll have two burgers and a vanilla goat sucker."

"With a side of fries," said Henry, lying on his back with his legs crossed, looking up at the ceiling.

"The only thing fried in that courtroom," I said, "was my case."

"It says chupacabras have gray fur and glowing red eyes," said Doug, "and they're found primarily in Mexico and Puerto Rico."

Henry sat up. "Didn't Althea come from Puerto Rico?"

"Yes, she did," I said. "But how did a Puerto Rican chupacabra end up in a pet store in Fishtown just when Mr. Topper was searching for a solution to his goat problem?"

"A mystery begging to be solved," said Charlie.

"I have to admit I miss Althea," said Henry. "She was a cool little fiend."

"What happened to her?" said Young-Mee, holding her fluffy white dog on her lap.

"Nothing good," said Henry. "She got the cage."

"The cage?"

"Oh man," said Natalie. "I hate that cage."

As soon as the chupacabra attacked the goat, as Goodheart knew it would, Ivanov came running from his post behind the door with his tightly buttoned uniform, his orange hat, and a net he used for just such emergencies. The net had come from the other side, he told me later, and could neutralize the supernatural power of any troublemaker that acted up in court. The chupacabra, in the middle of sucking the blood from the poor dying goat, lifted its head and snarled as Ivanov tossed the net on top of it.

In an instant the chupacabra turned back into Althea, sweet Althea, her cute little green face now smeared with goat blood.

"To the cage with you," said the judge.

"Noooo!" said Althea.

"Althea!" said Mr. Topper.

"What about due process?" I said, as if the words themselves would make my argument. "The trial isn't even finished. Mr. Topper has the right to be heard. Due process!"

"Mr. Topper has had all the process he is due," declared the judge. "Lock up that thing."

And just that quickly, Althea was shoved through the open cage door. The door was locked and the cage descended slowly, slowly, its chain creaking all the while, slowly into the hole in the floor. After a great flash of light the cage rose again, empty.

"Now," said the judge, "about those damages."

It was as brutal a defeat as a barrister could suffer in court. You know how they say there was blood on the floor? Well, this time there really was blood on the floor. As the judge calculated how much Mr. Topper owed Ms. Moss based on the current price of goat meat in something called the Kingston Jubilee Market, Ivanov mopped.

Even worse was the way my father looked at me through it all. Like his disappointment was more than disappointment, like he was embarrassed that I even existed. It was enough to make me want to quit the whole legal thing. But we weren't in Young-Mee's basement only to hash out my latest disaster in the Court of Uncommon Pleas. That was just for sport. We had more important matters to discuss.

Since this was the gang there at the beginning of the banshee case, I thought it only fair (after swearing them to utter secrecy) to bring them up to speed on everything that had happened since. They were amazingly cool about Keir's vampireyness—to his new friends, it seemed just another part of his essential Keirness. Now they were helping us figure out our next step. Like how to get hold of the contract that bound Keir McGoogan to the Château Laveau for all eternity. And what to do about the girl who tried to kill Keir. And then there was the peculiar Dr. Van and his Sedona Academy for Special Cases.

"It maybe doesn't look half bad," said Keir, paging through the full-color brochure Natalie had received from the academy, "for a prison."

"It's not a prison," I said. "It's a paradise."

From what we could tell from the brochure—and it was quite the brochure, thick with pictures of happy children frolicking and an ultramodern schoolhouse perched on a cliff with playing fields and pools and horses—the academy was like an amusement park for peculiar children. And did I mention the horses?

"They even have private chefs," said Natalie.

"Yum," I said. "What about butlers?"

"I don't see anything about butlers," said Keir. "But it says here that the staff caters to the students' every whim."

"That's a lot of whim," said Charlie Frayden.

"If I end up in boarding school," I said, "that sounds like the boarding school for me."

"Maybe for you, Elizabeth," said Keir, "but I've been locked up long enough. And I already told you Dr. Van gives me the creeps."

"He seems nice enough," I said. "And he saved you once already. What have you found out about him, Natalie?"

"Nothing," said Natalie. "Other than some stuff on the school's website. He's like a ghost. But I might have found out something about the girl who attacked us. It seems to be quite the tragic story, a real weeper. I'm thinking I should try talking to her mother on Saturday. You want to come with?"

"I suppose," I said.

"Maybe I should come, too," said Keir.

"I don't think that's such a great idea," I said.

"Why not?" said Keir.

"Safety?"

"But it's me she was after. I should be part of finding out why."

I looked at Natalie, who shrugged.

"Fine. And we'll bring Barnabas for protection. But what you really should be thinking about, Keir, is how to find that contract. My father is doing what he can to find a copy, but you said the original might still exist in the Château Laveau."

"If it's anywhere, it'll be in the countess's private library," said Keir. "But there's still the matter of the birds."

"You mean guards?" said Young-Mee.

"Birds," I said.

"I'll bring Kyu," said Young-Mee. She took hold of her little dog's face, turned it to her, and nuzzled the dog's nose with her own. "Kyu will scare them away, won't you, Kyu?"

"They'll eat your dog," said Keir. "And clean their beaks with its bones."

"Not my Kyu!" said Young-Mee.

"With the help of a crew, I can trick the birds and handle the countess's dogs, too," said Keir.

"We'll be your crew," said Doug.

"Don't be so quick to volunteer," said Keir. "It's scarier than you think."

"That's okay," said Charlie. "We like scary."

"No you don't," said Doug. "Remember that movie about the dead clown? You ran out after the first smile."

"Of course I ran," said Charlie. "There was a dead clown. But things are different now that we work with Elizabeth. She's way scarier than some dead clown."

"Was that a compliment?" I said. "That doesn't sound like a compliment."

"We're in," said Doug. "Both of us."

"Me too," said Henry.

"We're all in," said Natalie. She looked at Young-Mee, who nodded.

"Why would you all risk anything for me?" said Keir. "I don't have enough money to make it worth your while."

"Because we like you," said Henry.

"Don't be daft. No one does anything just because they like you."

"Now who's being daft?" I said.

I couldn't really imagine what a hundred years under the control of the countess had done to Keir, but I was starting to get the idea. What kind of person would only help a friend if you paid him? What kind of person would think the only way to get a friend's help was to pay for it? My mother might have been right to send Keir to school after all.

Just then there was a knock on the basement door.

We looked at each other as the door opened and we heard footsteps. We were imagining all the terrible things that could be coming down after us—Miss Myerscough, a chupacabra, a girl with a wooden stake—but it was only Young-Mee's mother carrying a tray with a plate of pastries and a pitcher of iced tea.

"I brought you down some *bungeo-ppang* to keep up your energy," said Mrs. Kwon.

"They look like fish," said Keir.

"But they taste like heaven," said Young-Mee, and she was right.

"It's wonderful to see you children so interested in Shakespeare," said Mrs. Kwon. "And I must say, unusual. Are you still discussing *Julius Caesar*?"

"We've moved on to *Hamlet*, Mrs. Kwon," said Charlie. "The ghostly parent, the son who can't make up his mind, the big sword fight at the end where everyone dies."

As soon as Charlie said that we all looked at each other nervously, as if a curse had been cast and some sad and brutal ending of this story had just been assured.

"How sweet," said Young-Mee's mother.

29

EMPTY GLASS

"Travis and Diego were the best of friends," said Natalie during our Saturday bus ride to the neighborhood where Pili grew up. This was the second of two buses— quite a journey. Natalie was in the row in front of Keir and me, turned around on her seat and leaning on her elbows as she talked. "They went to the same school, hung out at each other's houses. The obituary talked about them being closer than brothers."

"Obituary," said Keir, like he was trying to figure out how some strange fruit tasted.

"It's something they write after someone dies," I said.

"I know what an obituary is," said Keir. "It's just we didn't have much use for such a thing in the flophouse. The queen bee never allowed the jumper to come through the gates."

"Who's the jumper?" said Natalie. "A volleyball player? I've been thinking of joining the volleyball team."

"The jumper is what my mam called Death himself," said Keir. "In the château we could hear him rattling away, calling our names, but out he stayed. Though I guess he found those two all right."

"Best friends dead in house fire," said Natalie.

Barnabas was sitting in the back of the bus, his dark eyes scanning the aisle and streets, ever the protector. We had asked him to sit with us, but he'd declined. "I think it is better for everyone if I stay at a distance, Mistress Elizabeth," he said. "Danger can come from any direction." Even though his face didn't crack into a smile, I think he was enjoying the intrigue. My mother had been doubtful about this whole Saturday adventure until I told her Barnabas was coming along.

"When the obituary talked about the families of the dead boys," continued Natalie, "it said Travis had a sister named Pili. That's how I found it online. But it didn't explain why she was trying to kill you."

"Maybe she just didn't like your looks," I said to Keir.

"What's wrong with my looks?"

"Were you winking?"

"Or maybe there's a story behind the deaths that explains it all," said Natalie, "something tragic and full of horror. The articles told the basic facts, but there were gaps and I have questions, so many questions. It seems the more I learn about something, the more questions I have. I guess I'm funny like that."

"You're not funny like that in Mr. Armbruster's class," I said.

"Truth is, Lizzie, I don't really learn much in there."

"Who's going to be the one to tell Mr. Armbruster the sad news?" said Keir.

"He'll be crushed," I said.

"When you guys are done laughing," said Natalie as the bus slowed, "maybe we can start digging."

"For bones?" I said as I stood for our stop.

She smiled slyly. "Why not?"

I turned to Keir. "I told you she's a bulldog."

When we hit the street, Natalie let her phone guide us through the neighborhood of tidy streets and small houses. Above us the kettle of vultures wheeled through the sky, and behind us Barnabas walked with his hands clasped behind his back. It was quite a little army trailing after our ace private eye, Natalie Delgado, out to learn the story of the girl with the wooden stake. And now you're trailing after Natalie, too, as she makes her way across a ragged lawn and onto the rotting front porch of a little gray house, where she rings the doorbell.

Brrrring. Brrrrring.

There were cobwebs beneath the porch roof, and the shutter on the window beside the door was halfway to falling off. The house was dark and mournful, as if a funeral had just taken place. Natalie gave me a worried look as she waited for an answer. She rang again.

Brrrring.

Nothing. Until we heard the slight vibration of someone approaching the door.

"Who is it?" came a woman's voice, muffled by the still-closed door. "What do you want?"

"Mrs. Johnstone?" said Natalie.

"She's not here," said the voice. "And she doesn't have any money, so don't be coming back."

"We don't want any money," said Natalie. "We just want to talk."

A moment later the door opened slightly and a woman older than my mother, thin with dark skin and drawn features, appeared in the crack. "Why, you're just children," she said, seemingly confused. "What do you all want from me?"

"Are you Mrs. Henrietta Johnstone?"

"Maybe I am. Why?"

"We just have some questions, if you don't mind," said Natalie.

"Oh, I mind," said the woman before tilting her head. "Questions about what?"

"About your daughter, Pili," said Natalie. "And your son, Travis."

Natalie had replied with such brightness that it seemed impossible for the woman not to want to tell us everything about her children, to brag and boast. But the woman's face turned from tired to bitter, as if she was suddenly chewing on a piece of garlic.

"My daughter's gone and my son is dead," said the woman. "What more do you need to know?"

"Your daughter isn't really gone, is she?" said Natalie. "In fact, she attacked a friend of ours in the train station just a few days ago."

"My daughter is here?" said the woman. "You saw her?"

"I did," I said.

"How'd she look?"

"Strong," I said. "Fierce."

"That's her, all right," said Ms. Johnstone. "And back in the city. Imagine that. Who'd she attack? One of you?"

I looked at Natalie and Keir and then shook my head. "No, not one of us," I said.

"Him?" she said, gesturing out to the street where Barnabas, pale and tall, stood watching.

"No," I said. "Another friend, and she was lucky to get away."

"Do you mind answering some questions about your daughter," said Natalie, "and maybe why she's going around attacking people? We're worried about our friend's safety."

As the woman looked at the three of us, and there was something working along her features, like she was figuring things out. Then she looked up and saw the vultures perched on the trees. Her face hardened.

"Yes, I surely do mind," she said. "I mind very much. I've nothing more to say. And if you children are smart, you've got nothing more to ask. Now go on home and hide beneath your covers and clutch your stuffed dolls and hope you don't ever meet up with my daughter again. Go on. Scat."

She waved us away as if we were some foul thing stuck on her hand before slamming the door shut. It happened so quickly we were stunned. It all seemed a little strange, and more than a little rude.

"Maybe we should have asked for tea," I said.

Just then the door swung open and the woman was again in the gap, staring, first at Keir, then at Natalie and me.

"Let me tell you three just one thing more," she said. "That friend of yours you say my daughter attacked. She is not a friend, do you understand? The only thing she'll cause is heartbreak and loss, and then only if you're lucky. Not a friend. Mark my words."

And then the door slammed shut again.

POLEO-MENTA

O h, Travis, he was so sweet a boy," said Mrs. Acosta from the rocking chair in her living room. "He met my Diego the first day of first grade and since then it was always Travis and Diego, Diego and Travis. To find one you'd just have to find the other, on the playground, on the ball field, or at Mr. Jack's Soda Shop. Travis was so loyal, it made my heart to see them together."

As could be expected, Natalie hadn't heeded Ms. Johnstone's warning, which was pure Natalie. Tell her she can't wear that top with those shoes and then watch her pull it off.

After we were chased from the Johnstone porch, while Keir and I were feeling shaky about the whole get-some-answers thing—maybe clutching a stuffed animal and hiding beneath our blankets wasn't the worst of ideas—Natalie headed off to ask her next set of questions. A few blocks down was the house of Diego Acosta's grandmother.

"Even as they grew older and things turned hard with Diego, Travis never abandoned him. I blame myself for some of what happened. I couldn't watch him like I needed to. His mother would have done a better job, but when she wasn't allowed back in the country after going home to take care of her mother, and when my son died, things started to, well...I tried. I suppose that has to be enough."

"What kind of things started with Diego?" asked Natalie.

"He became quiet, withdrawn. He had different friends, too. When I asked Travis what was going on, he just said, 'Nothing good, Lita.' That's what they both called me, my two boys."

"What was going on with your grandson?" I said.

"I never knew for sure," she said, which I doubted. There didn't seem to be much that Mrs. Acosta didn't know for sure. "But Travis had the more sense of the two and I thought he could help Diego find the right path. Except Diego always had his own mind. He told me he had a plan. What could I say about that? How about school as a plan? How about a job as a plan? He would laugh and give me a hug and then he'd be gone again. Until that time he stayed gone."

Ms. Acosta had invited us in without knowing what we wanted, and after Natalie told her in a rush of Spanish what it was we'd come for, she offered us tea without our asking. She was old and blind and full of life. I offered to help in the kitchen but she said, "*No seas tonta*. I don't need help to make tea in my own house. You just sit and I'll be right back." And she was, with a tray and a teapot and four cups.

"Let it steep a bit while we talk," she said after she'd placed the tray on the coffee table—misnamed, don't you think?—and dropped down into her rocking chair. "Why again are you asking about my two boys?"

"It's for a school journalism project," lied Natalie with such assurance it was breathtaking. "We need to dig beyond the facts in an obituary, and I remembered reading about the sad story of the two best friends that was in the newspaper."

"It's tragic is what it is. But I don't mind talking about it. I think about it all the time, but the thinking gets so lonely. It's nice to share once in a while."

"So what happened when your grandson didn't come home?" I said.

"I grew worried, then I grew scared," said Mrs. Acosta. "And then I called Travis. They hadn't been together as much by then, different paths, but Travis told me he'd find Diego. He was that kind of boy, not the type to sit around and worry but do nothing. He would always do something. And wouldn't you know it, he brought my Diego home."

"Where had he been?" said Keir.

"They never said, neither of them. I have my suspicions now, after the fire, but then I was just happy to have my sweet boy back. And he always was—sweet, I mean. But after, he wasn't the same anymore. He was so sad, and with different habits, sleeping all day and heading out only at night. And it was like there was something burning inside him. I could smell it." She sniffed the air. "Why, I can even smell it now. Like a soul is on fire."

She gasped, as if some new horror had stepped into her house, but then said, "Oh my, I've been talking so much I forgot all about the tea. I'm sure it's ready by now."

I poured the tea into her porcelain cups and handed them around, placing Mrs. Acosta's cup in her hand. We sat in quiet for a few moments, sipping the rich minty tea. Occasionally Mrs. Acosta would sniff the air, as if she had a cold or something, and with each sniff, Keir would shrink back in his chair.

"The tea is delicious, Mrs. Acosta," I said.

"It's *poleo-menta*," she said. "Of course it's delicious."

"So what happened after Travis brought your grandson home?" asked Natalie.

"It wasn't long before he left again," she said. "And that was that. I never got another hug. I never got to tell him one more time how much I loved him. Travis went after him again, I know that because his sister and her friend came here looking for Travis."

"Pili?" I said.

"That's right. Little Pili would always be trailing after them when she was young, playing their games, drinking a float with them at Mr. Jack's. She even worked at Mr. Jack's when the boys outgrew it. She was as loyal to Travis as Travis was to Diego. I told her and her friend Olivia everything I told you, and she had that same sound in her voice that Travis had when I told him Diego was missing that first time. The sound of determination. I regret so much now telling her what I did."

"Why?" said Keir.

"Because she fell into the same hole as her brother. How

much better would it have been if I hadn't tried to meddle in what Diego was doing to himself? Then Travis would have been in college by now. And Pili would have still been drinking those root beer floats at Mr. Jack's. And Olivia would have been planning for the prom instead of spending all her days at Travis's grave. How much better for everyone would that have been, Diego included? Sometimes it doesn't pay to try to save those beyond saving. Sometimes it's better to just let them go."

We three sat there and watched as a tear fell from one of her sightless eyes. Then she shook her head and brightened.

"More tea?"

ROOT BEER FLOAT

Maybe we should stop," said Keir as we walked away from Mrs. Acosta's house. "Maybe we should just go home and forget about all of this."

"Pili Johnstone tried to kill you," said Natalie. "Don't you want to know why?"

"We know why, don't we?" he said as he walked, his head down, his hands stuffed in his pockets.

"But you haven't done anything to her or her brother," I said.

"It's not about what I did," said Keir. "It's about what I am."

"She's wrong about what she shouted at you," I said.

"It doesn't matter what you think, Elizabeth. Or what you think, Natalie. It matters what she thinks, or others like her. To them I'll always be an abomination. At least I was protected in the château. Maybe I should go back."

"What about your freedom?"

"It's funny," said Keir, "but right now, looking behind my back every step, I don't feel so free. And I'm sure neither does poor Barnabas, trailing after me like some mother hen."

"Then what about Dr. Van's school?" I said. "His academy might be a safe place."

"Or maybe just a prettier prison."

"But with horses," I said.

"Why don't we find a quiet place to sit and talk it over?" said Natalie.

"Why do I get the feeling," I said, "that you have someplace specific in mind?"

Natalie only smiled.

Mr. Jack's Soda Shop was a hole-in-the-wall between a carpet store and a warehouse, but a hole-in-the-wall with a soda fountain counter, which made it something close to paradise. We sat three in a row on the red leather stools.

"What can I get you children?" said the old man in the apron. He wore a white hat and his smile shone out from his long gray beard.

"How much is your root beer float?" said Natalie.

"The question isn't how much," said the man, "but how good."

"Then how good is your root beer float?" I said.

"Good enough that I'll start making three," he said.

"And another to go," said Keir.

"That's the spirit," said the old man. He rubbed his bent

and gnarled hands together before he pulled out three milk shake glasses from the cabinet behind him.

"Are you Mr. Jack?" said Natalie.

"That I am," said the old man as he started to scoop out the vanilla ice cream.

"A girl we met told us we had to have the root beer float at Mr. Jack's," said Natalie. "Her name's Pili, Pili Johnstone? Do you remember her?"

The old man kept working but something changed in his expression. "You met Pili?"

"In the train station," I said.

"Nice girl," said Natalie.

"She was," said Mr. Jack. "Not so much anymore, which is a sad shame, and a story to boot."

"We like stories," said Natalie.

"You won't like this one," said Mr. Jack.

And then, with a little prompting—but not too much, not too much at all, almost as if he had been waiting for us to come in, sit down, and ask—he stepped out from the counter, turned the OPEN sign to CLOSED, drew the shade over the window, and locked the door.

As he built our floats, and as we drank them with the slurping from our straws accompanying his words, he told us Pili's story. At first he echoed what Mrs. Acosta had told us about little Pili, trailing after her brother, Travis, and his best friend, Diego, spooning ice cream into her mouth at Mr. Jack's as she lovingly stared at her two heroes, and later working at the very same soda shop.

Then her brother vanished.

Mr. Jack had heard about the disappearances of Travis

and Diego, of course—the whole neighborhood had—but he figured they were just on a road trip or something. That was the way Mr. Jack had lived as a youth. But Pili sensed right off that something was very wrong. Their mother hadn't been well. Travis would not have just left. The police had been called but were doing nothing. Pili felt it was up to her.

"But she didn't know what to do about it," Mr. Jack told us. "At least until the Dutchman showed up at the soda counter."

"Eye patch?" I said.

"Pointy nose?" said Keir.

"Gray dog?" said Natalie.

"Trust me, children," said Mr. Jack. "That's no dog."

The man said his name was Dr. Rudolph Van and that Travis and Diego were both caught in a trap with some otherworldly beasts. He told Pili that his purpose in the world was to save children he considered special cases and that Travis was just such a boy. But he would need Pili's help to convince him to leave.

Pili, in truth, didn't trust the one-eyed man. There was something strange about Dr. Van, and his whole act seemed too noble to be believed. Not to mention that accent. But in the course of their conversation she learned where her brother was being held.

She quietly went to the address—not so much a house as an isolated collection of glass-clad boxes on a cliff over-looking the river—looked around, and made her plans. She only trusted one person to join her in the rescue, her friend Olivia, the star of the school soccer and basketball teams.

Mr. Jack remembered them getting ready in the store the night of the operation. The two of them were dressed all in black, with masks and flares and wire cutters in their backpacks.

He tried to stop them, to have them take what they'd learned to the police, or even get the help of that Dr. Van. But they had tried the police and didn't trust the Dutchman. They were scared, yes, but they weren't going to sit back and hope good things happened to their family and friends. They were going to make them happen.

It was like they both had become something new and strong. Pili and Olivia, heroes for a new age. Mr. Jack watched them stride out the back door of the soda shop and he felt such hope for the future.

"That was the last time I ever felt hope like that," he said.

"What happened?" said Keir.

"I never learned the details, never really wanted to know," said Mr. Jack. "All I know for sure is that when Pili came back to the shop her eyes were dead as marbles, and just as hard. And Olivia, though she made it back to her house, she never made it back to school or those teams of hers. She just stepped away from her life. As for the boys, the firefighters found their bodies in the wreckage."

"It's too tragic for words," said Natalie. "It's like a sad song."

Mr. Jack wiped at the counter with a rag. "I always thought if Pili had trusted in that Dr. Van at the start, had taken the help he offered, maybe things would have turned out differently. And not just for the boys. The doctor seemed to have a more humane approach. His spirit of generosity might have tipped Pili's heart in a different direction."

"What direction did it take?" said Natalie.

"It took a hard turn to hate. What had been good in her spun toward violence and vengeance. All she wanted was payback from those who had taken her brother."

"Payback from who?" said Keir.

Mr. Jack stopped his wiping and looked up at Keir. "You tell me, son. Because I surely don't know who was in that house. But with the way Pili turned out, and knowing her like I do, if I were one of them, I'd be more than worried. I'd be scared to my very bones."

THE SKINWALKER

"Ah, Fishtown," said my grandfather as he steered the Sturdy Baker through narrow city streets. "Can you smell the sea?"

"All I smell is this car," I said, leaning out my window.

"That's my air freshener."

"It's very fresh," I said.

"In the late spring they used to bring in so much shad from the Delaware River, the streets of Fishtown ran with scales and blood. Let me tell you, Elizabeth, there is nothing like a good plate of boiled shad with a drizzle of malt vinegar on top while you're ankle-deep in scales and blood."

"I believe it," I said, laughing. "Nothing."

This was the next Monday, when we had to suspend our investigation of the wooden-stake-wielding Pili so that

Henry, my grandfather, and I could try to figure out how Mr. Topper ended up with his goat-devouring chupacabra.

"What's that address again, young man?" said my grandfather.

Henry, in the back seat, looked at the piece of paper in his hand and read the address aloud for the fourth time.

"Yes, of course," said my grandfather. "Where else would she be? And why are we going to see her?"

"We have some questions," I said.

"Excellent," said my grandfather. "It's hard to get answers without a few questions. Ah, and here we are." He stopped the car and peered out the window. "Why, I barely recognize the place."

"That's because this isn't it," I said, looking at the numbers on the door. "I think it's on the next block, Grand-pop."

The right address, when we finally reached it, was a blocky brick building with narrow slots for windows, as if to keep something out, or, more worrying, to keep something in. A sign above the door read:

NASCHA'S HOUSE OF SPECIAL PETS: ENTRANCE BY APPOINTMENT ONLY!

My grandfather banged his cane on the door once, twice, and was about to bang it a third time when a salamander medallion on the door slid up and one brown eye appeared.

"Appointment only," said a rabbitlike voice.

"We have an appointment. I am Ebenezer Webster the Third, here to see Nascha on important business."

"What type of business?"

"Pet business, of course," said my grandfather. "I'm not here for the pastries."

The salamander medallion slammed closed, as if it was insulted, but a moment later the door opened.

"Come in, come in," said the burly man who greeted us. "And welcome to Nascha's."

Just inside the doorway was a large display window, where a couple of sweet young creatures were frolicking. I couldn't quite identify the species, half mammal, half bird, all cute. When Henry tapped on the window the creatures jumped about and spread their wings, delighted at the attention. Above them, wrapped around a fake tree, was a huge purple snake staring at the three of us.

"Does the snake look hungry?" I said. "I think it looks hungry."

"Nonsense," said my grandfather. "I'm sure all the special pets are well fed."

"With what?" I said. "That's the question."

The store beyond the display window was chock-full of terrariums and aquariums and little cages with fluffy balls of fur. Fish with lizard heads swam, and lizards with fish heads stuck out their tongues, and catlike creatures lay on shelves wagging their multiple tails and staring at caged birds that sounded like trombones.

"I'm sorry for the questions at the door," said the man. His skin was brown, his beard was brown, his suit and tie were brown. There seemed to be a theme. He leaned forward and rubbed his little hands together as his two oversized front teeth fluttered against his lower lip. "But we can't have just anyone wandering in. I am Clarence. Now, how can I help you this fine afternoon?"

"We've come to talk to Nascha herself," said my grandfather.

"Oh, I'm sure I can render whatever assistance you require," said Clarence. "So tell me, what kind of pet are you looking for?"

"Do you have a gremlin?" I said.

"A gremlin? You don't want a gremlin. Such disagreeable creatures. Now, we have those gryphons in the display window, which are just so adorable."

"Adorable is right," I said.

"But we only sell them in pairs. Two gryphons are a delight, one is a nightmare."

"Do you have puppies?" said Henry.

"Puppies?" said Clarence as if Henry had just yanked his beard. "We have no puppies. Do you know about the mills in which they are bred? Barbarous. We have chimeras, and mini-hippocamps, and a jackalope, if you are ready for such a thing, but no puppies. We can get you a cat, if you choose. Just let us know how many heads, how many tails. Wings are usually extra."

"What about a gremlin?" I said.

"Why on earth would you want a gremlin? Don't you know the trouble they cause?"

"That's sort of the point," I said. "You see, there's this goat in the neighborhood."

"A goat?" said Clarence. "A gremlin won't be of any use against a goat. Now, if there was a machine nearby making all kinds of noise, let's say an air-conditioning unit, well then, a gremlin would be perfect. It could even spoil a piano for you in a pinch if that downstairs neighbor insists on playing Mahler through the night. But a goat? How could a gremlin help you solve a problem with a goat?"

"Exactly!" I said.

"Hello, Ebenezer," came a melodious voice from behind us. We turned to see a woman approaching.

"Nascha," said my grandfather. "How nice to see you again."

"That is all, Clarence," she said. "I'll take care of Mr. Webster and his coterie."

Clarence nodded and bowed. "As you wish," he said before backing away from the woman. He kept backing away until he passed through a beaded curtain and disappeared into another room.

Nascha was tall and thin, skeleton thin, with cheekbones so strong they could wrestle a bear. She wore a patterned purple dress and was barefoot. Behind her we could see the tree in the window display, now without the purple snake. I remembered then that my grandfather had described her as a skinwalker, and I suddenly sensed what that might mean.

"Allow me to introduce my granddaughter, Elizabeth," said my grandfather.

"So you're the Elizabeth I've heard so much about," she said. "I thought you'd be older."

"I'm working on it," I said.

"And this is Henry Harrison," said my grandfather. "He was the wrangler for that gremlin you sold to Mr. Topper. You remember the creature, don't you?"

"I seem to, yes," said Nascha, her gaze still on me. There

was something about her eyes. It wasn't like she was look-ing into me as the countess had, it was like she was reach-ing into me and trying to rearrange things. I quickly looked away.

"Well, funny story," said my grandfather. "It was not a gremlin at all. Imagine Mr. Topper's surprise. It turned out to be a chupacabra."

"You don't say," said Nascha.

"I was wrangling a chupacabra," said Henry.

"That's quite impressive, young man," said Nascha. "And I see no scars. You must have had quite a helmet."

"No helmet," said Henry. "Just jerky."

"Astonishing," said Nascha. "We might be looking for some help around the store. Clarence is getting so . . . robust, and we could always use another hand."

"Would I get it back?" said Henry.

"My my, Ebenezer," she said. "Your friends are so charming."

"Who did you buy it from?" I said, still avoiding the woman's gaze.

"Buy what, dear?"

"The chupacabra."

"We didn't know it was a chupacabra," said Nascha. "We thought it was a gremlin."

"Maybe you did, maybe you didn't," I said. "And maybe we'll let the judge decide if our client, Mr. Topper, decides to sue you in the Court of Uncommon Pleas."

"On what possible grounds could he sue?" said Nascha.

"Breach of contract," said my grandfather as he put a hand on my shoulder. "It's really straightforward. You agreed to sell Topper a gremlin and sold him instead a dangerous beast."

"Or maybe fraud," I said. "That's a tort. And I'm not talking about apple pie."

"Does it get tiring being so clever, dear?" said Nascha.

"Yes, actually," I said. "It really does. But maybe it wasn't fraud, maybe it was a simple mistake on your part. Maybe, despite all your years of experience, you yourself were fooled. And that is why we are here and not in court. How did you end up with the chupacabra?"

"Look me in the eye, girl."

"I don't think so."

"Oh, Ebenezer. You must be so proud."

"More than you know," said my grandfather.

"A man came into the store carrying a cage," said Nascha. "An officious little man with a hat and a mustache. I thought he might be an accountant. He said he had recently come into possession of a gremlin, which he could not keep because it was agitating his goats. He said the gremlin was of a rare type he'd bought in Puerto Rico. I took a look. I had never seen that kind of gremlin before but took him at his word as to what it was. The man sold it to me at a very fair price. A few days later Mr. Topper came into the store with his sad story. I thought the gremlin would be perfect for him. That was the end of it."

"Did you get the accountant's name?"

"Fred, I believe it was."

"That makes sense," said my grandfather. "In my experience, all the best accountants are named Fred. Why, our firm's current accountant is Frederica Himmelfarb.

Deliciously clever with the numbers, I must say. Never skimp on your accountant, Elizabeth. That way leads only to misery."

"Fred what?" I said to Nascha.

"Abiz, dear," she said, and when she said it I couldn't help but glance her way. A victorious little smile lit her face, as if from the moment we had walked into her store she'd been waiting to give us this jolting little fact. "His name was Fred Abiz."

It wasn't so hard to decipher. I had guessed right away who might be the officious little man with the mustache, and when I heard the name I knew it was no man at all. I had met it in court when it was clothed in its accountant's garb, and suffered its threats when it took its truer form, a horned demon with clawed hands and hooves for feet. The demon Redwing, whose proper name was Abezethibou, had set up Mr. Topper so Mr. Topper couldn't interfere with the demon's plans to extend his dominion into our world. And for some reason he wanted me to know.

Was is a taunt? Was it a threat? Did it matter?

No, it did not matter. Redwing's horns were red and they blazed with fire. Either way I was toast.

SUNKEN SHIP

"It was a setup from the start," I said. "I was just a stooge."

"Find two more and you could have an act," said Natalie. "But that just means the fake gremlin's fate was sealed from the beginning. It's like a heartbreaking movie. The tragic heroine, the lovelorn boy left alone to wonder what might have been. None of it was your fault."

"Maybe so," I said. "But I still feel like I'm the goat. And the thing is—"

Just then Natalie shushed me as Mr. Armbruster peered at the two of us from the front of the classroom. Mr. Armbruster was showing us pictures of a boat called Lucy something that had somehow sunk and caused, like, a whole world war, but we had bigger fish to fry. Like why had the demon set up Mr. Topper? And what had really happened to Pili and her brother in that burned-down house? And when was the pink ever going to grow out of my hair?

"Give it time," said Natalie after the lifeboats had been launched and the boat had disappeared. "Pretty soon your hair will be half black and half pink, and that always looks kind of cool in a pathetic sort of way. Oh, and I think I found that Olivia."

"So quickly?"

"What's she saying about Olivia?" whispered Keir, who was sitting on the other side of me.

"Mr. McGoogan," said Mr. Armbruster. "Why don't you share with all of us your thoughts on the *Lusitania*?"

"Must I, sir?" said Keir.

"I think you must."

This was not a one-off occurrence, Mr. Armbruster picking on Keir as soon as he opened his mouth. It wasn't so much harassment as intense interest. Like Keir was a puzzle the teacher was trying to solve. The problem was, even with the bow ties cutting off the circulation to his brain, Mr. Armbruster was just smart enough to maybe succeed, and then where would we be? Down in the deep with Lucy.

"Come now, Keir," said Mr. Armbruster. "Don't keep us in suspense."

Keir gave me a look, like it was all my fault—which, I had to admit, it was—then stood, took his baseball cap off, and placed it over his heart.

"They told us there were one hundred and twenty-eight Americans dead when the Germans sank that boat. They sang angry songs and waved flags. It was all part of the march to war that sent our fathers and brothers over there to fight and die. They didn't tell us then how many millions of bullets were in the belly of that ship, how many tons of shells and shrapnel. That might have muddled things, you see. We the people need to be spoon-fed our stories without any inconvenient facts when we're sending our loved ones someplace distant to die. We need to be stirred, you see. I guess one hundred and twenty-eight was stirring enough. The end."

When Keir put his cap back on and sat down, there was a moment of quiet in the classroom, like everyone was embarrassed for him. I mean, what kind of kid gives a speech like that about some stupid boat? And Mr. Armbruster just stared, like he was on the edge of figuring everything out.

"Couldn't you have just said it was a boat and it was, like, torpedoed?" I whispered when Mr. Armbruster went back to his little slide show. "Sometimes too much is too much."

"It went over, though, didn't it?"

"It did not go over."

"I stunned them with my words."

"I think they were stunned by something else," I said.

He looked at my face and then looked away. "I know, I know. Keep my head down."

"Your oral reports on the Progressive Era are due next week," said Mr. Armbruster after he turned off the projector. "I'll have a schedule on our class page by the end of this week. While it is not required, I'm encouraging each of you to talk to me about your project. I might be able to give you some guidance about appropriate reference materials. Once again I want to warn you, you cannot just read something off the web."

The bell rang and the quiet of the class was suddenly overtaken by burbles of conversation and the sounds of books being stuffed into backpacks. And then above this everyday meaningless noise, Mr. Armbruster said,

"Oh, and Keir? Can you see me before you leave the classroom, please?"

Natalie and I stood outside the classroom, waiting to learn what was going on behind the closed door. What had Mr. Armbruster discovered and what was he going to do about it? I kept expecting to see a pack of police storming down the hallway. I could already see the headline: HUNDRED-YEAR-OLD VAMPIRE CAUGHT IMPERSONATING MIDDLE SCHOOLER. And the cops, if they came, wouldn't just be taking in Keir. I'd be with him in the big house, hoarding spoons. For some reason something about prison always made me think of spoons.

"What is taking so long?" I said.

"Don't worry so much," said Natalie.

"You know, you might end up in as much trouble as Keir and me," I said.

"You'll keep me out of it," she said.

I looked at my friend Natalie and then turned away. "You're right, I will. So what's this about Olivia?"

"I joined a group chat of some kids at her school."

"Really? Did you know any of them?"

"No."

"Then how did you do that?"

"I lied, naturally," said Natalie. "And it turns out that

someone was at a funeral of an aunt and saw Olivia at the cemetery, just sitting beside a gravestone."

"Did she say hello?"

"She was too freaked. But I remembered Mrs. Acosta said the same thing. I got the name of the cemetery, too."

"It sounds creepy."

"I know. Cool, right?"

"No, not cool," I said. "Just creepy."

Right when I said it, the door to the classroom opened and Keir sauntered out. That was the thing about Keir, he was a saunterer. You couldn't tell what was going on from his walk. Good or bad, great or dreadful, he just sauntered on. The only way to learn what was happening was to ask.

"So?" I said.

"So nothing much," he said.

"He just wanted to chat?"

"Sort of. He said he likes my comments in class. He called them inspiring. He said he sees a lot in me."

"I bet he does."

"But he fears I'm not working up to my potential."

"Oh man, if I had a nickel for every time—"

"And he's upset that I'm not handing in my homework."

"Why aren't you handing in your homework?"

"Because you told me I couldn't pay my friends to do it for me."

"So it's my fault."

"Exactly so," said Keir. "And that's what I said to Mr. Armbruster. But I told him you'll try to do better from here on in. He's looking forward to our presentation."

"Our presentation?"

"Well, that's the story. And you'd better get to working, Elizabeth, if I'm going to have anything to say at all."

Natalie looked at Keir and then at me as I sputtered with frustration, then back at Keir. "I think Mr. Armbruster is wrong, Keir," she said, a wide smile breaking out. "I think you're working fully up to your potential."

"Why, thank you, Natalie. So what's this about that Olivia?"

"Natalie thinks she found her," I said. "At a cemetery."

"Dead?"

"Not yet," said Natalie. "We're going to talk to her this afternoon."

"I can't make it, sorry," said Keir.

"What do you mean you can't make it?" I said.

"I have a thing about cemeteries. I avoid them is what I do. It's worked out for me so far. Besides, I have plans."

I gave him a look. "Plans? What kind of plans?"

"Just plans," he said, avoiding my eyes.

"Make sure Barnabas comes with you."

"I will," said Keir. "I'll meet him outside the school as always. I'll be back at the house by dinner."

"Maybe Henry can join us, then," said Natalie. "Three's a good number when visiting at a cemetery."

"Any number's fine," said Keir, "as long as you're not the one they're visiting."

34

THE CEMETERY

We took Henry's car service to the cemetery, which, let me tell you, sure beat the two buses and the long walk. If I couldn't have the pool or the butler, maybe I'd settle for a car service. But only if I didn't have to get up at five like Henry to make morning swim practice. When the car let us off at the cemetery gates, I stopped for a moment and looked around. It seemed oddly familiar.

"Wasn't this where we reburied Beatrice?" I said.

"I think it was," said Henry. "Yes, right over there. Maybe I should pay my respects. Let her know I'm still thinking of her."

"She knows," said Natalie. "Trust me. First let's find out if Olivia is here."

We wandered around the cemetery looking for a lost girl spending her days among the tombstones. It didn't take us long to find her, sitting cross-legged on the ground, playing with the petals of a ragged bunch of flowers.

She was older than we were, tall and lanky, with curly red hair that was long and loose and a bit wild, almost like a mourning veil around her head. She looked like she belonged right where she was, beside a grave with a marble marker that read TRAVIS JOHNSTONE.

We quietly walked to the graveside and stood in a row until she looked up at us through her curls. Her face wasn't sad or mournful, like Barnabas's face, it was just flat. As if nothing got through, as if nothing mattered.

"So let me guess," said the girl. "You're the middle school kids they're talking about, the ones who have been asking all kinds of dangerous questions. The ones my mother told me not to talk to."

"That's us, all right," said Natalie proudly.

"Why are our questions dangerous?" I asked.

"The fact that you don't know is dangerous enough. You three should just play with your dolls and forget about all of this."

"How come everyone thinks we still play with dolls?" said Natalie.

"You don't?" said Henry.

"I didn't say that, it's just—"

"Why did you stop going to school?" I said.

Olivia looked at me for a moment and then turned away. "After what I'd been through, was math going to save me?"

"But math rules!" I said.

"The whole school thing seemed so unreal after what happened, I couldn't bear it. The doctor told my mom I just needed time, so she lets me come here, hoping the phase will pass. But it's not passing, and a century won't be enough for me to feel like I belong in school anymore."

"And you belong here?" I said.

"With him, yes," she said. "And Diego. And my dad, just three rows down."

"What happened at that house?" said Natalie.

"If I snapped my teeth and hissed," Olivia said in her dead voice, "would that send you running? It should."

"But it won't," I said. "I'm sorry, but just like you, we have a friend in trouble. And the trouble he's in is from Pili."

Olivia went back to picking at her flowers. "Then he's in a world of trouble."

"Tell us about the doctor," said Natalie.

"Which doctor?" she said.

"With the eye patch," said Henry.

"And the dog," I said.

"Oh," Olivia said in her flat voice. "That doctor." She picked at the flowers more violently and then started twisting the stems as she said, "He told us it would be bad."

Natalie knelt down and gently took hold of the mangled bouquet. She straightened what stems she could straighten and arranged what was left of the petals until they almost looked like flowers again. Then she carefully laid them in front of the headstone with Travis's name.

"Go ahead," she said.

"He told us it would be bad and we had to do it his way," said Olivia. "But Pili didn't want to do it his way. Who would? That wasn't the kind of girl she was, at least not then. We figured we knew what we'd find. Drugs. Crime. We'd seen enough movies. Travis and Diego were caught in a trap, but we could get them out. Our way. Sneak in, sneak out. We could do it ourselves. We'd seen the movies." She paused for a moment and closed her eyes. "But this wasn't like the movies."

"What was in the house?" said Natalie.

"A nest," said Olivia. "A nest of monsters, horrid beasts in human form, all teeth and nails, slithering around in the shadows like snakes and feeding themselves on the blood of their living victim, who was hung like a trophy on a wall."

"Which one was on the wall?" said Natalie.

"Travis," said Olivia as she stared at the headstone. "Still alive. Crazed with fear and pain."

I tried to imagine the scene painted by her words, but I couldn't. I had seen ghosts and demons and the very strange Court of Uncommon Pleas, I had seen a chupacabra suck the life out of a goat, but this was too much. This gasp of horror was beyond my imagining.

"Just the sight of it was enough to convince us both that all our movie plans were ridiculous," said Olivia. "We backed away from the window, keeping our gaze on the monsters as we stepped quietly away. But we didn't step quietly enough. Burning-red eyes turned in our direction, two of which belonged to Diego. Then came the inhuman howls. And then came the dogs."

I looked up just then, looked around. The snap of danger that had chased Pili and Olivia was still in the air. I could hear the monsters howling and the dogs charging. Then I spied a strange figure standing at the cemetery entrance, as if summoned by the story. It was tall and thin and still and sad, a little like Barnabas. With a start I realized it was Barnabas. I had told him where we were going that afternoon, but why was he here?

"What happened next?" said Natalie, still kneeling next to Olivia.

"Something charged right past us, a fierce gray thing that leaped straight into the pack of dogs that were about to tear us to pieces and sent them scattering like bowling pins."

I looked up into the sky, high and blue and clear. Clear of clouds, clear of vultures. If Barnabas was here, where was Keir?

"As the dogfight continued," said Olivia, "the doctor appeared like a ghost out of the darkness. He had come to save us, he said. He had come to end the horror."

I pulled my gaze from the sky and stared at Olivia as she continued her story.

"They went back in to finish what needed finishing. The doctor, and his gang, and Pili, too. She decided that the only way to save her brother was to do it the doctor's way. When they went in, I sat on the ground, hugging my knees. And then, as the fire raged, I ran. I didn't know what else to do. When I was finally home safe, I went right up to my room and crawled under my covers. Who could I tell what I'd seen? Nobody. So that's who I told. And in truth, I still haven't come out from under the covers. And I haven't seen Pili since."

"You said Pili tried saving Travis the doctor's way," I said. "What was Dr. Van's way?"

She turned her head and looked at me. "Who is Dr. Van?"

"The dude with the eye patch and the dog," said Henry. "His name is Dr. Rudolf Van."

"Van is just part of his last name," said Olivia. "His full name is Van Helsing. Dr. Rudolf Van Helsing. And his way is to hunt the monsters and kill them. To stick stakes into their hearts and burn their corpses until not one of them remains on the face of the earth. And that night Pili joined the vampire slayer's crusade."

As soon as the implications of Olivia's story slipped through my thick skull, I knew right away what had happened to Keir. He had said he had plans, which meant avoiding Barnabas after school and slipping away to find his own path to safety. He thought maybe it lived in a full-color brochure, but what he would find instead was...was...

I spun toward Barnabas and started running.

35

VAN HELSING

What was left of the house was perched on a cliff high above the Schuylkill River. It had once been sleek and modern, with huge windows and a pool. Yeah, a pool. It would have been something like my dream house—please, Mom, please, just this once—if it hadn't been a burned-out wreck. The windows were vacant holes between bare pillars of stone. The roof was gone. Even the pool was filled with charred trees and sodden furniture. Gasp! The pool! So why were we there?

The kettle of vultures flitting between the trees might clue you in.

Charlie Frayden had used his bird-watching forum to find the latest sighting of the great flock of turkey vultures that had invaded the area. And once we had the general location, Olivia was able to guide us to the exact piece of land. It was the same property where she had seen the nest of monsters that Dr. Van Helsing had destroyed. Van Helsing had returned to the scene of his crime, or his victory, depending on your point of view.

Now, in the twilight, we stood in a line before the burned-out hulk. There were five of us: Henry and Natalie and Barnabas and me, along with Olivia, who had felt obligated to come along because Pili was part of it all. We were there intending to save Keir McGoogan from the clutches of the vampire slayer, if there was anything left to save.

"He's not here," said Henry. "There's nothing here."

"The vultures say he is," I said.

"Maybe they jammed a stake in his heart and then brought his body here," said Natalie. "Maybe we're too late and poor dead Keir lies somewhere in the rubble."

"I don't think so, Mistress Natalie," said Barnabas, "or that creature wouldn't still be standing guard."

Barnabas pointed to the far edge of the cliff, where the gray wolf-dog stared at us with her pale eyes. La Loba. The sight of her sent a prickle up my spine even as the hairs on the animal's back rose at the scent of us.

"There was another small building a little way down the cliff," said Olivia. "Maybe that wasn't destroyed by the fire."

"But how do we get past the animal?" said Henry.

"As calmly as possible, Master Henry," said Barnabas. "Wolves are like the nobles of my time, pouncing on fear. Sadly, there's little for me to be afraid of."

Slowly, bravely, Barnabas made his way around the pool and through the rubble toward the gray beast at the edge of the hill. When he reached her he stooped down, started talking too softly for us to hear, and held out a hand for the beast to smell.

La Loba leaned forward and snarled.

Barnabas reached past her bared teeth to rub her neck. A moment later La Loba was on her back as Barnabas scratched her belly. The beast let out a contented moan.

"Hurry, children," said Barnabas, his attention still on La Loba. "We might not have much time."

We hurried in a single file toward the hill, Henry in the lead. We kept Barnabas between us and the moaning animal as we reached the edge. A stone stairway led down to another structure, a large box of cement and glass, singed by the fire but still intact. A soft light glowed from inside.

When we reached the bottom we could see through the windows into a single large room, lit by portable lanterns, with a desk at one end and upholstered chairs arranged around a low table at the other. And hanging from the wall above the desk, duct-taped in place with a crazy splatter of thick silver bands, was Keir.

That's right. Keir McGoogan was duct-taped to the wall. He actually looked good in silver—it nicely set off his hair.

Pili was standing off to the side in her leather jacket, looking up at the boy on the wall. And standing in front of Keir, with his cape and cane, his back turned to us, was the vampire slayer himself.

Somehow we needed to get into that room and save Keir. If Barnabas could keep La Loba distracted, and if Natalie and Henry could create some sort of diversion that would lure Van Helsing away, then maybe Olivia could hold up

Pili, giving me enough time to free Keir so that we all could run, run away. It seemed like a plan, a weak wack-brained plan that relied on impossible stealth and abilities I didn't have, but a plan all the same. I was still working out the details when Van Helsing, as if he'd known we were there all along, slowly turned to face us.

And he was smiling.

Just then we heard the snapping of a branch behind us. We spun around to see a tall woman in a green overcoat standing next to a squat bruiser with a red bandanna atop his bald head. The man held some sort of rifle. The woman held a great silver sword.

So much for plans.

36

A STRANGE PROPOSITION

Welcome, my friends," said Dr. Rudolf Van Helsing as the four of us were forced inside the office. "Welcome to the battle between the living and the undead."

We weren't tied up or duct-taped like Keir. Instead, the woman in the green overcoat flicked her sword in the general direction of the chairs facing Keir and we dropped right down, quickly and quietly.

A moment later, the final member of Van Helsing's gang, gripping two old dueling pistols in his gnarled hands, escorted Barnabas in as well. Even with his pale face, Barnabas didn't seem as frightened as the rest of us. I suppose being immortal has some advantages.

On either side of Keir now stood the members of Van Helsing's vampire-hunting crew, who he introduced with a great flourish. Along with Pili there was Mrs. Calabash with her long gray hair matching her silver sword. And there was Dolp, with his red bandanna. And, surprise surprise, there was Mr. Jack of the soda shop, whose false story had helped dupe Keir into seeking Dr. Van on his own.

I gave Mr. Jack my angry face and he shrugged, but I couldn't hold his lies against him. His loyalty was to Pili, and I could admire that. In fact, I could admire the way this whole plot had played out so neatly. From the first moment I had spied Van Helsing, and you remember when that was, he had been planning just for this.

"So this is your Sedona Academy for Special Cases," I managed to say.

"It's smaller than it looks in the brochure," said Natalie.

"And there are no horses," said Keir from the wall.

"The deceit was unavoidable. Once I learned of the court order allowing this little monster to leave the Château Laveau, I figured a special school with horses and private chefs was just the right kind of lure. All we needed was a proper introduction, which Pili provided, and then a full-color brochure full of lies, which we sent straight to Ms. Delgado. Nothing sells like a full-color brochure full of lies. But here is a truth for you. At the Sedona Academy for Special Cases, we teach our students the one thing they cannot learn on their own: how to die."

"Sweet school," I said.

"It is good to see you again, Olivia," said Dr. Van Helsing. "I know Pili missed you. She hoped you would finally agree to join us. You, as much as anyone, know the horror that we are fighting."

"I don't see a horror taped onto the wall," said Olivia, "just a kid."

"He's one of them, O," said Pili. "And not so young. He's almost a hundred years older than we are."

"He's still a boy, frozen in time from the moment he was bitten," I said.

"And you put him on the wall," said Olivia, "like they put Travis on the wall."

"Payback to the monster," said Pili.

"He's not a monster," I said. "He's our friend."

"These things have no friends," said Pili, "only victims."

"These things, as you call them, are humans, young miss," said Barnabas. "With names. And friends. And families. It was a mother's love that caused him to be turned from one type of human to another. We are all more than our conditions."

"Quite sentimental of you, Mr. Bothemly, considering," said Van Helsing.

"What do you know of me, Dr. Van Helsing?" said Barnabas.

"I know you work at the Webster law firm and that you have been protecting the monster. But I also know your history. You are as undead as he is, *ja*, just without the fangs. But my family has been hunting these creatures for generations. We know full well the dangers they pose for humanity. Which is the only reason why this specimen is still alive."

"He wants me to spill on the flophouse," said Keir. "How to get in, get out."

"It is a nest we intend to destroy, as we destroyed the nest at this location. And there is a particular monster who has been loose for more than a century, spreading her poison like a plague upon the land. We will not leave until she is dead."

"They're hunting Miss Myerscough," said Keir.

"Myerscough is one of the original few infected by Dracula himself during his time in London," said Van Helsing, "before my great-great-grandfather Abraham finally put him down. Since then, the crimes she has committed are innumerable. We have been chasing this fiend from London to New Orleans and finally to here. It has fallen upon me to finish it. I tried many years ago, and lost an eye to one of those foul vultures in the process. But now I am determined to end her reign."

"And you don't want to help them, Keir?" I said, surprised. There was an angle for Keir to play here, but Keir wasn't playing it. How unlike him.

"I might have helped once," said Keir. "But it all looks different to me now."

"She made you a monster," said Pili.

"To save my life," said Keir. "I won't help you kill her for that."

"And that is why, my friends," said Dr. Van Helsing, "I am glad you have joined us. Maybe you can convince this monster of the rightness of our cause. Or maybe he might give us what we want to protect you from, let us say, your own unfortunate fate."

Ahh, there it was. I was only surprised it had taken so long. Dr. Rudolph Van Helsing, the great protector of humanity, was ready to sacrifice a few humans so he could go on killing the unhuman. I looked around for some sort of a plan to get us out of this. There had to be something we could do. We're not just lobsters in the aquarium, waiting to be boiled. There's always something.

"So this is what it's come to, Pili?" said Olivia. "You'll kill me if this boy doesn't talk."

"No," Pili said, looking down now. "I won't let that happen to you."

"What about the others?" said Olivia. "And what about the boy? Your brother would be trying to protect him, not kill him."

"And that's why Travis is dead, O," said Pili. "That night when we went back, we had saved Travis. Dr. Van Helsing and Dolp and Mrs. Calabash, we all had gone in, fought the demons, and brought him out with us as the fire we set burned. Diego was inside, of course. He had been turned. You saw what they were, what he had become. He needed to die in that fire. But still, Travis fought free of us and went back in to save what he thought was his friend. He never came out again."

"Yet you learned nothing from his heroism," said Olivia.

"What I learned," said Pili, "was that mercy is weakness when it comes to them."

"It is not about mercy, miss," said Barnabas. "Nobody here is asking for mercy. And it would be a futile request of the likes of Van Helsing, I have no doubt."

"Then what is it about?" said Pili.

Barnabas glanced my way and then I saw it, a plan, desperate and stupid, but a plan. And all it required was remembering the words told to me by my father and grand-father, by Barnabas, and even by the judge over the course of this misadventure, and then tossing them out like a hooked worm.

"It's about due process," I said.

"Very good, Mistress Elizabeth," said Barnabas.

"What is this due process thing, young lady?" asked Mr. Jack.

"It's about having a fair trial," I said. "Not just a pretend thing with fancy rules that gets the result you want, but a really fair trial with all sides being heard."

"A trial, you say," said Van Helsing, like a fish snapping at the bait. "What a marvelous idea! What fun!"

He spun around as if searching for something and then pointed his cane at Keir, still taped to the wall.

"Let us try McGoogan for being an undead monster who feasts on human blood. *Ja?*"

"A trial in the Court of Uncommon Pleas?" I said. "Yes, that's a great idea."

"Not in the Court of Uncommon Pleas," said Van Helsing. "We'll do it here. Now."

"But there's no courtroom here," I said, "no judge, no jury."

"This will be the courtroom," said Van Helsing. "And we don't need a judge. Judge Jeffries is a pompous windbag. Things would run better without him. My crew can serve as jurors, with Mrs. Calabash as the foreperson. It will be Van Helsing battling the famous Elizabeth Webster for the life of Keir McGoogan. Are you ready?"

"No," I said. "Absolutely not. If anyone is to try the case, it has to be Barnabas."

"But Barnabas is not a licensed barrister, are you, Barnabas?"

"No longer," said Barnabas, "as well you know."

"I wouldn't dream of putting Mr. McGoogan's fate in the hands of an unlicensed barrister. Nay, Elizabeth, it must be you."

"Go ahead, Elizabeth," said Keir on the wall. "I'm willing to bet on you. No one else I'd rather bet on. Well, maybe Barnabas, but you're second, I promise."

"He's willing," said Van Helsing. "How can you turn down the opportunity? A match of wits and law to save the thing you claim as your friend? Are we on?"

37

Mock Trial

Mr. McGoogan," said Dr. Van Helsing in a loud and dramatic voice, "you were close to dying on the dark and stormy night a hundred years ago when your mother took you to the Château Laveau, *ja*?"

"So I'm told," said Keir.

"And on that date, to save your life," said Dr. Van Helsing, "Miss Myerscough bit your neck and turned you into the monster you have become."

"Objection," I said. "Calling Keir a monster kind of gives the game away, don't you think?"

"It's what he is, my dear," said Mrs. Calabash before slamming her sword on the desktop. "Objection overruled."

The office had been transformed into a mock-up of the Court of Uncommon Pleas. The four jurors—Pili, Mr. Jack,

Mrs. Calabash, and Dolp—sat at the desk in the front of the courtroom. There was an area before the desk where the lawyers stood while Natalie and Henry and Barnabas, along with Olivia, sat watching from the chairs behind the low table. Beside the desk was a witness chair, which was now empty, as Keir, who had sworn to tell the truth while Mrs. Calabash's sword was at his neck, remained taped to the wall.

Up there he looked a little like the ram on the wall behind the judge's desk in the real courtroom, although Keir wasn't chewing a licorice twist.

This wasn't the plan that had flitted through my mind when Barnabas gave me his glance. I had thought we would buy time before a proceeding in the real Court of Uncommon Pleas, with all its rules and regulations. In this room, with a jury as rigged as one of those old-time ships with all the ropes, due process for Keir seemed as far away as Fiji. But in desperate situations, a girl has to take what she can get, and this was what I had. And was it weird that I felt almost at home in the made-up courtroom, as if somehow this had become my arena?

"So, to continue where we were before the interruption," said Dr. Van Helsing, "on that fateful night, Miss Myerscough turned you into a monster. And there are scars on your neck as proof, *ja?*"

"I admit to the scars."

"And in the hundred years since, Mr. McGoogan," said Dr. Van Helsing, "you've been a blood-eater, is that not correct?"

"I eat what I'm served," said Keir. "At the Château Laveau it was usually gruel. At Elizabeth's house it is sometimes dead generals."

"Dead generals, you say? And how do they taste, Mr. McGoogan?"

"Sweeter than you'd expect," said Keir, giving me one of his winks.

"But you hunger for blood," said Dr. Van Helsing, "human blood, day and night, *ja?*"

"Yes," said Keir, "there's no denying it."

"You could try," I said.

"The blade I swore on was mighty sharp, Elizabeth."

"Smart lad," said Mrs. Calabash.

"And you think of human blood, constantly," continued Van Helsing. "You dream of it. You sicken without it, *ja?*"

"All of that, yes."

"And when your schoolmates stroll past you in the halls of Willing Middle School West, you are thinking of all the blood burbling though their little bodies, is that not true?"

"That, yes," said Keir, "along with the jangle of coins in their pockets."

"You are a blood-eater, and will always be a blood-eater, as long as you are allowed to walk this earth, is that not correct, Mr. McGoogan? Oh, there is no need to answer. We all know the truth." Van Helsing turned and bowed to me. "I have no more questions, Ms. Webster. Your witness."

No more questions? My witness?

I had been waiting in dread for what Keir, in his suddenly chatty mood, would end up answering to Van Helsing's most obvious questions. How had Keir gotten the blood he craved? What crimes had he committed to satisfy his unholy hunger? I was actually as curious as the jury about what he would say.

But Van Helsing had stopped before getting that answer. Was he stopping before asking the one question too many that might destroy his case? Or was he hoping that I, thinking he was afraid of the answer, would ask the one question too many that would destroy my case? It seemed to me like a flip of the coin on which Keir's life would depend. Keir might have appreciated the bet, but it had me tumbling in uncertainty.

Then I remembered what this case was about. It had little to do with Keir. And when I focused on that, I knew exactly what to do.

"I have no questions for the witness," I said.

"No questions?" said Van Helsing. "How strange. And unexpectedly cowardly for the famous Elizabeth Webster. Well then, I have just a few more of my own."

"That is not permitted, Dr. Van Helsing," said Barnabas.

"Not permitted?" growled Van Helsing.

"Your direct examination was completed," said Barnabas calmly. "You can only ask more questions of your witness to clarify something brought up in Mistress Elizabeth's cross-examination. As there was no cross-examination, you are finished with Mr. McGoogan. Those are the rules."

"Whose rules?" bellowed Van Helsing.

"Are there no rules?" I said, facing the jury, spreading my arms out wide. "No rules?"

"There should be rules," said Pili.

"Every game has rules," said Mr. Jack.

"I never liked rules," said Dolp. "Like brushing your teeth every night. Is that a rule?"

"Yes," said Mrs. Calabash. "That is a rule. And rules are rules. No more questions for this witness from you, Doctor. Do you have another witness?"

Van Helsing lifted his cane and pointed it at Keir, then lowered it again. "Fine," he said. "I've proven enough. No other witnesses needed. Call whomever you please, Ms. Webster."

Everyone in the made-up courtroom looked at me, wondering what I had up my sleeve. I was wondering, too. I took a breath and then said,

"I call Dr. Rudolf Van Helsing."

There was the inevitable commotion—the doctor shouting, Keir laughing, Mrs. Calabash banging her sword on the desktop. As it continued, I looked at Barnabas. He nodded at me, as if I had made the only possible call, and then he glanced at the jury. As Van Helsing sat in the witness chair and swore, at the point of Mrs. Calabash's sword, to tell the truth, I gave the jury a more careful look.

How was I to win them over? Pili had been the one to say there should be rules, Mr. Jack had backed her up, and the other two had gone along. In this house, where Pili's quest to kill the undead had been born, she seemed to be the route to Keir's freedom.

As the courtroom quieted, I turned to the witness. "Dr. Van Helsing, you said your family has been hunting what you called 'these monsters' for generations."

"That is right. We are protectors of humanity."

"Do you believe there is any humanity left in Keir?"

"What existed once has been devoured by what he has become."

"So there is no possibility for friendship," I said, looking at Pili.

"When a monster like Keir McGoogan looks at a human like you, Ms. Webster, it sees only prey."

"How long have you been hunting Keir?"

"I have been hunting Myerscough my entire life. McGoogan is one of the monsters in her nest, so for him it is the same length of time."

"And in all that time, have you ever brought a case against him in a court of law?"

"Such beasts obey no law."

"Have you ever asked a court for and received a warrant for his arrest?"

"Not for him specifically, nay."

"So you've been hunting him on your own supposed authority."

"Someone must hunt them or they will devour us all."

I looked at Pili, sitting at the desk with a stony face. My eyes still on her, I said, "Like you hunted those who died in the fire at this house?"

"It was a great victory for our cause."

"How many died in the fire you set, Dr. Van Helsing?"

"All of them."

"So you don't know how many died. And you don't know the names of the dead. But still you are so certain that all of those you burned into ash deserved their fate."

"The brother of Pili was hung on the wall as they tried to drain him dry."

"What kind of inhuman monsters would hang someone on a wall, I wonder?" I said, glancing up at Keir. "And you were sure that none inside that house were actually trying to help Travis? Like, for example, Diego Acosta? Could he have been trying to save his friend?"

"He had been turned and he was there, so the answer is nay. I told you they have no friends."

"But Travis seemed to think otherwise. Travis ran back into the fire to try to save Diego, didn't he?"

"He was deluded."

"Maybe his friend had been secretly helping him. Or maybe Travis simply believed that his friend deserved the benefit of the doubt. That his friend was innocent until proven guilty in a court of law. See, that's what I've been learning due process is all about. We are always so certain and then, when we ask enough questions, sometimes we find that we were wrong. That's why we need witnesses. That's why we have trials in courtrooms with all kinds of rules. That's why we don't just go around killing because our daddies did it."

"Is there a question in your babble?" said Dr. Van Helsing.

"How about this one—how are you so certain that Keir is not our friend?"

"Because he is a monster, with nothing but darkness in his heart. Let me ask you this, Elizabeth Webster. Has Keir McGoogan ever done anything to help you or his other new schoolmates? Has he ever done anything other than lie and deceive you? Has he done anything other than take?"

I didn't have to answer his question. In fact, my grandfather had told me a lawyer should never answer a witness's question. It shows weakness to give up control of a cross-examination. But when I looked at Pili, there was something in her eye, as if she was looking for hope in my answer. I was wondering whether I could give it when I lifted my head and looked at Keir.

He turned his face away from me, as if he was embarrassed by what he had become, and it broke my heart.

He was a boy struck down by an illness, turned into a blood-obsessed vampire, and then imprisoned for a hundred years in a castle with the most brutal of keepers. I had seen up close the wounds all that had caused, as he played dice games to take a friend's money, as he manipulated others, me included, to do his bidding. Yes, he took and took and took. But there was more than darkness in his undead heart, wasn't there?

Wasn't there?

"You're suddenly very quiet for a lawyer," said Dr. Van Helsing, with an ugly laugh.

I turned to look at Olivia, knowing that Pili would be following my gaze. "I'm just thinking about what makes someone a friend," I said.

Arguments were supposed to come at the end of the trial, but he had asked his question and I could tell that now was the time. I turned to face the jury and spread my arms wide once again.

"A friend shares, and Keir has certainly done that with me and Natalie and Henry. Maybe not his money—he does like his money—but he shares his games, his adventures, and his past. When he shares memories about things like sunken ships and rich old guys, history comes alive for us in a way no book can match.

"And a friend lets you see your world through his eyes. Keir didn't have to go school with us, but he wanted to. He cherishes being with the other kids, the things he can learn, even the ways he can show off. And he does show off. A lot. But when I look at middle school through his eyes, I suddenly feel so lucky to be there. How is that possible?"

"I asked for an answer," said Dr. Van Helsing, "not a speech."

"You asked and she's answering," said Mrs. Calabash, banging her sword on the desk. "Let her finish."

"Thank you," I said. "A friend also makes you feel good about yourself. Keir does that for all of us. I don't know how he does it, maybe it's a cunning little trick of his, but when we're with him we somehow feel like we can do more, be more. Like we're worth more. If it is only a trick, it's the best trick a friend can play.

"And finally, a friend tells you the truth. I know that Keir hasn't told me everything—I can only imagine the horrors he's been through. But the only times he's lied to me, he let me know he was lying so I could figure it out if I wanted to. And whenever he's made me a promise, he's kept to it.

"So when I look at Keir, I see a friend. As do Natalie, and Henry, and even Barnabas." As I said their names I looked at them in turn, and in turn they each got up so that we stood together, a legion of friendship. "We're all his friends," I said to the jury, "and we all came to this place out of friendship to try to save him, despite the danger. Just like Travis tried to save his friend. Does that answer your question, Dr. Van Helsing?"

There it was, my little speech, like the closing argument at a trial in the Court of Uncommon Pleas.

I looked up at Keir and saw a sea of emotion washing across his face. I smiled at him and then examined the jurors for the final time. I thought I saw a couple of encouraging nods. Then Mrs. Calabash said, "You're finished, I hope. Another long speech and I'll be cutting off Dolp's ears just for sport."

She turned around to look at Keir on the wall. "I think we've all heard enough. How say the rest of you? Are we ready to make our decision?"

"I am," said Pili, who was looking at Olivia.

"I'm with her," said Mr. Jack, who was looking at Pili.

"When's dinner?" said Dolp, who was looking at his thumb like he had never seen it before.

It was time to stop. That's one thing the goat incident taught me: stop when it's time to stop. But something Dr. Van Helsing had said was scratching at my brain. Is it scratching at yours, too?

"I have one more question, if that's okay with the jury."

"Go ahead, miss," said Mr. Jack with a kindly smile.

"Dr. Van Helsing," I said. "When I asked about a warrant, you said you had no court-issued arrest warrant specifically for Keir. That answer implies that you hold a valid warrant for someone else. Whose arrest warrant do you have?"

The answer would send us all back to the château.

38

TEA, FINALLY

As dusk fell, Keir McGoogan and I stood side by side before the great iron gate of the Château Laveau.

Keir wore his plaid jacket and blue cap, his green pack slung over one shoulder. He had just announced his presence into the speaker and asked for the gate to be opened so he could come back home. I stood gripping a briefcase I had swiped from my stepfather's home office. I needed to look like a lawyer, and I thought a briefcase would do the trick.

As the sky darkened, the motor started churning churning and the gate slowly swung wide.

I glanced to the left of the stone arch, where Charlie Frayden, wearing goggles, oversized rubber boots, and yellow rubber gloves, gripped a giant cable cutter. Doug Frayden stood beside Charlie, leaning on a shovel. He had dug up the wire feeding power to the gate as Keir and I stood and waited. At the moment the gate was opened to its widest, Charlie squeezed the handles of the cable cutter.

A bang and a burst of sparks sent Charlie sprawling backward as the moving gate died. The cutter was still in his hands, its blackened and twisted blades pointing now at the sky. Charlie's hair stood on end. And was that smoke coming from his boots?

Still on the ground, Charlie smiled and waved to let us know he was okay.

Keir gave him a nod, and then Keir and I passed through the frozen gate and began our long walk up the drive. Against the darkening sky we could see the kettle of vultures circling over us as we started climbing the hill. In the distance the dogs howled.

When we reached the trees, I looked behind and saw Henry hurriedly pushing a wheelbarrow through the open gate. Henry was followed by Young-Mee and Natalie, the two looking quite stylish in yellow raincoats and rain hats as they lugged heavy buckets. In the wheelbarrow was the carcass of a deer for the birds. In the buckets were livers and hearts bought from a butcher shop for the dogs. Everything had been doused with animal tranquilizer.

When we emerged into the open area before the mansion, the sky was clear. I wondered what was currently filling the sweet dreams of the turkey vultures. Bright skies? Dead chipmunks? Cranberry sauce?

Egon was waiting for us at the red front door. "Welcome back to the château, Keir McGoogan," he said in that high-pitched voice. "I've made up a spot for you in the attic."

"I won't be staying in that cursed attic," said Keir.

"You said you were coming home."

"With conditions," said Keir. "That's why I brought the lawyer. We'll be hammering out my future with the countess."

"The countess is unavailable for hammering."

"Then some other time," I said. "Let's go, Keir. I told you this was a waste."

"Don't go," said Egon. "What about your tea, Elizabeth Webster?"

"Tea?"

"We know that Elizabeth Webster loves her tea. And freshly baked biscuits."

"Biscuits?"

"He means cookies," said Keir.

"Cookies?"

"Please stay for tea and biscuits," said Egon. "And I'll see if the countess can be roused."

"Well, since there's tea," I said.

As Egon waited, bent over in that bow of his, Keir and I entered the house. Egon closed the door behind us and turned the lock with the telltale snap-click. "This way, please," he said as he began to lead us down the center hallway.

"I have to tell you, Egon," said Keir, "it is so good to be back!" He said the last part with such enthusiasm that his voice masked the snap-click of me turning the lock open again.

"We're glad to have you back, too, Keir McGoogan,"

said Egon as he kept walking. "We missed you somewhat." He turned his head stiffly to catch me hurrying to Keir's side. "And maybe we'll find room for your lawyer, too."

The checkerboard floor. The coffin-shaped birdcages where, beneath the covers, I could hear the winged hunters shifting and stirring. The great portraits of the Countess Laveau dressed all in black, with the fierce Miss Myerscough always standing behind her.

"Miss Myerscough is waiting for you both in the sitting room," said Egon as he led us beneath the soaring staircase. "When she heard Keir McGoogan had returned, she couldn't wait to greet him."

"Did she bring the chains with her?" said Keir.

"Only her joy," said Egon, in a voice as joyful as rock. "I'll be bringing the chains."

Miss Myerscough was standing before the fireplace. Her hands were clasped tightly, her braid of hair lay on her shoulder like a dead snake, her smile was dangerous. We sat on the couch in front of her.

"It is so lovely to see you again, Keir," said Miss Myerscough. "And you, too, I suppose, little Elizabeth."

"We've come to discuss the terms of my client's return to this house," I said.

"Terms, terms, terms," she said. "What care I about terms? All I know is one of my children has come home."

"I'm coming back on my own terms or not at all," said Keir.

"Of course you're coming back," said Miss Myerscough. "Whatever else could you do? The hunger grows, doesn't it, my dear? It gnaws at the bones. And we can't survive on little animals forever, can we? How long would it be before you inflamed the mob? But you are always safe in the château."

"The first term you must agree to," I said, playing my role as lawyer in our little play, "is that Keir will be able to come and go from this house as he pleases."

"Oh no," said Miss Myerscough, shaking her head. "That can't be allowed. Safety demands that we have control over our wards, both for their sakes and for yours."

"And there will be no more chains or sessions in the attic," I said.

"I don't see why not," said Miss Myerscough. "Rules are rules, and they must be obeyed or there will be consequences. Anything else is anarchy. You are not an anarchist, are you?"

"And Keir will no longer do your bidding against the other members of this household," I said.

"Of course he will," said Miss Myerscough. "We all must do our share. If you knew how hard I work, day and night, night and day, to keep this house of mercy running, you would be ashamed of your efforts to allow Keir to shirk his duties."

"Those are the terms," I said. "I have an agreement in my briefcase for the countess to sign so that the settlement can be approved by the Court of Uncommon Pleas."

"Have you not heard me, girl?" said Miss Myerscough. *"There will be no terms!"*

An instant later she was back to the calm and smiling Miss Myerscough. "Oh, look, Egon has come with the tea."

Egon entered with a silver tray covered by the large silver

dome. You remember what was squirming beneath the lid last time I visited, don't you? As he placed the tray on the table in front of the couch, I was braced for mayhem.

But the only thing escaping when he yanked up the silver dome was steam from the blue ceramic teapot. Along with the pot were three cups on saucers, a bowl of sugar, a pitcher of milk, dainty silver spoons, and, yes, cookies. Finally!

Miss Myerscough sat down in a chair beside the table and asked, "How do you take your tea, Ms. Webster? Do you prefer arsenic or strychnine?"

"Sugar?" I said.

"Pity."

I watched as she lifted the pot and poured, so focused on what she might be adding to my cup that I didn't notice the goings-on in the hall.

"Egon," said Miss Myerscough without looking up, "go check on the birds."

"As you wish," said Egon, before leaving the sitting room.

It was then that I heard the cawing and shuffling, as if some great disturbance had just walked through the front door. And while you know what that disturbance was, Miss Myerscough simply continued pouring and serving the tea, unconcerned about the fuss, until Egon rushed back into the sitting room.

"It's him!" said Egon in his high-pitched warble.

"Who?" said Miss Myerscough. "Collect yourself, Egon. Calm down and speak up."

"It's Van Helsing!"

She suddenly stood, dropping the teapot so that it smashed into bits. Hot tea washed across the tray as she turned to me. "What have you done, child?"

"He has a warrant for your arrest," I said as calmly as I could. "He has promised you a fair trial."

"A fair trial, you say? There will be no fair trial. *He will kill us all!*"

"He's only coming for you," said Keir. "The rest will be left alone. He promised."

"*The only thing he promises is death!*" she shouted, hatred spilling out her suddenly red eyes like the tea spilling off the tray, before she spun into a great fat bat and flew out of the room.

We were so shocked by the whole scene that we sat and watched it all in silence, until Keir said, "She didn't take it so well."

"And what about our tea?" I said. "Why is it so hard to get a cup of tea in this place?"

THE LIBRARY

As soon as Keir ran for the open door of the sitting room, I grabbed the briefcase and followed. When we reached the doorway, we slowly stuck our heads through the gap.

Van Helsing and his crew were in a tight defensive circle as hawks and ravens, falcons and owls swerved and swooped above them. Mrs. Calabash pointed her sword, Dolp swung his shotgun loaded with silver pellets, and Mr. Jack cocked his pistols loaded with silver balls. Waving two flaming torches, with a trail of black smoke rising from each, were Pili and Olivia, shoulder to shoulder. Van Helsing himself held the two fancy knives that were used to kill Count Dracula over a hundred years ago.

And outside the circle stood Barnabas with his hands behind his back, calmly watching it all.

After the jury had voted to free Keir—a win for *moi*, how surprising is that?—Van Helsing showed us the arrest warrant for Miss Myerscough, issued by the Court of Uncommon Pleas for the District of Great Britain. If Keir helped him get inside, Van Helsing promised to capture, not kill, Miss Myerscough and ensure she had a fair trial in the court that had sat for centuries in the upper reaches of the Tower of London. Olivia had joined his crew to once again stand with the great friend of her childhood. And Barnabas was there as a noncombatant to make sure Van Helsing kept his word.

As Van Helsing and his crew shuffled in formation toward one arm of the stairway, Egon pulled off the cover of a coffin-shaped cage and opened the cage's door. The condor stuck its head out of the opening.

The great bird looked left, looked right, and then flapped itself free before landing heavily on top of its cage. It stared at us as it preened its wings, like a costumed supervillain about to go into battle. Then it jumped off its cage and circled just under the high ceiling. It grunted once, whipping the swarm into a frenzy, before it attacked.

"Follow me!" shouted Keir over the hiss and caw, the shouts and the gunfire. He hustled across the hallway to a black door and pulled it open. I sprinted after him and found myself at the foot of a dark staircase that Keir was already climbing. I climbed quickly behind him. As the two of us approached the door at the top, we slowed down, sneaking up the final steps together.

Beyond was a commotion of sorts, something loud, fierce, and definitely unhealthy.

"Wait here while I check it out," whispered Keir. He opened the door, crept through, and closed it behind him.

The seconds it took for him to come back felt like hours, like days. And when he did return, shutting the door quietly behind him, his forehead was creased with worry.

"The fight made its way upstairs," he whispered. "Miss Myerscough's and Van Helsing's crews are battling to the right. The countess will be there, too. Avoid that side like the plague. Trust me, Elizabeth, the countess would snatch your heart and feed it to her birds before you knew something was missing."

"She certainly has the nails for it," I said.

"The countess's library is down the hall to the left. Look for the word *Private* on the door."

"You're not coming with me?" I said, panic turning my voice into a squeak.

"It's gone bad," he said. "I need to help. Miss Myerscough convinced the rest of those she saved with her bite to join the battle. She has them believing Van Helsing is after them, too. But they might listen to me. After your little speech, I don't have any choice. They're sort of friends, too, I suppose."

"So it's my fault."

For a moment his sly smile returned. "Don't you know, it's all your fault, Elizabeth. Find the contract. I'll come when I can. If you find it before I show, you know what to do."

"But I don't," I said. "See, that's the thing. I don't know what to do."

"Grab it and run," he said.

And with that, he was gone. I couldn't decide if I was impressed with what Keir was doing to help the others, or foot-stomping angry that he was leaving me alone.

I was frozen for a moment, and then, before I realized it, I was through the door and racing down the hallway to the left with the clatter of the fight behind me. The bloodred wallpaper was flickering with the reflection of firelight. The old dead people in the paintings were staring down at me like I was a scurrying cockroach with a briefcase. As I ran, I glanced behind me.

Birds flying, swords swinging, walls burning.

When the hallway turned to the left, I leaped and landed right in front of a door with the word PRIVATE printed on a plaque. Somewhere inside the library might be the contract that was the key to Keir's freedom. I hesitated a moment and took a deep breath—I didn't know legal discovery could be so terrifying—and then I turned the knob.

The air inside the room felt somehow alive, like it was breathing and waiting, waiting and breathing, hungry, angry, scratching at time itself. My hand shook as it bounced around the wall beside the door, looking for the light switch.

Click.

Light flooded the large room and my heart seized.

It wasn't the old books that caused my little heart attack, or the wooden file cabinet where old contracts might be kept, or the desk on top of which a rodent with gorgeous brown fur was pawing at the floor of its cage.

No, it was the woman sitting in the winged chair facing the door, her chin high, her black suit buttoned tight, a paisley scarf around her throat, holding in her hand a large piece of vellum covered with red writing.

"How unsurprising to see you again, Elizabeth," said the Countess Laveau. "I assume you've come for this."

40

THE COUNTESS

Was I scared? Terrified, actually. The image of the Countess Laveau reaching her long-nailed fingers into my chest and pulling out my beating heart remained thumbtacked to my brain. But I was there to save Keir, so instead of running, I dropped into the chair across from her, holding the briefcase as a shield.

"I would ask if you wanted tea," said the countess, "but I believe the servants are all otherwise occupied."

No surprise there, right? I mean, instead of Château Laveau they should have called this heap of stone the House of No Tea. I gestured to the document in her hand. "Is that the contract you said was destroyed in a fire?"

"As a matter of fact."

"So you lied in court."

"I was...mistaken. But knowing how important the

document was to Keir, I took another look. And voilà. Here it is."

"Voilà?" I said. It's pronounced *vwahlah*, in case you're interested, accent on the *lah*, and according to the dictionary every time you say it you have to pretend you just pulled a rabbit out of some lady's pocketbook. "Is that what you'll say after you feed the contract to the rat in the fur coat? Voilà?"

She leaned toward the cage and ruffled the animal's neck with one of her nails. The rodent showed its sharp little teeth.

"Minks will eat anything," said the countess, "even vellum. But no, Elizabeth, I am not going to destroy Keir's contract. Instead, I'm going to give it to you."

"Just like that?"

"Just like that," she said. She gave the mink a final scratch and then dropped the document on the table between us. "Voilà."

"Is this a trick?"

"Put it in your cute little briefcase, dear, before I change my mind."

And I did exactly that, grabbing it off the table and giving it a quick glance to note the squiggly signature of Caitlin McGoogan on the bottom before snapping it inside the briefcase as if it was one of the countess's birds about to fly away.

"I guess I'll be on my way, then," I said, standing. "See you in court."

"I won't be in court," she said.

I had already taken a step toward the door when I stopped and swiveled my head. "No court?"

"Despite the promise made by his mother when we saved his life all those years ago, I am setting Keir free."

I turned around and faced her head-on. "Why?"

She looked down and brushed a bit of lint off her perfect black jacket. "Whimsy, I suppose."

I stayed frozen for a moment right there, in front of the door of my escape. Maybe it was because of the countess's strength and bearing. Or maybe it was the way she wasn't pretending to be happy to see me, unlike the always-smiling and ever-frightening Miss Myerscough. But most of all it was because the countess was as hard and as real as a diamond and I couldn't leave her with that word, that soft little careless word, hanging in the air.

I walked back toward her and sat down in the chair. "You're the least whimsical person I've ever met."

"And that bothers you?"

"I like it," I said.

She tried to fight her smile and finally succeeded. "We've been keeping careful watch on our Keir."

"With your birds," I said, nodding.

"And we get reports."

"Reports? From who?"

"It doesn't matter from whom," she said, waving away my question like it was an annoying fly. "Keir has...surprised us. We thought the only way to protect him, and the people he would come in contact with, was to keep him here. Forever. But we hadn't counted on one thing."

"His inner decency?"

She laughed. "He has no inner decency, dear, at least he didn't when he lived here. What we hadn't counted on, Elizabeth, was you."

"But I didn't do anything."

"We respond to our environments. We knew how Keir responded to the environment we created for him here. But he responded to you and your friends in a way we could never have expected. It forced us to reconsider many things."

"To reconsider the way you treated him all these years?"

"Yes, that, too, of course. I've lived long enough, Elizabeth, to have more than my share of regrets. But I was thinking of something else. I had a daughter. Her name was Linette. She was the dearest of creatures. And then she died."

"I'm sorry for your loss," I said. That's what you say when you don't know what to say. I've even said it after a Debate Club debate. *I'm sorry for your loss.* But it felt so small just then, and when the countess winced as I said it, I felt small, too.

"I unwittingly brought Miss Myerscough to America to be Linette's tutor," she said. "I didn't know then what she was. But in the yellow fever epidemic of 1905, when my daughter's gums started bleeding from the saffron scourge and the doctors had no solutions, Miss Myerscough offered her...services. There was a decision to be made. I had a chance to save my daughter's life, but at what cost?"

"What did you decide?"

"It doesn't matter. By the time I did decide, it was too late. She was gone. As I laid my head on her silent chest and wept, I knew in my bones it wasn't the fever that had killed her—it was me. Whether because of my decision or my hesitation, I was the cause."

The countess put a hand to her throat, as if the scarf was there to hide a wound.

"I tried to join my daughter, but Miss Myerscough found me before I succeeded and wouldn't let me die. She told me I had to stay alive to preserve Linette's memory. That's why I allowed Miss Myerscough to save as many as she could. After my loss, in Linette's memory I wanted to heal the world. But there was a darker purpose, too, I can admit now. For each time I saw the horror of the life those like Keir lived, I felt somehow more elevated, purer, for not having subjected my daughter to that. I was congratulating myself, even as I was part of the horror."

I started to say something, some bland piece of assurance, as weak as *Sorry for your loss,* but before I could even get a word out, she thankfully waved me quiet.

"And so now, to make up for my cruelty," she said, "and because he has shockingly earned it, I'm giving Keir a chance for something other than this. And I'll leave him enough of his precious money to pay your bills, with some left over for his room and board and creature comforts. Keir does like his creature comforts. And to you, Elizabeth, I give the responsibility for his life, and for the damage he does."

"Wait, what?"

"Oh, my dear, the moment you went into the Court of Uncommon Pleas to give Keir his freedom, you were taking it upon yourself to make sure he doesn't succumb to the beast Miss Myerscough put within him."

"We're just lawyers. It will be the law that gives him the freedom to make his own choices. And then it will be his responsibility."

"There was a young woman named Rachel who became one of Miss Myerscough's favorite children. She was sweet and quiet and devoted. We trusted her. When she escaped, none of us were too worried. She would grow hungry, she would come back, she was so sweet. A few months later we starting reading of a series of mysterious deaths in Chicago. We sent Miss Myerscough on the train to fetch her back, but Rachel destroyed herself before she arrived. A stake through her own heart. Can you imagine the agony she must have felt at all she had done?"

"No, I can't."

"Well, dear, maybe you should."

"Keir's better than that. He wants to do right."

"Are you still playing the lawyer, or is this the clear-eyed friend speaking? He might need the second more." The countess rose. "It is time for me to stop the foolishness in the other wing."

"Van Helsing brought guns and torches," I said. "They started a fire."

"He is always so boringly predictable. He has come for Miss Myerscough, but only Miss Myerscough, or so I've been told. A trial has been promised. Maybe it's for the best. I thought it crucial that all her precious children always be under her thumb, but Keir might have shown us another way. Wait here for Keir to find you. Don't leave without him, it would be terribly unsafe. But when Keir comes for you, don't linger."

"I won't, trust me."

"Surprisingly, I do, Elizabeth. She was very sweet, my Linette. I have to admit, when I see you I think of her."

"I'm not sweet," I said.

"She would have grown out of it, too. At least I hope so. Our time here is over, I fear. We'll find someplace new. I hear Iceland is quite popular these days. Perhaps a cottage by a thermal pool. I could use a long bath. And maybe there we'll do things differently."

"And maybe there you'll lose your regrets."

"Oh, my dear, dear Elizabeth. I don't think they ever go away, and who would want them to? They're like a string of pearls that lets us know we've lived a life. I'm sure you'll have your own lovely string. Let's just hope Keir isn't one of them."

As she was leaving, I stood and faced her. "How did you do it?"

She stopped, turned around. "Do what, dear?"

"Become you?"

She smiled. "In my hometown of New Orleans, as the poor daughter of a former slave, I was always underestimated. Men thought they saw a girl they could take advantage of, and I let them see just that as I took advantage of them."

"It must have felt great."

"Of course it did, but you know that already, don't you, dear? You're the girl who faced down the demon in court. Women like us, we never let anyone else define our limits."

She paused just a moment as if she had something else to say, but then turned and pulled open the door. The shouts, the clash of metal, the clatter of battle. The lights in the hallway were out and her silhouette, outlined only by the twisting orange of a distant fire, was tall and regal.

The Countess Laveau.

A puff of smoke leaked into the gap where she had been before she closed the door behind her. I coughed. The mink hissed.

I felt, just then, small and terrified, powerful and reckless, and full of tears. Keir had been right—somehow the countess had reached into my chest and pulled out my heart, yet my skin was untouched. I was still trying to figure it out when I heard a knock on the door.

I waited in silence, too scared to answer.

"Elizabeth?"

I jumped to the door and yanked it open. Keir, his face smudged with soot and his cap askew, stood in the doorway gripping a lantern. His large front teeth glowed white.

"Did you get it?" he said.

I lifted my briefcase.

"Then what are you waiting for?"

"You," I said.

I should have been frightened by this thing in front of me, I should have felt the terror that the countess had tried to slip into me like a knife between my ribs. But I wasn't afraid of Keir. Instead I leaped forward to give him a hug. The fear on his face as I grabbed hold made me laugh. Why I was laughing I couldn't figure, but the sight of him, still alive, still full of possibilities, just brought it out of me.

And maybe I began to understand my father a little bit better.

"Enough of that," Keir said, pushing me away. "You'll ruin my hair. There's a tunnel to the outside beneath the house. Let's go."

I swiveled my head toward the table. "What about the mink?" I said.

He looked at the cage. "That little rat's been nothing but trouble its whole life."

"Like you, huh?"

He looked at me and gave his half-cocked smile before he ran over and unlatched the door. The mink slipped out of the cage and hissed for effect before jumping off the table and sprinting out the door.

"Now, Elizabeth," Keir said, "can we get out of here? Please?"

41

EMANCIPATION

"O yez, oyez, oyez," called out the ram on the wall, and with that licorice-scented command the Court of Uncommon Pleas was called into session. I was at the barristers' bench in the front of the courtroom, standing next to Josiah Goodheart, as the puff of smoke burst behind the judge's desk and the red-eyed judge appeared, coughing and waving his hands as if at a swarm of bumblebees.

"That's all," he said between waves and coughs. "Be seated. It is time to wield the sword of justice, so be careful one and all that ye don't get skewered."

We all sat. As the judge asked for emergency motions, Josiah Goodheart tilted toward me. "I need to apologize, I think," he whispered, "about that goat."

"You should be apologizing to the goat," I whispered back.

"I suppose you're right. Talk about getting skewered with the sword of justice."

"Well, I sure learned my lesson," I said.

"And what lesson is that?"

"When dealing with someone with *good* and *heart* in his name, expect the worst."

He laughed. "A fine lesson that is. And you haven't even met my brother, Uriah."

"Ms. Webster!" shouted the judge, staring angrily at me with those red eyes.

I nervously stood. "Yes, Your Honor?" It was like I was back in social studies class, getting yelled at by Mr. Armbruster for talking to Natalie. I mean, was it always my fault that the person sitting next to me wanted to chat?

"Are you and Mr. Goodheart having an enjoyable time there on the front bench?"

"We're discussing goat recipes, Your Honor," I said.

"Am I supposed to be amused?" barked the judge. "Next time you bring a chupacabra into this courtroom, you keep it in its cage. The bloodstain is still on the floor, not that it doesn't give my courtroom a beneficial air of severity. Now, where is your father?"

"Somewhere on the other side, still searching."

"Then I'll ask you. In the matter of *McGoogan v. Laveau*, did your firm get hold of the contract?"

"The contract was not properly filed with the Prothonotorius," I said. "Or maybe the contract was destroyed by unknown agents on the other side."

"I am sorry to hear that," said the judge, sounding oh so

not sorry. "Another Webster failure." He raised his gavel. "In the matter of—"

"However," I said, interrupting and causing the judge's red eyes to pop, "I was handed the original contract by the Countess Laveau herself and am prepared to present that to the court."

"Indeed? The original? From the countess? How surprising. And I suppose, with your father indisposed, you'll be handling tonight's hearing."

"Yes, sir."

"Is that agreeable to your client? After the fiasco of your last appearance in this court, I would think Mr. McGoogan would want you to stay as far from his case as possible, lest he end up like the goat."

Just then Keir stood up in the back of the courtroom and said, "I'm with Elizabeth, Judge. For better or for worse."

"The worse could be worse than you imagine, young man," said the judge. "Then let's see it, Ms. Webster. And no more of your tricks."

"No, sir," I said.

I lifted my briefcase, snapped it open, and took out the piece of vellum, now rolled and tied with a pretty bow. I put the briefcase down on the bench and carried the scroll to the judge.

He untied the bow, unrolled the scroll, and peered at it with his red eyes. "Interesting, quite interesting. Clerk, call the case."

"*McGoogan v. Laveau!*" shouted out the tall green clerk in her strangled voice. I took my place at the table and motioned for Keir to come forward. He slid out of his seat and started his slow saunter to the front of the courtroom.

As you and I wait for Keir to take his place beside me, you might be wondering how ended the fight at the Château Laveau. Very well, thank you, for all concerned but the château itself. According to Keir, the battle was still raging when the countess arrived. With one wave of her hand the birds stopped their attacks, the residents stopped defending Miss Myerscough, and Van Helsing and his crew stopped swinging their blades and torches.

In the calm, Van Helsing swore that he would ensure Miss Myerscough had a fair trial in the Tower of London, and his crew, which now included Olivia, swore that they would hold Van Helsing to his pledge. Miss Myerscough screamed and hissed, but when Van Helsing asked the countess for permission to take his prisoner, she nodded, and that was that. The whole hunting party, Barnabas included, made it out safely.

But the fire that had started in the battle grew out of control. Even as Miss Myerscough was bound with a rope made of garlic and wolfsbane, the fire was climbing up the walls, burning the main stairway, devouring the great paintings hanging in the center hall. By the time Keir and I had made our way out through the underground tunnel to greet our waiting friends, the roof was already in flames.

"At last you've made it, Mr. McGoogan," said the judge when Keir was finally standing beside me. "Next time maybe settle into a row closer to the front." The judge turned to stare at the barrister standing at the other table in front of the bench. "Mr. Locksley, where is your client?"

Barrister Locksley simply put his hands over his mouth.

"Still following orders, I see," said the judge. "Prudent of you, Locksley. What say ye, Ms. Webster?"

"I don't think the countess is coming, Judge," I said. "At least, when she gave me the contract she said she wouldn't be coming. And when we tried to serve notice of this hearing at her residence, we found the Château Laveau in ruins after a mysterious fire of some sort and the grounds deserted."

"Any idea where the countess might have gone off to?"

"She mentioned something about Iceland?" I said.

"Out of our jurisdiction, then. How delightful. I've had enough of her insolence. Now, Mr. McGoogan, I'm ready to make judgment."

This was the moment that the banshee had sought from the beginning. This was the moment that would define the rest of Keir's life.

"In light of Ms. Webster's startling procurement of the contract," said the judge, "and the failure of the defendant to appear in court, I find the contract by its terms to be void. I therefore find judgment against the defendant and declare the plaintiff, Keir McGoogan, now and forever emancipated."

As soon as the gavel slammed, a cheer went up from the spectators, and the babies on the ceiling twittered and laughed. It would have been a joyful moment if Keir himself hadn't dropped down into a chair as if the weight of the world had just then fallen on his head. He wasn't overcome with happiness, he was just overcome, and in the face of his emotion, the courtroom quieted.

"Mr. McGoogan," said the judge.

Keir dragged himself to his feet. "Yes, Judge?"

"You have just obtained the most valuable thing known to man or woman. Freedom! So answer me this. What do you intend to do with it?"

Keir stared down at the table for a moment. "Well, Judge," he said finally, "I've been pondering on that more than you might expect, and this is what I came up with. I'm going to the beach to spy the ocean for the first time in my life."

The judge pulled back in surprise. "The beach? That's the best you could come up with?"

"Aye," said Keir. "And while I'm there, I think I'll eat some chocolate."

The judge leaned forward and stared at Keir McGoogan like he was staring at a frog, and then he said, "Splendid idea. Just splendid. Clerk, call the next case."

THE GREAT PARADE

My mother roasted a big knob of meat for our celebration dinner, which for some reason meant that all afternoon the house smelled like a barn animal had settled into the living room and was scratching itself.

"Nice lamb, Melinda," said Stephen. "Very tasty. Gosh, it's almost too tasty."

"It's not lamb, dear," said my mother. "It's mutton. I thought Keir would appreciate a tastier meat."

"And I do, Mrs. Scali, more than you could imagine," said Keir, chewing and chewing. I think he would have spit out the piece in his mouth, but my mom was smiling at him and his napkin was already full.

"At least the potatoes are good," said Petey. "And the kale. Yum."

"Since when do you like kale?" I said.

"Since Mom started making mutton," said my brother. "What's mutton, anyway?"

"It's a lamb all grown up," said my mother. "Like you will be if you eat your kale."

"No more kale, then," said my brother. "Ever."

"Elizabeth," said my stepfather as he cut his mutton, working so hard he would have been better off with a hacksaw, "I think I found something of yours in my briefcase. While searching for a patent application, I picked up a file that contained an agreement between someone named Ina Brathwaite and what must be a company called Azibeth-something-or-other. I have no idea what it's about, but it seems to be right up your alley. Do you want it back?"

As my throat tightened, I looked at Keir. He was moving mutton around on his plate. I looked at my mother. She was holding the kale dish, offering it to my brother. I looked at my brother. He was pushing away the kale. It seemed that no one understood what my stepfather was talking about. But I did. And you do, too, I know. How did something like that get in there?

"My grandfather's secretary must have put it in the briefcase," I said, trying to act like it was nothing. "Thanks, I'll bring it back to her. My grandfather is sure to be looking for it."

"Good," said my stepfather. "So, Keir, now that you've won your case, what are your plans?"

"Don't know yet, sir," said Keir. "I'm still trying to work it out."

"Can't Keir stay here, Mom?" asked Petey. "He's like the perfect roommate because he plays video games with me but he doesn't stay in my room."

"I think I'll be moving on, Petey," said Keir. "It's been grand here, it has, but I've put your folks out too much already."

"You know you're welcome to stay as long as you want," said Stephen. "Gee, it's been fun having you."

"Where will you move on to?" said my mother.

"I'll figure it out as I go," said Keir. "There is so much I haven't seen. The ocean. The mountains. And what about Ohio? I hear wonderful things about Ohio."

"From who?" I said.

"At least that means you'll be done with school," said Petey. "I don't know much about Ohio, but I bet it beats school."

"Don't be so sure," I said.

"I rather liked school," said Keir. "I'll miss it almost as much as I'll miss you people. In fact, before I leave school I have one more thing I need to do."

"What's that?" said Stephen.

"My oral report. For Mr. Armbruster. It's due tomorrow and I wouldn't want to disappoint him. Have you got it worked out for me yet, Elizabeth?"

"Uh, no," I said. "I've been a little busy with, like, things."

"Well, you have all night," said Keir. "If we want to be done on time, you'd best get cracking."

Funny, huh? But even though Keir was pretty persuasive for a hundred-year-old vampire, I didn't crack.

"Mr. Armbruster is going to explode," I whispered to Natalie. "I mean, Keir's got nothing. He didn't read one Wikipedia page. Nothing."

"He'll come up with something," said Natalie. "He's Keir."

"Then why was he begging me to prepare his oral report for him?"

"Because he's Keir," said Natalie.

"And to think I almost felt guilty!" I said.

It was report week in Mr. Armbruster's social studies class. Which meant you were bored to tears except on the day you had to give your report, when you were a bundle of nerves, worrying about your hair, your teeth, your pronunciation of the term *laissez-faire*, which was some sort of economic thing that nobody knew how to say. *Lazy fairy? Lasso furry?* You tell me.

Juwan stood in front of the class and did a little slide presentation on a rich guy named Carnegie who gave out libraries like they were dimes. We all clapped.

And Prisha did a slide show on a reporter named Ida B. Wells who wrote about injustice to African-Americans and once said, "The way to right wrongs is to turn the light of truth upon them." We all clapped.

And Natalie stood up and spoke about Oliver Wendell Holmes Jr. and his book. She said he fought for the North in the Civil War and that his Supreme Court decisions protected workers' health, freedom of speech, and due process rights. She also talked about how pretty his wife was and how all his clerks were like his children, which she got from watching an old movie called *The Magnificent Yankee*, which was funny because I didn't even know he played baseball. But most of all she talked about his mustache. It was quite the mustache. We all clapped.

And then Mr. Armbruster called on Keir.

Keir stood up at his desk. "I'm sorry, but I don't have a slide show prepared for our class today," he said.

I gave Natalie a wide-eyed look, waiting for the explosion.

"I'm disappointed," said Mr. Armbruster, hands now on his hips. "What happened to your slide show, Keir?"

"Elizabeth ran out of time," said Keir.

There was the sound of chair legs scraping the floor as everyone and their mothers turned and looked at me with accusing glares. I lowered my head onto my desktop but misjudged the distance and banged the desk loudly with my forehead. When my head jerked back up from the pain, the eruption of laughter made me feel just perfect. And was there a red spot on my forehead? I was pretty sure there was a red spot on my forehead.

"But if it's all right with you, sir," continued Keir over the laughter, "I could say a few words about a very special parade that happened during that Great War we've been talking so much about."

"That would be fine, Keir," said Mr. Armbruster. "Who doesn't love a parade?"

While Keir took his time sauntering to the front of the class, I rubbed at my forehead. "Is there a spot?"

"Of course there's a spot," said Natalie. "You look like you've been hit by a bus."

"Probably the one I was just thrown under. I really need to work on my face plant."

"Leave it to the experts," said Natalie.

"Class," said Mr. Armbruster, meaning Natalie and me, "quiet down, please. Let's all pay attention while Keir tells us about his parade."

Keir stood now in front of the class. He was wearing his plaid coat and blue baseball cap. He took the cap off, pressed it against his heart, and looked down for a bit, like he was trying to remember the words. Or maybe the thing itself.

"It was in September of 1918," he said finally, "and we were winning the war, that was clear, and my father, somewhere in the trenches over there, would soon be coming home. So my mam made sure I was dressed fine and then we took the train into Philadelphia to see the great parade. The parade was partly to celebrate our men in uniform, like my father, but mainly to sell more Liberty Bonds. When there's a war, the two things they're always looking for are men and money.

"They expected ten thousand would show up for the parade, but twenty times that shoved themselves onto Broad Street as the soldiers marched and the bands played and boats on wheels floated by. And whenever the parade halted, the men came out huckstering for their Liberty Bonds. One of them asked our part of the crowd who had a husband overseas and my mam raised her hand and he pointed at her and said, 'This woman gave her all. What will you give?' Mam blushed from the attention, and then there was a bayonet drill, and then the marching continued.

"At the end of the parade, we all pushed together on the south side of City Hall, where a model of the Statue of

Liberty stood, and the muckety-mucks talked about win-ning the war. Planes flew overhead and giant guns fired shells into the air and we did a lot of cheering, jammed so close we were cheering into each other's faces. On the train ride home my mam kept saying, 'Wasn't that some-thing, Keir? Wasn't that something?' 'Aye,' I replied, 'it was something.'

"Within two weeks, seven hundred were dead in the city. The next week, over two thousand more. It was the flu, the Spanish Lady, they called it. She moved quick and killed fast. The following week, the Spanish Lady claimed another forty-five hundred souls. It seemed as if the whole of the city was sick. The funeral bells kept ringing and ringing until all you wanted to do was rip the iron things straight out of their steeples and toss them into the river.

"And then the Spanish Lady came for us.

"My mam, she caught it first, but I got sicker faster. It started with a chill, and then a fever, and then so much pain you couldn't stand, you couldn't eat, all you could do was cry, but then you couldn't even cry because your lungs were already filling up with something wetter than air. And your ears turned blue, and then your whole face. My mam could barely sit up, but she cared for me like an angel even as she grew sicker herself. The doctor signed the certificate of my death three weeks after that parade. My mam died the very next day. I still cry for her. And though we didn't know it, my father was already dead, killed by a bullet in the throat on the Somme. It was a grand autumn, it was, for the McGoogan clan.

"And you want to know the kicker? The city fathers,

they knew the flu was in the city, brought in by a bunch of navy men come south from Boston. The papers the very day of the parade reported a policeman dead from the flu. They were warned that bringing so many people together could lead to disaster. But there was a war to finance, and quotas to meet, and the rich couldn't be bothered to pay their fair share, and the Liberty Bonds, the Liberty Bonds weren't going to sell themselves.

"Ah, but it was a grand parade, it was. The best I ever saw. The end."

We didn't clap after Keir's little speech. We didn't say a word. We just sat there, a little dazed. What just had happened?

As Keir sauntered back to his seat, I checked out the room. We had all been through something similar in our own time, so his big parade story hit the room like a storm of sadness. Natalie was wiping a tear. The other kids were looking down or around, sniffling. Mr. Armbruster was staring, like the mystery of Keir McGoogan was all coming clear to him. And why wouldn't it be, considering Keir had just told the true story of his almost-death a hundred years ago?

How fast would Mr. Armbruster get on the phone to the FBI, to the CIA? He was Mr. Armbruster, after all, he could get the president on the phone if he wanted. Didn't I tell you he went to Harvard? How soon would agents in black suits and sunglasses come swarming? Talk about a mess.

When Keir sat down, he leaned toward me. "I think that went over," he said.

I didn't have time to respond before the bell rang, which was a good thing. I mean, what was I going to say: *I'm sorry for your loss?*

And then Mr. Armbruster, above the ringing silence of the still-quiet class, said, "Keir, could you see me for a moment before you leave?"

Of course he did.

Keir gave me a sad smile, like he knew the jig was up. And then he leaned toward me and said, "Elizabeth? Can you do me a favor?"

"Bring you a spoon in the prison they're going to throw you into?"

"Why would they send me to prison? And why would I need a spoon?"

"To eat your pudding?"

"What I need is to see my dead mam again," he said. "Can you arrange that?"

"What? No. I don't know."

"Please try," he said. "I suddenly miss her like a missing hand. I have a choice to make and I need to see her before the decision comes due."

A LONG STARE

Is my grandfather in?" I said to Avis when I stepped into the offices of Webster & Spawn that afternoon. "I really need to talk to him."

Avis stopped the peck-and-hunt, hunt-and-peck of her typing. "He's seeing a client right now, dearie, and...and maybe it's not the best time to disturb him."

"Okay," I said slowly, a little weirded out by her hesitation. Avis *never* hesitated. "Is my father in?"

"No, dearie, he's still on the other side. Very important business, he says."

"Keeping away from me?" I asked. "Ha ha, just joking."

But was I? Was I wrong to think my father's disappointment in me was so great that he had run through the Portal of Doom to get away from me?

"No, dearie, your father loves working with you. There

WILLIAM LASHNER

was just something he had to do. Maybe Barnabas can help you."

I looked over at Barnabas sitting at his tall desk. "I'm sure he can," I said.

As I walked toward Barnabas I had to pass through the waiting clients. Sandy, with the blond hair growing like weeds all over her body, gave me a bright smile.

"We heard about Keir," she said. "We're all so happy for him. And it's so encouraging. It gives us hope."

"I'm all for hope," said Mildred, the young girl in red shoes who was not young and not a girl. "I'm hoping for a cigarette."

"Is he happy?" said Sandy. "Keir, I mean. Free at last, right?"

"I guess so," I said. "I also think he's scared."

"Of course he's scared," said Mildred. "There's nothing easy about being free. Too many choices. I had six husbands."

"Six?" I said

"Too many choices," said Mildred.

Barnabas put down his feather pen and stared mournfully at me when I finally reached his desk. "It is especially gratifying to see you this afternoon, Mistress Elizabeth. The broom in the storage room was getting lonely."

"The broom's going to have to wait," I said. "I have a bigger issue."

"Bigger than sweeping the office?" said Barnabas, raising an eyebrow. "I daresay you exaggerate."

"Keir wants to see his mother again," I said.

"Ahh, how tender. I expect the banshee will show herself

292

to her son any day now." Barnabas's eyes grew blurry and he looked off into the distance. "Such reunions between the two sides are sweet and much desired."

"But it was the contract that allowed her to come over once a month," I said. "Because of us, the contract's been declared void by the judge."

Barnabas shook his head, as if shaking the image of his fiancée, Isabel, from his mind. "Interesting point, Mistress Elizabeth. Quite astute of you. By following our client's directives, we might have blocked her access to her son. It's just such a shame about your gremlin case. Mr. Topper would have been much more amenable to allowing a parental visit than Portal Keeper Brathwaite. But the verdict in *Moss v. Topper*, I'm sad to say, was quite damaging to his candidacy. He's discussing his options right now with your grandfather."

"So that's why Avis was acting so weird."

"We all thought it best not to include you. Feelings are still a bit raw. I'm sure you understand."

"Believe me, I do," I said before looking around, leaning forward, and lowering my voice. "But what would happen if I had proof of an improper agreement between Portal Keeper Brathwaite and Redwing?"

"That type of scandal would change everything," said Barnabas. "But such a thing certainly wouldn't exist in writing."

I opened my backpack, took out the file my stepfather had found, and reached high to place it on Barnabas's desktop. "Voilà," I said.

"Voilà?"

"Exactly," I said. "Voilà."

"How did you get hold of this?"

"I don't know," I said, though I had a pretty good idea. And you do, too, probably. I mean, when did I ever leave my stepfather's briefcase alone, even for a moment? But I decided just then to keep my suspicions to myself. "It just showed up."

"Astonishing," Barnabas said as he opened the file.

It took only a few moments for Barnabas to read over the entire document before he snatched the file from his desktop and started hurrying to my grandfather's office. He was at my grandfather's door when he stopped and turned to me.

"Well?" he said.

"I'll stay right here while you tell them," I said.

"Don't be silly, Mistress Elizabeth," said Barnabas. "It is your find. You must present it to your client. Come, come. We all must face our defeats head-on. Hurry now, I won't go in without you, and time is of the essence."

I slumped my way over to the office door as Barnabas knocked. When the door was flung open, my grandfather stood in the doorway.

"What is the matter? What?" said my grandfather, before he saw me standing nervously to the side. "Oh, Elizabeth. Maybe we can meet later—"

"Elizabeth found something of great importance regarding Mr. Topper's candidacy for the position of Portal Keeper," said Barnabas. "May we come in?"

"I'd like to say yes," said my grandfather before glancing behind him, where I could see Mr. Topper sitting on a chair in front of the fireplace. Then my grandfather said in a whisper, "But now is not the time."

"Trust me on this, Mr. Webster," said Barnabas. "Now is absolutely the time. Mr. Topper will be quite pleased by what Mistress Elizabeth has discovered, and he'll know exactly whom to thank."

"And whom will that be?"

"Why, Mistress Elizabeth, of course."

"Ah yes," said my grandfather. "Well then, Barnabas, your say-so is always good enough for me. Come in, both of you, and let us hear the news."

As Barnabas and my grandfather stood inside my grandfather's office and discussed the written agreement between the current Portal Keeper and Redwing, Mr. Topper stared at me.

Was it my hair? Was a piece of kale stuck in my teeth? I turned to look at my grandfather as he talked with Barnabas, but all the time I could feel Mr. Topper's gaze. It was so cold it made me shiver.

And then, finally, Mr. Topper spoke.

"As you must be aware, Ms. Webster," he said, his mouth pursed in disappointment, "losing Althea was one of the most distressing moments of my life."

"Let's not go on about that now, Topper," said my grandfather. "This document Elizabeth found changes everything about your case with the Stygian Transit Authority. We must move on this immediately, or sooner. Let us focus on the future."

"I want her to know this first," said Mr. Topper. "To see something so precious disappear from my life so quickly was a trauma. I tried to blame that nasty Mr. Goodheart, who brought the goat into court, but he was just doing his job. I had to wonder, Ms. Webster, if you were doing yours."

"I'm sorry for your loss," I said. Oh sure, like you would have come up with something better.

"I continued to wonder, until your father came to my house one night to offer his condolences."

"My father?" I said.

"Yes, your father. He told me you had violated the cardinal rule of trial practice. He said you were hoping the evidence you presented would help, instead of being sure of it."

I nodded. "My father." Of course he had gone to Mr. Topper to complain about me. Maybe the guy who sells him his coffee in the morning was sick of hearing it and his dentist wasn't in the mood. So he went to Mr. Topper to complain about his daughter so the two could have a why-is-Elizabeth-ruining-my-life party, swapping disappointments over a pot of tea and a plate of cookies.

"But then, Ms. Webster," continued Mr. Topper, "he told me that your gambit in the courtroom was one of the bravest pieces of lawyering he had ever seen. Based on the law, he said, if you'd played it safe the only thing you could have been sure of was defeat. Most lawyers would not have dared what you attempted, your father included, but they would have been wrong, because your maneuver was the only possible way to win the case."

"But we didn't win."

"No," said Mr. Topper, "we did not. But only because Althea was not what we thought she was and our opponent knew it. I don't know the ins and outs of the law—and frankly, who would want to?—but I can tell when a father is proud of his daughter, and that was clear."

"My father?"

"And that's when he told me what you had discovered with your grandfather at Nascha's House of Special Pets, that I was maneuvered into buying that chupacabra by Redwing himself to torpedo my candidacy for Portal Keeper. Which meant there was nothing that could have saved our case. Althea was going to the other side one way or the other, but you, at least, gave her a chance."

"Indeed," said my grandfather.

"And so what I want to say," said Mr. Topper, "what I have wanted to say since your father's visit, is thank you. Thank you for being so brave in court in your attempt to save my Althea. And thank you for continuing to work for me even after the case was closed, interrogating Nascha and now finding this document your grandfather is so excited about. If there's anything I can do for you, just let me know."

I was so flabbergasted, my jaw had dropped. I pressed it closed with my fist.

"You should be very proud, Ebenezer," said Mr. Topper.

"I am," said my grandfather. "More than you could know."

"And just to put your mind at ease," said Mr. Topper, "I've been looking in on my Althea with the Lens of Fate. She is doing wonderfully on the other side. She has found herself a pack of chupacabras to play with and she is frolicking. Yes, frolicking. She is happier there, I can see it, and that makes me happy. And here's a secret: they eat goat every night. *Goat*—that scamp!"

I looked at my grandfather, and he was beaming. Beaming.

I looked at Barnabas, and he was staring. Staring. Then he raised an eyebrow and the idea struck me at once.

"Actually, Mr. Topper," I said, "there is one thing you can do for me."

44

S'MORES

We took the Sturdy Baker to the Portal of Doom.

"It was quite an honor having a Lens of Fate in the office," said my grandfather as he drove, leaning forward in his seat, barely able to see above the dashboard while he stomped pedals and pushed levers. I sat beside him, buckled tight in more ways than one. "That was the first time, and I daresay the last, for such a grand opportunity. And we owe it all to you, Elizabeth."

I was too busy staring out the window to respond.

"I have to admit I peeked in on our great ancestor Daniel Webster himself," said my grandfather. "He was giving a speech. A real stem-winder, from the looks of it. Apparently there are lectures on the other side given by the greatest orators of all time. How thrilling that must be."

"Did you hear that, Keir?" I said, still looking out the window. "There are lectures on the other side."

"Be still, my beating heart," said Keir from the back seat.

Of course Keir was in the back seat. Why else would we be going to the Portal of Doom? And of course we were both in a mood. Inside my pack was Keir's death certificate and a transit permit authorizing him to pass to the other side to reside with one Caitlin McGoogan. A one-way ticket.

"Be sure to give my regards to your mother, Keir," said my grandfather. "And you can assure her that all her fees have been taken care of by the funds the countess left. Regards to your father, too. It must have been something to see him after all this time."

"It truly was, Mr. Webster," said Keir. "A sight for sore and misty eyes. They'll be mighty gratified for all your help in getting me back to them."

"Well, you were a wonderful client. And we'll miss you mightily. Won't we, Elizabeth?"

"Can we, like, not talk for a bit, Grandpop? Please."

"Of course, dear."

"Thank you."

He waited a beat for effect, just to show that, yes, he was trying, and then he couldn't help himself. "But Keir will be surrounded by his loved ones. And he hasn't seen his father since the Great War. What I wouldn't give to—"

He stopped talking when I finally looked right at him. I wasn't in the mood for my grandfather's chitchat. I wasn't in the mood for anything other than my own sadness. I should have realized this was the inevitable destination from the very beginning. I mean, it wasn't as if the banshee hadn't told us what she was after from the start.

"Are you going to do what your mother wants?" I had asked Keir as we were sitting in my grandfather's office, waiting for Mr. Topper to bring in the Lens of Fate so Keir could see his mother on the other side.

"What do you mean?"

"I'm talking about your mother's plea to me in the courtroom before she disappeared."

"I told you, it was just her thanking you for all you did."

I looked at him out of the corner of my eye and his head bowed.

"I should have known you'd figure it out," he said. "You look smart, Elizabeth Webster, but you don't look half as smart as you really are."

"It wasn't so hard. You can translate Klingon on the web if you want to."

"What's Klingon?"

"A lot less common than Irish, is what it is."

And this is what the banshee Caitlin McGoogan had pleaded to me before she vanished to the other side. *Send him across*, she had said. *Send my little boy back to me.* After a hundred years of missing her son, she wanted Keir to join her on the other side. Freedom was choice, and Keir now had to choose. This side or the other side. What was a young vampire to do?

"Well?" I said as we waited for Mr. Topper. "Have you decided?"

"I'm thinking on it," he said. "It's why I need to see her."

"What about working on that thing Mr. Armbruster suggested? That might be a reason to stick around."

After Keir's Spanish Lady speech, I was sure that Mr. Armbruster was onto him, and I still think he was. But instead of putting Keir in handcuffs as a fraudulent middle school student, the teacher did something much more devious and Mr. Armbruster–like: he encouraged him.

"He says he never had a student perform little plays about history before," Keir said after sauntering out of the classroom that day. "He wants me write my stories down and create more. He told me it would take a lot of work, but it could be a book and he would help me get it published. I could be an author, imagine that! Maybe I'll get myself a pipe."

Deep down, I hoped Keir would write his book, *Keir McGoogan and the Great Parade*. He would surely ask me to ghostwrite it for him—who better? But it also might be a reason for him to stick around for a while, and for some reason I really, really didn't want him to leave. I suppose by living with my family, he had become like part of my family.

When Mr. Topper brought in the Lens of Fate, Keir spent a long time in my grandfather's office peering through it. I wondered at what he was seeing, what he was feeling. But when he came back through the doorway I wasn't wondering any longer. His decision was written as if in ink on his face, and it nearly broke my heart.

So now, as we drove to the Portal of Doom, I couldn't help but sift through my memories. Keir with the rake at the Château Laveau. Keir sauntering down the hallways of Willing Middle School West. Keir duct-taped to the wall. Keir on the beach.

That's right, on the beach.

I had promised Keir I'd take him to see the ocean, and that was a promise I wouldn't break before he vanished to the other side. So after the final court hearing, a bunch of us had headed east, through the wilds of New Jersey, to a state park on a spit of land just north of Atlantic City. It was too cold to swim, of course, but the sun was shining, and the ocean was big and blue, and the wind was stiff enough to set the waves crashing and send the kites Charlie and Doug brought high into the cloudless sky.

We took off our shoes and slapped around in the freezing-cold water, laughing and running away from the surf as it came for us. We built castles in the sand and walked up and down the beach with the kites, yanking on the strings when they turned and started to dive. While I took my turn with the spool, I looked down the shoreline and saw Keir and my mother talking, talking as if they had been talking together for a long time.

After Stephen lugged the wood out of the rental van, Petey helped Young-Mee build a bonfire and we huddled around it eating sandwiches my mom had made and drinking hot cocoa from thermos bottles. Natalie played her guitar and Henry banged his bongos and Juwan blew his harmonica and we sang songs that Keir didn't know. Then we taught him the words to "Yesterday." By the end he was singing like he had paid the Beatles to write the song just for him. His voice was high as a bird's and surprisingly sweet.

Then it was time for the chocolate. We had to show Keir how to do the marshmallow-graham-cracker-and-chocolate thing, especially the roasting-the-marshmallow-without-burning-it thing, but he got the hang of it, except

for the eating-it-neatly thing. We all laughed at the white
and the dark and the light brown crumbs smeared all over
his cheeks.

"What do they call this little treat again?" he asked.

"S'mores," we told him.

"Why do they call it that?"

We laughed and laughed and never told him. And when
it was over and we were back home in Willing Township,
Keir had a moment with each of his new friends. He hugged
them and told them he was off to live with relatives, but
he'd keep in touch, and he made a joke here, and a touching comment there, and tears were shed, a few even by Keir
himself.

To be honest, it was a little unfair taking him to the
beach just before he was about to pass into the other world.
Like taking a kid to Disney World before moving her to
Ohio. But a promise was a promise, and as Keir would have
said, it seemed to go over.

"It is something, it is," he said as we stood, just the two
of us, with the sun setting behind us and the orange light
spreading across the rough surface of the water. This was
just before the bonfire, when we grabbed some time alone.
"What did you say about the ocean, Elizabeth? You said
the waves are telling you a story that you can't understand,
but that you know is perfect. It sounded like nonsense to
me then, but not now. Now I might use it in my book."

"Then stay and write it," I said, surprising myself.

"I can't," he said.

"You can. I'll even help you do it."

"Then it wouldn't be my book. Don't look so shocked

there, Elizabeth. Maybe I learned something in middle school after all. Me staying might sound good now, but for how long? You'll grow older and have a life of your own and I'll still be the boy forever. That would just be sad."

"You'll be Keir forever. That would be wonderful."

"I made a promise, Elizabeth. My mam, she didn't come to you on her own. I begged her to get me out of that old creepy house. I promised her I'd pass over to be with her. That was the point."

"I thought it was about freedom."

"Ah, that was your father saying that. And maybe, to be truthful, that's what I had in mind when I convinced my mam. Staying on this side, but no longer under Miss Myerscough's thumb. That sounded like a plan until...until..."

"What happened?"

"You."

"I'm that terrible?"

"And them," he said, waving his arm at our friends playing with the kites or building the bonfire. "Leaving you and them is the hardest thing I'll ever do, but I am what I am, Elizabeth. And the hunger, when it comes, it takes me over. In the flophouse they were able to keep it at bay, but on my own I would become the worst thing in me."

"You could fight it," I said.

"Until I couldn't. I'd sooner pass over to the other side than do something bad to you, or to them, or anyone like you or them, which I suppose is everyone. There are enough bloodsuckers loose in the world as it is. I don't want to be one of them. The end."

"Nice speech," I said, and it was.

"Maybe I'll put it in the book," he said.

Even though there were tears in my eyes, I started laughing. But he was right, and I knew it in my bones. It was what everyone had been telling me through this whole adventure. Still, none of that made our trip to the portal any easier. All I wanted was for this stupid drive to never end.

"Ah yes," said my grandfather. "At last. We've arrived."

THE PORTAL OF DOOM

Here you are," said my grandfather, waving a hand toward the doorway to the portal about fifty yards away. I can't tell you where it is, rules are rules, but my grandfather had driven us right past it before he parked the Sturdy Baker and stepped out with us onto the street. "Go on," he said. "No use dillydallying."

"Aren't you coming, Grandpop?" I said.

"Oh no. Not me. Even when young I couldn't handle the tipsy-turvy of the portal. You can take it from here, Elizabeth."

"I don't think—"

"Exactly. Nothing to it. And good luck to you, Keir. All I can say to you as you begin your journey is to be ready for surprises, for there is more to be gained in the detours than you could ever imagine."

"I'm getting the idea," said Keir. He turned and shook my grandfather's hand. "Thank you, sir. You've been most kind."

"Hurry, now," said my grandfather. "Never keep the Portal Keeper waiting."

As Keir and I started walking toward the entrance, I swiveled my head to look back at my grandfather. He gave me an encouraging smile that was the saddest encouraging smile I had ever seen.

"When we say goodbye," I said to Keir, "nothing sappy. I couldn't bear anything sappy."

"I'll be as stoic as a statue."

"Good," I said, "even though I'm not sure what that means."

On the other side of the doorway we found ourselves in a small frigid room with fluorescent lights and green walls. A wooden desk was set against a wall. A huge ledger was cracked open on the desktop. And, of course, behind the desk sat a clerk. Remember what I said about paperwork? The clerk was wearing a uniform with bright buttons along with a familiar orange knit hat with a fuzzy ball on top.

"Name of traveler," said the clerk.

"Ivanov?" I said.

"Ivanov who?" said the clerk.

"No, I mean, hello, Ivanov. It's me, Elizabeth? Elizabeth Webster?"

"I need the name of the traveler," said Ivanov coldly.

"Uh, okay, sure," I said. "Keir McGoogan."

"Documents?" said Ivanov.

"A death certificate from 1918 and a transit permit allowing the passage."

I zipped open my pack and took out the papers. Ivanov looked them over with his stern face and then from a drawer took out a stamp with a big wooden handle. He pounded the stamp into an ink pad and then onto the death certificate. Pound pound. He did the same to the transit permit. Pound pound. Then he took out a small red slip of paper and filled it out with a feather pen.

"Sign here, Mr. McGoogan," said Ivanov, offering the pen and pointing at a line on the red paper.

Keir stepped forward and signed.

Ivanov examined the signature, compared it to the large ledger propped open on his desk, and stamped the red slip twice before handing it to Keir.

"This is your ticket," he said. "Don't lose it."

And then he smiled broadly at me. "Hello, Elizabeth. Sorry for all that rigmarole, but I must maintain my professional face when dealing with the paperwork. Nothing is more important than the paperwork."

"Ivanov, what are you doing here?"

"This is my day job," said Ivanov. "I'm only needed at the court when it is in session, and that is so infrequently the position barely pays for the pool."

"You have a pool?"

"You think I would do all this if I wasn't paying for a pool? Mr. McGoogan, good travels to you, sir. I expect you haven't eaten too big a breakfast."

"Just some pancakes," he said.

"I hope they were small."

With that Ivanov pressed something beneath his desk and the wall behind him swung open, revealing a passage leading to a brightly lit elevator with a folding brass gate for a door.

"Come now," said Ivanov, jumping off his chair. "The time is at hand."

I looked at Keir. Keir looked at me. My breath caught in my throat.

"Nothing sappy, Elizabeth, remember?" said Keir.

I was trying to figure out what to say without bursting into tears when I turned to see Ivanov standing on a stool in the elevator, smiling at us.

"You can come, too, Elizabeth," said Ivanov. "Barristers of the Court of Uncommon Pleas are allowed to accompany their clients to the mouth of the portal."

Keir and I looked at each other, a little embarrassed, and then headed to the elevator.

Ivanov waited for us to step inside before leaning forward to pull the gate shut. As he flipped a large brass lever, he said, "Going down."

The elevator shook and dropped, dropped and shook.

A wall of rough rock rose on the other side of the gate as we descended. My heart sank as fast as the elevator, and yes, I started crying. No one said anything, maybe they didn't notice, or maybe they were just being polite, but there it was. I wiped my eyes. I wiped my nose. How do you say goodbye to a friend you'll never see again as long as you live? The rock wall rose and my heart fell and we went down, down.

Finally the elevator settled and stopped within a huge

cavern with spears of rock pointing up from the ground and down from the domed ceiling. But the thing that caught the eye, the amazing thing, was in the far wall: a hole the size of a truck surrounded by a thick ring of steel. The steel had all kinds of strange symbols marked in gold, symbols that looked like an eye, a staff, a sword, a ram, a bolt of lightning. But it wasn't the rim that most fascinated, it was the hole itself, quivering with light.

"Welcome to Portal Nine of the Stygian Transit Authority," said Ivanov as he leaned forward and opened the gate. There was a path carved into the stone floor, a path that meandered between the stalagmites on its way to the portal. "Go on," said Ivanov. "The Portal Keeper is expecting you both."

Right after Keir and I stepped out of the elevator, Ivanov pulled the gate closed, waved once, and began to rise. When he disappeared out of the cavern, Keir and I looked at each other before starting down the curving path.

As we approached the portal, the light grew brighter and the amazing patterns within it became clearer. Have you ever put your eye to a kaleidoscope and spun the tube so that the different colors started dancing? Yeah, that was what the portal looked like, a dancing kaleidoscope pointed at the sun.

There were two people at the side of the portal. One wore a uniform and a cap, operating a console of some sort. When he turned and looked at me through his goggle glasses, the familiar face smiled.

Yes, Mr. Topper was the new Portal Keeper. With the evidence we had found, he had made his case to the STA and been appointed Keeper of the Ninth Portal, the position his father had held and the job he had wanted his entire life.

The demon Redwing, when he learned that his plan to send armies through Portal Keeper Brathwaite's portal was foiled, had bellowed out my name in anger, or so we had been told. That was a nice little nugget to keep me up at night, and it made me wonder what Josiah Goodheart was up to when he slipped that file into my stepfather's briefcase at the barristers' bench. A mystery for another day.

But now, when Mr. Topper smiled at me, it was like he was smiling with everything inside him. It would have been something to warm my sad little heart, but my attention was stolen by the second figure, standing beside him.

A woman with dark hair and a familiar posture. I knew who it was even before she turned and tilted her head at me.

"Mom?" I said.

She was about to respond when a great sucking sound came from the portal and the shifting kaleidoscope of light and color began to shake and shimmer, as if its surface was being beaten on the other side like a drum. Mr. Topper and my mother both turned to the portal, whose middle grew bright and brighter until it was as if it had been set on fire. As the fire spread to the edges of the portal, the middle now became clear and we could see a strange shimmering scene on the other side.

Inside a cave, much like the cave in which we stood, a half woman half horse in a Portal Keeper's uniform was standing before a console of her own. And beside her a group of people surrounded someone, as if saying goodbye.

When the group parted, Keir and I both gasped.

Keir gasped because he could now see his mother holding hands with a young man in a green uniform, who I assumed was his father. Standing beside them were two older women—his aunties? And alongside was another man who looked very much like I imagined Grady to look as he drove the carriage through the dark and stormy night.

"Glory be," said Keir. "Isn't that a thing."

And the reason I gasped was that the person they were saying goodbye to on the other side, the person in a suit and holding a briefcase, was my father.

MASSACHUSETTS

The next time I was called to the office out of social studies class, accompanied by the usual chorus of oohs and aahs and squeaks, it wasn't my father waiting at the front desk.

"Mom?" I said.

"I'm sorry, sweetie," she said when she saw me, "but you have another appointment with Dr. Fergenweiler that I completely forgot about. Get your coat and let's go. I don't want to be late."

I looked at Mrs. Haddad sitting in front of her computer and shrugged in apology.

"Dr. Fergenweiler?" I said to my mom as we were heading to the car.

"I wanted to be consistent with your father's pathetic excuse," said my mother.

"Mrs. Haddad is going to think I have a disease."

"But you do, dear," said my mother. "You're a Webster. I packed us both a bag. Now get in and don't ask where we're going."

"Where are we going?"

"Elizabeth," she said.

With the radio playing, we swept out of Willing Township and onto the highway north. You know what's north of Willing Township? New York and Connecticut and then Massachusetts. And you know what they have in Massachusetts? Boarding schools. It's a state of Pilgrims and boarding schools, and I wasn't in the mood for either.

But whenever I grew exasperated with my mother these days—and I still often did—I calmed myself by remembering how I'd felt when I saw her standing beside the Portal of Doom. I thought, weirdly, that with her there, everything would be all right. That my mother had the power to fix anything. And I sort of think she does, but that day it wasn't Mom who had done the fixing.

When my father recovered from his trip through the portal—which included using a special trash can kept by the Portal Keeper for just such moments, a box of tissues, and a small bottle of mouthwash—he pulled Keir aside for a talk.

"Your father was on the other side talking to your banshee," said my mother as Keir and my father huddled together over a document my father had taken from his briefcase. "He wanted to let Keir's mother know how he was doing in school."

"Like a parent-teacher conference?" I said.

"Exactly. And also to give her the opportunity to let Keir stay here for a while. Your father drafted a guardianship agreement that allows Keir to remain on this side in order to continue going to school. It also allows his mother and father to visit once a month. On the fifteenth of the month, as a matter of fact."

"Did she sign?"

"She didn't want to at first, she misses him so," said my mother. "But your father can be very persuasive, and Keir's father so wanted his boy to have an education. Eventually they both signed. Now it's up to Keir to decide if he wants to stay. He has to agree to the terms, too."

"He won't agree," I said. Keir had his arms crossed, his head down. "He's afraid of what he might do if he stays."

"He's right to be afraid," said my mother. "But I think we can make it work."

I turned and looked at her. "You were the one sending reports to the countess, weren't you?"

"She was…concerned. And I needed to know all the details of his transformation."

"Then you know he can't stay."

"The countess gave me the recipe for a special shake to keep Keir fed and healthy without the need for blood. The ingredients are boggling—something gross, something rare, kale, and something so weird I don't want to talk about it—but as long as he drinks one each and every day, she says the hunger will be under control, like it was in the château."

"And who would be Keir's guardian?"

"I would be," she said. "And Stephen."

"Does Stephen even know about Keir?"

"Of course he does, Elizabeth. Your father suspected what Keir was right away, and I told Stephen. In fact, after I told him, *he* was the one who convinced me to let Keir stay at the house. He said every kid needs a chance."

"And Keir would stay with us?" I said.

"I guess we'd lose our guest room for good. And I so liked having a guest room."

"But we never have guests."

"True. But I suppose we will now. On the fifteenth of every month."

I couldn't help myself. I hugged my mother then and there. She let me for a moment, before she pushed me away and brushed the pink hair out of my eyes.

"He still might want to join his mother and father and aunties, Elizabeth," she said. "He still might want to pass through the portal. But at least he now he has a real choice."

I looked over at Keir. As he talked with my father, he was kicking at the rock floor of the cavern. Then he turned to stare at the portal, looking at his mom and dad, imagining his life over there. When he aimed his gaze at me, his eyes were rimmed with red and his jaw shook.

It was time for Keir to choose.

Choice. It seems like such a great thing, doesn't it? Should I have this breakfast cereal or that Pop-Tart? Which book should I pick out of the hundreds in the library? Simple, right? I'll have that muffin. I'll take a mystery for now and leave the manga for later. Usually, it doesn't really matter. But what happens when it does really matter? What happens when the whole curve of your life depends on a choice?

I was thinking about Keir's choice when I realized what this trip to Massachusetts was all about. My mother was taking me away so that I could make a choice of my own.

My grandfather wanted me to dedicate myself to the family business even if it meant blowing off school. I needed to get my priorities straight, he told me again and again. But somehow looking at school through Keir's eyes made me appreciate it so much more. Maybe it was time to actually make it more than just this thing in my life I suffered through. Maybe it was time to beat school like a kettledrum.

And then there was my mother, who from the start had wanted me to turn away from what she called the Webster ghostly foolishness and pay attention to the things that really mattered, like family and friends and school. And truth was, in my time with Webster & Spawn my grades had taken a dive like those kites on the beach. But there was something that maybe she didn't understand.

I had a moment with my father at the portal while Keir was making his decision. "None of this would have mattered," said my father, "if you hadn't saved Keir from Van Helsing and then gotten that contract."

"We were lucky to get out alive," I said.

"This time," he said. "I'm scared for you, Elizabeth."

"That's funny, because I'm scared for me, too."

"It's not funny," he said. "I'm thinking that maybe you should hold off on the law stuff. There will always be the dead and the undead. You can back off and finish school before you decide about joining the firm. Your mother says your grades are slipping."

"Like a marching band on a hockey rink," I said. "But something happened that I need to tell you about. Something weird. This was in the château, when I had just gotten the contract from the countess. Keir showed up, and we had to run to escape the fire and the fight, and in the middle of it all I started laughing. It was so strange. I just started laughing."

He looked at me, his face somber as a wet rock, because as soon as he heard it he knew. Of course he knew. When he had said the work filled him, I wasn't sure what he was talking about, but when I looked at Keir, I realized it filled me, too.

So I had a choice. And then and there, in that car, it was time to choose. As my mother and I drove north on the New Jersey Turnpike, I snapped off the radio and said, "I'm not going to boarding school."

"Good," said my mother. "Because that's not where we're heading."

"And just so you know, despite what you and Dad want, I'm not going to quit the firm. Whatever I have to do to be a great barrister in the Court of Uncommon Pleas and help people like Keir, I'm going to do it. Which means I'll be sweeping a lot of floors. But I'm going to be the best floor sweeper they've ever seen. Those floors are going to glow. And I'm sorry about my grades in school, but whatever I have to do to raise my grades, I'm going to do that, too."

I put my head down and stared at my hands and thought of the Countess Laveau and the way she made me feel.

"I know you and Dad and Grandpop want me to choose one or the other," I said, "but I choose not to choose. I'm not going to let anyone limit what I am, even those who love me the most. I can be more than any of you think. I'll just have to show you."

"Oh my," said my mother as she drove on, a slight smile breaking out.

"So that's that, then, right?" I said. "We can go back home?"

"I have another idea," said my mother. "Stephen mentioned something about a go-cart track? Petey was jumping up and down when he heard and Keir said he had never driven anything with a motor before."

"I love go-carts!" I said. "Let's join them."

"I thought instead, while they're driving around in circles, we could have a mother-daughter weekend. At a spa."

"A spa?"

"We'll do some yoga. We'll get pedicures. And maybe we'll do something about your hair."

"What's wrong with my hair?"

"Nothing. I like what you and Natalie did with it. But you've been fussing about it so much I thought maybe you'd be ready to try something new. They have books you can look through. Whatever you choose, they'll create it for you."

"Can they make me look like Yuki?"

"I don't know who that is."

"From *Vampire Night*. Her hair is this beautiful reddish-brown color, wild and spiky at the same time."

"We'll find a picture online to show them."

"Yes!" I said, pumping a fist.

"See, it will be fun. And sometime during our stay,

maybe, if you want, I'll tell you the story of how your father and I met."

"Wait, what?"

"I told you I'd tell it to you when you were ready."

"You'll really tell me? All of it?"

"Well, most of it," she said.

And she did. Alone in the hot tub, during our sprout-and-tofu dinners, as we lay with our heads touching on the one big bed in our room, she told me the whole terrifying and yet romantic tale of her journey to the other side and back, which was, in its own way, my origin story.

And trust me when I tell you, it's legendary.

ACKNOWLEDGMENTS

Every book needs a great editor and this book had two, the brilliant Tracey Keevan at Disney, who pointed out the horrifying gaps in my horror story, and the incredible Alexandra Hightower at Little, Brown, who polished this thing to a high sheen. Writing this was a group effort, and if the book sings it's because of their voices.

I also want to thank Mary O'Callaghan, the language program coordinator for the Department of Irish Language and Literature at the University of Notre Dame, for helping me with the banshee's Irish. I had no idea what the ghost was requesting of Elizabeth until Professor O'Callaghan graciously agreed to lend a hand. Before that I thought she maybe was asking for a pickle.

My agents Wendy Sherman and Alex Glass have been

with me every step of my Elizabethan journey and I will be forever grateful to them for making it happen.

My family is my support and inspiration, especially my children, who seem to keep appearing in the books.

I also want to thank all the school librarians who hosted me in the last year and all the middle school kids around the country who talked to me about Elizabeth, the law, and the writing process. I write these books to teach, entertain, and inspire, and these students have done exactly that for me. The main struggle in writing for younger readers is to keep up with such an amazing audience.

Finally, this book is coming out in the midst of a pandemic that eerily echoes the influenza outbreak of 1918 that sickened Keir and killed tens of millions worldwide. Keir's stories of the 1918 pandemic were enhanced by two excellent books, *The Great Influenza* by John M. Barry and *Pandemic 1918* by Catharine Arnold. History continues to teach us that no matter what we face, we are stronger when we face it together. Elizabeth has taught me that nothing makes us stronger than a Legion of Friendship. Welcome to my Legion.